Special Books by Special Writers
The Book:

UNDER ONE ROOF

One of the most moving, honest and *uplifting* stories you'll
ever read. And it's just plain *romantic*, too!

The Characters:

Spencer Coburn. Overstressed physician, divorced father.
He's currently the sole emotional and physical support of...

Stacy Coburn, his teenage daughter——his *pregnant*
teenage daughter.

Gina Banning. Hardworking, divorced schoolteacher and
only child. She's currently the sole emotional and physical
support of ...

Joe Banning, her eighty-three-year-old father——her seriously ill father.

The Author:

Two-time RITA Award finalist and *Romantic Times*
Reviewer's Choice winner, Shannon Waverly has fans world-
wide. Shannon wanted this, her tenth book for Harlequin,
to be a very special one. *It is.*

Dear Reader,

When I'm asked if my stories are based on real people or actual events, I usually say no, they're fictional creations. And that's the truth. However, the emotional journey my characters take is usually one that I've traveled myself, at least in some small way. The journey that Gina and Spencer take in *Under One Roof* is no exception.

Gina Banning and Spencer Coburn are caught in the middle of things. They're middle-aged (and facing dreams unmet). They're in midcareer (and wondering where they're going). And, most significantly, they're in the middle of a "generation sandwich" and feeling pressure from both sides. Not an easy place to be, especially when those sides are a fifteen-year-old daughter who's pregnant and a senile father who's dying.

Writing this book, my tenth for Harlequin, I felt a special affinity with Gina and Spencer, because I, too, am smack in the middle of things. A few years ago I also lost my father.

However, *Under One Roof* is not a story about dying. It's about living, about the forward-moving thrust of life and joy renewed, because while Gina and Spencer must say goodbye to one generation, they must also say hello to another—as I did, with the birth of my granddaughter.

Above all, *Under One Roof* is a love story. And *that,* finding the miracle of love in the midst of adversity and sadness, is the real story I wanted to tell, the journey I want to share with you. I hope you enjoy the ride.

With love,

Shannon Waverly

P.S. I enjoy hearing from readers. Please write me at:
RWA/New England Chapter, P.O. Box 1667,
Framingham, MA 01701-9998

Shannon Waverly

UNDER ONE ROOF

Harlequin Books

TORONTO • NEW YORK • LONDON
AMSTERDAM • PARIS • SYDNEY • HAMBURG
STOCKHOLM • ATHENS • TOKYO • MILAN
MADRID • WARSAW • BUDAPEST • AUCKLAND

ISBN 0-373-70703-7

UNDER ONE ROOF

UNDER ONE
ROOF

CHAPTER ONE

"DAMMIT, MOOKIE! Now you see why I told you to use condoms?" Spencer Coburn's voice carried through Tucker Street Walk-in like the crack of a pistol. Everyone in the clinic froze.

That included the nineteen-year-old who sat in front of Spencer, gaping at him. Spencer wanted to smack the kid.

"Hell, Doc, what am I gonna do?"

You're gonna die, Mookie, Spencer thought. *You're gonna friggin' die.* Red-hot and blind, he flung his clipboard. It toppled a jar of tongue depressors before banging the wall and clattering to the floor.

The privacy curtain suddenly slashed along its pole.

"Spencer."

He pivoted, his stethoscope swinging away from his tattersall shirtfront with the force of the movement. Doug Ferguson stood in the doorway. The younger physician had spoken calmly enough, but his eyes were hard and bright.

"You've got a phone call."

Spencer blinked, trying to clear the heat from his brain. "Who? Stacy?"

"Uh...yeah. I'll take over here."

Something wasn't right. Spencer looked at his patient for a clue. The kid was shaking. But then, so was he. He frowned, looking past Doug to a knot of staff people standing in the corridor. Some of them had been with him since the beginning, when the clinic was little more than a swept-out pizza joint. Good people, dedicated to caring, no matter who the patient. They were looking at him now as if they'd never seen him before.

"Oh, hell," Spencer muttered under his breath. He broke out in a sweat and for a moment thought he might be sick. He shouldered his way around Doug, and although he already knew there was no phone call, strode off to his office. It lay just beyond the staff lounge, the very last compartment in the long warren of rooms that made up the clinic. He often thought of the walk-in as the belly of Jonah's whale, and his office, its deepest recess.

He rounded his desk and fell into his leather chair. His insides were still shaking. He took a deep breath, closed his eyes and tried to think calming thoughts. Instead, he imagined Doug Ferguson's cool, rational voice explaining the options open to that poor son of a bitch, selling him the "every reason to be optimistic" package.

What *he* should've done.

Suddenly Spencer surged forward, grabbed a fistful of darts from a chipped coffee mug on his desk and hurled them at a dart board. All but one tumbled to the floor. Then he picked up the mug and flung that, too. He didn't bother to clean up the pieces. What was the point? The world was full of broken things. What was one more useless mug?

He considered throwing something else, the lamp, or maybe that pile of unread medical journals. But throwing things was starting to look pretty dumb, so he just sat back and tried to shed his remaining anger with a few more slow breaths.

Doug walked into the staff room across the hall a few minutes later. Spencer heard him open the refrigerator.

He took another deep breath, exhaled it and managed to calmly ask, "Is the kid okay?"

"As well as can be expected." Doug stepped to the doorway and popped open a small can of juice. "How about you?"

"I'm fine." Spencer leaned far back in his seat, one foot pushing against the edge of his desk, propping him in a pose of calculated ease. "The kid'll probably sue," he said on a brittle laugh, "but I'm fine."

Doug tipped back the can and took a swallow, then came into the room and stood at a glass case, studying the items within. Sports trophies, won mostly at community-league basketball. Tributes from civic organizations and government officials. On the shelf below those gleamed Spencer's collection of antique paperweights, in the forefront of which stood a rough plaster weight shaped like a Dixie cup and embedded with beach glass and a couple of tiny fingerprints.

Still looking into the case, Doug said, "Do you want to talk about what just happened?"

Talk was the last thing Spencer wanted to do. Not because he made a policy of keeping a professional distance from his staff. Hell, Doug was also a friend. Spencer just felt uncomfortable discussing his personal life with anybody. In his experience, most men felt that way. Someone should've informed Doug Ferguson. The guy had missed his calling. Should've been a shrink, or maybe a priest.

"What can I say? I messed up." Spencer pressed the desk with his foot and made the chair rock, trying to look unconcerned. Inside he was a wreck. How could he have forgotten to check on that kid's blood work? He was supposed to have called him two days ago with the results. If he'd remembered, he would've had time to compose himself, frame his words and phone Mookie properly. Instead, the kid had walked in off the street, chasing down the results himself, catching him off guard.

He added quietly, "I'll stop by Mookie's at lunchtime, have a talk with him and his mother."

Doug walked over to a chair and sat down. "You've been doing a lot of that lately, messing up."

Spencer had to admire the guy. Where the rest of the staff cowered and tiptoed, Doug came right at him, ignoring his status.

At his continued silence, Doug asked, "Have you given any further thought to what we talked about last week?" He finished his juice and set the can on the floor.

"Sure, I've thought about it." Spencer lowered his foot and let the chair nudge him forward. "And I still say I'm not depressed. Not clinically, anyway."

Doug's face, still round and cherubic at thirty-two, relaxed into a smile. "Well, why the hell not? Everyone else around here is."

Spencer chuckled, then pushed himself up from his chair and headed for the coffee machine in the staff lounge.

From within the office Doug continued, "Even your common, low-grade blues should be attended to if they persist. You know that."

Spencer concentrated on filling a mug, spooning in sugar.

"Just the fact that you haven't been sleeping should tell you something. You've lost your appetite, too, I've noticed."

Spencer focused on pouring in milk, stirring.

"I know it's a hard notion to accept, a doctor being depressed. People expect us to handle all sorts of crap. Not only handle it but fix it, too."

Spencer returned to the office.

"But, hell," Doug continued, "we're only human. And fixing things around here can get pretty overwhelming, especially when a person cares as much as you do."

With a rueful snort, Spencer crossed to a window that looked out on a back alley, a window he always kept closed, even on warm May mornings like this one, because of the foul smell and traffic noise out there.

"Spence, you've got to do something. You owe it to your patients. Hell, you owe it to yourself."

Spencer let out a long breath that seemed to empty more than his lungs. "I agree."

A hesitation, then, "What did you say?"

Spencer turned from the window. "I agree with you. I'm gonna take a break, Doug. You know, a vacation?" The words floated from him like surprised, released ghosts.

The younger doctor's expression shifted from perplexity through astonishment to relief. "Good. That's ... good. You've been working much too hard lately. Rumor has it sometimes you even stay through the evening shift."

Spencer shrugged. That was nothing new. He'd been working the occasional evening shift since his divorce four years ago. The good old American work cure.

"It's been a discouraging year for you, too, starting with that break-in and robbery here on New Year's Day. Then the financial plug being pulled on the preschool immunization program and the fiasco at the state house. I can understand how you'd be feeling a little down. And, oh hell, your father dying. I just remembered."

Spencer sat on the windowsill and shrugged again. He was no stranger to break-ins or ended programs or confrontation with bureaucracy. And as for his father's dying, well, there hadn't been much to that. A heart attack that had taken the elder Dr. Coburn with blessed speed; no pain or lingering illness, just a few brief days in the hospital, with no excessive strain on the family. The only inconvenience to Spencer was the funeral, and even that had only taken him away from Boston for a day.

Spencer involuntarily shivered, remembering that day. Mid-February in northern Illinois, a snowy Wednesday with a sky like iron. Two hundred people turned out anyway.

For one clarified moment Spencer saw himself standing there again in the snow-covered cemetery, with his mother on his right, his sister and her family on his left. For that moment, he *was* there, listening to the minister's dolorous voice, his sister's sniffles. There, staring at a cold mahogany casket that refused to take on meaning no matter how much he wanted it to. And all around him, the hissing of snowflakes falling through the empty trees.

Spencer gave his head a small shake and returned to the present. "It isn't that, Doug. My decision to take a break has nothing to do with my father's death or the robbery or the hours I put in." He paused, rethinking what he'd said. "Sure, those things haven't helped. But my lousy moods and even lousier behavior are coming from somewhere else."

"Stacy?"

Spencer looked at his colleague in mild surprise. "I guess it's no secret. Ever since she started high school, she's been a major worry—hanging out with a bad crowd, letting her schoolwork slide." He turned and stared out the window again, at a discarded, mildewed mattress in the alley. For a moment he considered not saying any more. The words were too painful. But Doug had to know. "And now," he said in a voice that didn't sound like his, "now she's pregnant. She called me last night to tell me."

From behind him, he heard a hitch in Doug's breathing. "But...she hasn't even finished her first year of high school."

Spencer raised his coffee mug and forced his jaw to unclench. He sipped and somehow swallowed. "It'd be wiser not to remind me of that right now."

Doug swore under his breath. "How far along is she?"

Spencer turned to face the younger physician. "About six months, she thinks."

Doug winced. "Too late for her to terminate. What's she going to do?"

Spencer stared at the carpeted floor and fought a burning in his eyes. He'd been awake all night, wrestling with possible solutions, dozens of them.

"I need a favor, Doug. Two favors, really."

"Anything. Name it."

"For starters, I could use that farmhouse your parents own in the Berkshires. Stacy moved in with me last night and—"

"Moved in?"

"Mmm. Maureen says she can't handle this." Anger tightened Spencer's chest, but he didn't want to get into slinging blame. God knew enough could be slung at him. "Anyway, I'd like to take Stacy someplace where she can finish out her pregnancy in peace and privacy. I don't want her staying around Boston, everyone at school finding out and talking about her. I'd prefer keeping Maureen's family out of it, too, especially her parents." Spencer returned to his desk and sat, placing his coffee on the stack of unread journals. "So I was wondering, are your folks still looking for a tenant for the farm, or have they decided to sell?''

Doug settled back, crossing his legs, folding his hands over his waist. ''Well, they've definitely decided to stay in Arizona, which means, yes, they're planning to put the farm on the market, but they want to have some repairs done first to make the place more salable. In the meantime, I'm sure they'd appreciate having some money coming in. I just can't guarantee how long you'll be able to stay.''

''As I said, we'll only need it for the summer, until Stacy has the baby.'' Spencer finished off his coffee, felt an acid burn in his stomach and realized he hadn't eaten anything yet that day.

''Spence, I have to warn you, the place is pretty remote. Most people, when they think of the Berkshires, think of Stockbridge or Williamstown, the bigger, touristy places. But Bingham is nothing like that. It's just a small rural village in the middle of nowhere.''

''Great. That's perfect.'' Nowhere was exactly where Spencer wanted to be for a while. ''So, do you think your folks'll let me have it?''

''I don't see why not. They hired a realtor to manage it for them. I'll give him a call. When do you want to move in?''

''Ten days, two weeks maybe. I'm pulling Stacy out of school, so I'll need some time to get her work together and arrange for a tutor out in— What's the name of that town?''

''Bingham.''

''Bingham,'' Spencer repeated, nodding. ''I need to talk to her guidance counselor, too. I'm planning to send her to boarding school in the fall and need some recommendations. After that there'll be adoption arrangements to make. Who knows how much time that'll involve." He sat back in his creaking chair, already feeling better just thinking he was on the road to mending the situation. "I need to look up some obstetricians out in the Bingham area, too, and I have to take Stacy shopping for maternity clothes. Two weeks maybe. Tell the realtor two weeks."

Doug nodded reflectively. "So what's the other favor? You said there were two."

Spencer liked how Doug refrained from asking about the father of Stacy's baby. Probably knew he didn't want to even think about the father.

"I want you to take over the clinic while I'm gone."

The younger physician sat straighter. "Are you serious?"

"Hey, somebody has to know how to take over when I quit and open my office in Newton."

Predictably, Doug smiled. Opening an office in the affluent suburb of Newton was an ongoing joke between them, sort of like running off to Tahiti.

Something in Spencer's face, however, chilled the smile right out of Doug. "No, I'm not serious about leaving," Spencer assured him, "though God only knows why. Here I am, forty-two years old and still driving a glorified bicycle to work."

Doug relaxed visibly. "Hey, I like your car."

"I'll give it to you, right after I open my new office."

In reality, leaving Tucker Street for private practice was an idea Spencer had been tinkering with a lot lately. He had expenses. Besides salaries for fifteen people and crushing premiums on malpractice insurance, there was Maureen's alimony every month, maintenance on the house he'd left her and, of course, supporting Stacy.

Boarding school wouldn't come cheap, and in a couple of years there would be college.

But his preoccupation with leaving the clinic wasn't based just on financial concerns. Spencer studied his hands, curled over the edge of the desk, hands that had set innumerable fractures, stitched unspeakable wounds, probed thousands of throats, written a million prescriptions, delivered untimely babies and closed the eyes of the untimely dead. Those hands were trembling now because the simple truth was he didn't care about the clinic anymore. He just didn't give a damn.

What really frightened him, though, was the suspicion he was losing his interest in medicine altogether. He'd lost his compassion for his patients, lost his joy in his work. Nothing came from the heart anymore. A dead weight seemed to have settled where his enthusiasm and ambition had once burned. And if that was the case, he couldn't see himself practicing medicine anywhere.

Trouble was, if he didn't practice medicine, what would he do? He'd never wanted to be anything but a doctor. At his age would he even be able to pick up a new field?

Spencer closed his eyes, feeling shaky and exhausted. He needed a rest, needed time alone to sort this out, to find out if it was a case of permanent burnout or just an offshoot of his despondency over Stacy. Although he hadn't admitted it to Doug, the farm would be as much a retreat for him as for his daughter.

Across the room, Doug gave a dry chuckle. Spencer glanced up. "I don't mean to minimize what you're facing, Spence, but she's only pregnant. She doesn't have a terminal illness—nobody's died. Things'll get better."

Spencer let his gaze touch the myriad framed photographs cluttering his desktop, every one of them of Stacy.

One had fallen over. He leaned forward and righted it. Second grade, must've been. Two front teeth missing. Smiling, anyway. His heart broke a little more. "You don't have kids, do you, Doug?"

"I hope not." He chuckled again. "I've never been married."

Spencer nodded. The guy didn't have a clue. Spencer didn't question that things would get better. Of course they would. He was determined to spend the summer making sure they did. Out in the quiet Berkshires, he would do his best to put his daughter's life back on track. But no one could tell him things would ever be the same as they once were or as good as they could have been.

Just then the receptionist knocked on the door frame. "Sorry for interrupting, but the waiting room is beginning to look like Grand Central."

"We'll be right out, Bev," Spencer said. The woman left. "Go on, Doug. I'll be right behind you."

But the younger doctor remained in his seat. "Look, Spence, I know you say you're going to the farm because of Stacy, but while you're there, try to relax and enjoy yourself too."

"I intend to."

"Good. If you were a patient of mine, a summer at the farm is exactly what I'd prescribe. It'll be good for you to get away and not think about patients or medicine or anything. In fact, I'd recommend you not even take anything medical to read. Just get away completely."

Spencer refused to admit it, but the thought had already crossed his mind. "Sounds good to me."

"Another thing," Doug added as he got to his feet, "while you're there, get out in that fresh mountain air and do something physical. Get those old endorphins moving."

That, too, had occurred to Spencer. "I will. Thanks for the suggestion. Now go, or Bev'll be back with reinforcements."

Finally Doug Ferguson left him alone.

Spencer remained where he was, slouched in his chair, gazing at the gallery of photographs on his desk. Stacy at every age, opening like a blossom of limitless beauty and promise. Somewhere outside the back window, a robin was trilling in the warm May sunshine. Spencer closed his eyes and tried to listen, tried to find optimism in the voice of that bird, who sang in spite of traffic noise and alley smells and the futility of fixing what was irrevocably broken. He failed.

He sat in his office and shivered, listening to a robin's song but hearing, instead, the hiss of snowflakes falling, falling through empty trees.

CHAPTER TWO

GINA BANNING felt the first flutters of anxiety when the door opened before she'd turned the key. She was certain she'd locked up before heading out to the market.

She entered the apartment on tiptoe and, after placing her groceries on the kitchen table, crossed the sitting room and nudged open the bedroom door. When her gaze met the empty bed, her anxiety escalated to full-blown alarm.

"Dad?" she called, even though she could see quite clearly he wasn't there. An oscillating fan on the bureau stirred the warm June air trapped in the room, smelling faintly of lilacs and stale bed linens.

Gina wheeled off the threshold and rapped on the bathroom door. "Dad?" she called before pushing open that door, too. The only trace of him was the nicotine-stained stub of an unfiltered cigarette on the rim of the sink.

She turned, her troubled gaze combing her father's apartment, the three tight rooms she'd been sharing with him for the past four days. Damn! She shouldn't have gone out, not even for the few minutes it had taken her to run down the road to get those groceries. She should've been content to sit here averaging her final grades and gone shopping later when her father could accompany her. Granted, he usually napped for an hour in the afternoon, but usually didn't mean always, and she should've remembered the times he didn't, the times he awoke after just a few minutes and refused to settle again.

Slinging her purse strap over her shoulder, Gina hurtled out the door and down the stairs, heedless of the ice cream she'd left melting on the table. He was probably just in the yard, she told herself. He probably just wanted to get some air and look at the flowers.

But when Gina looked out the back door of the house, her heart sank. The yard was deserted. She searched it again. Still came up empty.

She rounded the house at a run, heading for the front gate. On the way she happened to glance toward the garage and noticed the doors were open. That stopped her short. The next moment her pulse was roaring in her ears. Joe's old Chevy was missing.

How could that be? she wondered. She thought she'd hidden all the keys. Groaning, she clutched her head and for once regretted not having more hair to pull. Her father had no business behind the wheel of a car. Good Lord, he didn't even have an active driver's license anymore. She raced to her own car, parked out front, and set off in pursuit.

Gina drove up and down the maple-shaded streets of Bingham Center, searching for her father. His car was nowhere in sight. She zipped down Route 112, past Buffington Antiques and Auction Barn, past the Wooden Bucket Sugar Shack, Hobbs Hollow Falls and the Red Rooster Inn, all the way to the sign that marked the town line—Bingham, Massachusetts, Established 1703, Population 680. Still nothing.

With a deepening sense of urgency, she retraced her route to Bingham Corners, where Route 112 and Emerson Brook Road intersected. She slowed just long enough to double-check the library and church grounds. Nothing. Neither was her father one of the old men sitting on the porch of the Bingham Corners General Store.

Gina set off again, her tires squealing as she turned onto the long country lane she should've taken first time by. Why hadn't she? she reprimanded herself harshly. This was where neighbors told her they usually found her father when he went wandering, at the old family farm on Emerson Brook Road, roaming the fields, trying the doors. Hadn't she wanted to believe them?

Lord, she'd better hurry, too. She'd heard that new tenants had moved in. Nobody from the area. Nobody who would recognize Joe Banning and understand. "Damn!" Gina swore, as she pressed the accelerator.

She barreled down the narrow, winding road at breakneck speed, past mossy stone walls and newly planted cornfields, past the homes of old neighbors and friends. Only the covered bridge over Emerson Brook slowed her beeline race, and even then the wooden planks clacked with the startling rapidity of a drumroll.

Yes, she could believe her father might be at the farm. These days he was always at the farm, at least in his mind. She only hoped she got to him before some stranger did.

STACY COBURN should've been studying algebra. The tutor her father had hired was planning to test her tomorrow. Instead, she sat in the middle of her saggy double bed, playing a game of solitaire and listening to an alternative band that irritated even her.

She didn't know why she still had the stupid CD on. Her father couldn't even hear it anymore. After ordering her to turn off "that noise" and hit the books, he'd gone out to the garden and was tilling the same dirt he'd been working for almost a week now.

She tossed down a jack of hearts on the pink chenillē spread and muttered a curse. Boy, did she hate living here, in this strange house, in this strange part of the state. Although it was only a couple of hours' drive west of Boston, she'd never even heard of Bingham until two weeks ago.

Little wonder. It was the pits. There was nothing to do here, nowhere to go. The house didn't even have cable TV. They really needed it, too. The mountains made mincemeat of reception.

With an angry lunge toward her nightstand, she snapped off the music.

Maybe she'd run away, she thought, returning to her card game. Sure, she could do that. She could probably pack a bag, raid her father's wallet, slip out the front door and catch a Greyhound before he even looked up from his stupid plowing. Then he'd be sorry. They'd all be sorry. Her mother. The kids at school. Todd.

Yeah, right. And just where did a fifteen-year-old run off to when she was six and a half months pregnant?

Stacy tossed aside the deck of cards and with a disconsolate sigh sank back on her bed pillows. She'd really messed up this time, she thought, placing a hand on her rounded stomach. Under her palm the baby kicked. Usually the feathery movement filled her with amazement and made her smile. Today, however, she only felt sad, sad for herself, sad for the baby she'd never get to know. Nobody wanted them, not even the people closest to her, people she'd been counting on for support.

She'd been able to hide her condition from her mother for more than five months, partly because she'd worn loose, layered clothes, partly because her mother had been too preoccupied, once The Jerk had moved in.

Stacy wished she'd been able to hide her condition indefinitely. Her mother had gone postal. She'd even hit her. Stacy couldn't ever remember being hit before.

Why had she done it? her mother wanted to know. Couldn't she have waited to have sex? Why hadn't she used birth control? Why hadn't she told her sooner, when there was still time for an abortion? Stacy'd had no answer except *I don't know. It just happened.*

"And just what do you intend to do now?" her mother had inquired.

Stacy had been especially lost for an answer there.

"I'll tell you what you're going to do. You're going to call your father and let *him* handle it, let *him* see what I've been going through these past four years alone."

"My...Dad?" Stacy's breath had whooshed out of her. "I can't call Dad."

"Why not? Do you think he's never going to hear about this?"

That was exactly what Stacy had been thinking, or at least hoping. "Please, Mom. I'll die of embarrassment."

"Fine. Go live with your boyfriend, then, or with one of your slutty girlfriends. Just don't expect to stay here."

"You're kicking me out?"

"You got it. I'm at the end of my rope with you, girl."

Stacy had already known she couldn't live with Todd. He'd broken up with her as soon as he'd understood he was going to be a father. And she didn't really want to live with any of her friends. She knew she'd become their main topic of gossip. And so, faced with the prospect of homelessness, she'd called her father.

Dialing his number, she'd prayed his reaction wouldn't be anger—and it wasn't. It was silence, followed by, "Oh, Stacy." Only that, but spoken in a voice so ragged with disappointment she wished he *had* gotten angry. She would've preferred being beaten black and blue to hearing that disappointment.

That night, after settling into his apartment in the city, Stacy had wanted to talk. She'd wanted to tell him how scared she was of this pregnancy, how hurt by Todd's and her mother's reaction, how sorry she was for disappointing him. She'd needed to hear him reassure her that she wasn't in this alone, that everything would work out fine and he still loved her. But he'd made it abundantly clear he wasn't in the mood for talk. He was tired, he said. Said he needed time to adjust to her news.

That had been two weeks ago. Stacy was still waiting.

Exactly what she was waiting for she wasn't sure. He'd certainly adjusted to her news. By the very next day he'd had her entire life mapped out for her, from an appointment with the adoption agency right down to the way he expected her to dress. Sometimes when she thought about how bossy he'd become, she wanted to scream.

Stacy rolled onto her side and tucked up her knees as far as they would go. The white half curtain on the window by the bed billowed softly in the warm breeze, then flattened against the screen with an abrupt out-draft.

What she was waiting for, she supposed, was for her father to tell her she was still loved. But apparently she wasn't. By becoming pregnant she'd made herself unlovable. Now he didn't want her in his life any more than Todd or her mother did.

Of course, he hadn't said that to her in so many words. What he'd said was, in the fall he intended to send her to some boarding school in Pennsylvania. He claimed he only wanted to help her make a new start, but she wasn't dumb. She could read between the lines.

A small noise downstairs momentarily drew her out of her thoughts. She lifted her head off the pillow, listening with heightened attention, but after a length of silence, she gave it up and lay back again. She'd lived in three different houses in her lifetime, and each had possessed its own peculiar noises—pipe clanks, shutter rattles, floor squeaks. This house undoubtedly had its own repertoire of sounds.

Stacy let her gaze roam her room. Reluctantly she admitted she didn't really hate the house. Actually it had a great feel to it, one of permanence and durability. She just didn't like *why* she was here.

Her father claimed he wanted to minimize the damage to her reputation, spare her grandparents and move her to a quieter, safer place than his neighborhood. But she couldn't help feeling he had other, less supportive, motives. Embarrassment, for example. He was probably so embarrassed by her that he'd do anything to hide her from the people he knew, even leave his practice for an entire summer—and medicine was his life.

She thought she could live with his embarrassment— she was pretty bummed herself—but his aversion to her was something else. He never joked with her anymore, hardly even talked, except for surface conversation. And when he looked at her, she got the feeling he was looking through her, as if she wasn't really there for him.

Well, screw you, Stacy thought, swiping hard at her tears. She'd tried to cooperate, tried to please him. But apparently he couldn't be pleased. It was like she'd died or something, or at least changed so much he was never going to feel the same about her again. Well, fine. She didn't need him, either.

A creaking sound—on the stairs?—drew her out of her thoughts again. "Dad?" she called, propping up on an elbow. Instantly she recognized the absurdity of her calling to him. The tiller was still rumbling.

It had to be her imagination. No one else was in the house.

Maybe it was the real-estate agent, come to show the apartment in the attached barn to a prospective tenant.

But why would the real-estate agent be inside the main house? Why would he be bringing a client by at all when he knew her father wanted the apartment to remain unoccupied?

It was her imagination, then.

But it wasn't her imagination. She distinctly heard another step on the creaky stairs, a slow, labored step, accompanied by heavy breathing. Her heart stopped—and then began to speed. "Dad?" she called again.

Silence. Why didn't the person out there answer her?

The top step squeaked. Stacy couldn't move. Panic immobilized her. Maybe it wasn't a person, after all. Maybe that was why "it" didn't answer. The house was certainly old enough to have a few resident ghosts.

Adrenaline rushed through her. Did she have enough time to slip under the bed? In her condition, was she even able to fit? Should she try for the closet, instead?

Before she could reach a decision, a grizzled head popped around the door frame. Stacy jumped, letting out a scream. Simultaneously the head echoed her reaction, bellowing and retreating.

Stacy didn't wait to see if it reappeared. She scrambled off the bed and dashed to the window. "Dad!" she called as loudly as she could. "Dad, help."

The tiller continued to chug along. Behind her, the shuffling footsteps entered the room.

"Dad!" she tried again, her throat hurting from the force of her effort. Obviously her father couldn't hear her. Obviously he wasn't going to help. No one was.

With nowhere to hide, she pivoted and faced the intruder, hoping boldness would throw him off balance at least long enough for her to run past and out the door.

The man she found standing there was old and gaunt, with a wide, knobby forehead and thin, center-parted hair as gray as cobwebs. In spite of the day's warmth, he wore a long-sleeved flannel shirt buttoned at cuff and neck, and dark green work pants that, without suspenders, surely would fall around his ankles.

"Margaret?" he said, his voice weak and scratchy.

Stacy took a stealthy step toward the door. Her heart was racing. "Who are you? What do you want?"

He continued to stare at her, searching her features. "Margaret?"

"What's the matter with you?" She took another step. "I'm not Margaret."

"Yes, Margaret." He perked up, as if she'd finally understood him. "She came up here a little while ago."

"Up here? You're..." Stacy almost said "crazy" before good manners intervened. "You must be mistaken. I've been up here for hours, alone."

He took a step closer, pulling his left leg along as if it was asleep. His droopy-lidded, deerlike eyes fixed on her in a way that made her shiver. "Where is she, then? I've been looking and looking." His voice began to catch and break. "But I can't find her anywhere."

Good grief, he *was* crazy. He was stark raving mad, Stacy realized, just as his hard, bony hand lifted and touched her cheek.

GINA'S CAR jiggled down the hard-packed dirt driveway
that led to the farmhouse. Her heart was in her throat
because she could already see her father's Chevy parked
by the front porch steps. Actually, "parked" was too
generous a term. He'd nosed the front bumper right into
the bridle-wreath bush she used to like to shake when she
was a child to see it "snow."

She eased her car to a stop behind her father's, turned
off the engine and gazed up at the simple, sturdy, two-
story frame house. She ought to be feeling something
more than anxiety, she thought. This had been her
home—where she'd eaten thousands of meals, slept
thousands of nights, played and laughed and cried,
dreamed dreams and seen some of those dreams come
true—and she hadn't been back since her parents had
sold it thirteen years ago. You'd think a person could
drum up a few sniffles after such an absence.

At the moment, however, Gina had no room for sentimentality. Her father wasn't in his car, and the front
door of the house stood wide open. "Oh, Dad." She
winced. "What've you done now?"

She slid out from behind the wheel and unglued her
skirt from the back of her thighs, all the while framing
the apology she would offer the new tenants. That was
when the rumble of machinery caught her attention. The
sound was coming from behind the house. She paused,
head tilted. Was the land being farmed again?

Hope spiraled within her. Maybe the person operating
that machinery hadn't heard her father drive up. Maybe
she could slip inside the house and get him out before
anyone even realized he was there. That would be wonderful. No embarrassing encounters. No halting expla-
nations.

She hurried up the steps, tiptoed across the deep porch and gave the open door a light knock. "Hello?" she called, but softly, just to cover herself in case someone was inside. "Anybody home?"

When no one answered, she entered the narrow front hall. Everything inside the house was different, yet fundamentally unchanged. That was her only observation, and it faded immediately into her overriding anxiety to find her father.

Swallowing her trepidation, she peered into the room on her left—the parlor. Her father wasn't there. She gazed up the staircase, then shook her head. Her father had trouble climbing stairs. She'd leave searching the second floor for last.

She moved on down the hall, balancing on the balls of her feet. Just outside the kitchen she paused again. "Hello?" The only sound that came back to her was the growl of machinery outside.

She stepped into the bright, south-facing room, and even while she was relieved no one was there, she grew increasingly worried. Where in heaven's name was her father?

Quietly she pressed open one of the swinging café doors that divided the kitchen from the dining room. Her father wasn't there, either.

She turned, surveying the kitchen once more. Suddenly her gaze came to rest on a door so unobtrusive she'd forgotten it existed. The door provided access to the woodshed. Was it possible he'd gone that way? She looked over her shoulder to make sure she was still alone, then tiptoed forward.

The structure on the other side of the door was, in reality, much more than a woodshed. Gina's parents had called it that because it was where they happened to store, among other things, their firewood. But it was huge, more than half the size of the house itself.

Gina had her hand on the door latch and her mind on the mischief her father might be getting into when someone behind her cleared his throat. She froze. Simultaneously she realized the rumble of machinery was gone.

Oh, hell! The worst had happened. How was she ever going to explain this?

Slowed by the weight of dread, she turned.

The first impression she got of the person standing inside the back door was size. Sunlight streamed over a frame that was strapping and solid and at least six feet tall.

Her second impression was attitude. This person wasn't the least bit happy. He stood in a stance of aggression with his fists cocked on his hips and his mouth set in a scowl. She really couldn't blame him.

"Can I help you?" His voice was deep and as dark as a moonless night.

"I'm s-sorry," she stammered. She never stammered. "This must appear awfully strange, my coming into your house like this."

"You got that right." A muscle jumped along his jaw.

"I knocked. For quite a while," she exaggerated. "But no one answered."

"So you figured you'd open the door and walk in, anyway?" He pinned her with a look so sharp she felt nailed in place.

"I'm sorry. I just didn't know what else to do." To show her goodwill, Gina stepped closer, close enough to pick up his scent: sweat and soil . . .

And Patchouli?

She frowned as she took in the work-honed musculature of his arms, the dirt ground into his jeans . . .

And athletic shoes that probably cost more than her car?

What sort of farmer was this?

Without releasing her from his steel-trap gaze, he slowly pulled a red bandanna from his back pocket and wiped it across his brow and down his temple, where his rich brown hair feathered into gray.

As awkward as she felt, she met his gaze head-on. In fact, she couldn't have stopped staring if she'd tried. He had the most unusual eyes—a striking shade of violet-blue. But it wasn't their color that drew her. It was something deeper, deeper even than the caution and anger that infused them. Weariness perhaps? Whatever it was, she got the feeling those eyes had seen everything there was to see, even though their owner didn't appear to be much older than she was.

He pocketed the bandanna with slow care and set his fists on his hips again—a wall of a man determined to keep her corralled. "Would you mind telling me what you're doing here?"

The last thing Gina wanted was to stand here explaining herself. She had to look for her father. But she supposed this man deserved an explanation. "I think my father may have come in here. I'm looking for him."

"Your father is in this house?" He sounded doubtful.

"I believe so."

His eyes narrowed. "Why would your father be in this house?" His dark brows lowered, lending his eyes an intensity that, under different circumstances, Gina thought she might find attractive. Right now, she only felt intimidated.

"He..." She considered lying but couldn't come up with a single excuse that would hold water. She drew a deep breath and met those intense eyes squarely. "My father has arteriosclerosis—hardening of the arteries. Sometimes not enough oxygen gets to his brain and his behavior becomes slightly...well, inappropriate. He's often forgetful and sometimes he wanders. Most often he ends up here. This is where he was born and raised."

The man didn't wait for further explanation. Muttering a string of curses, he turned and bounded down the hall. "Stacy?" he called.

Curious and fairly alarmed herself, Gina followed.

CHAPTER THREE

"STACY?" SPENCER TOOK the stairs two at a time, driven by images of his daughter having to fend off an aggressive, maybe even violent, intruder. Not all old people with impaired brain functions were docile. For that matter, the woman downstairs might be lying. She and her "father" might have entered this house with less than lawful intentions, and that story about hardening of the arteries . . . well, con artists had come up with crazier notions.

"Stace, are you still up here?"

"Uh-huh."

The shakiness of his daughter's voice deepened Spencer's anxiety. Breathing the fire of paternal protectiveness, he leapt the top step, crossed the hall and in a flash reached her room.

He found her standing at the foot of her bed, as pale as the sunlight pouring through the windows. He followed her frightened gaze to the old man who'd somehow walked into the house undetected. The fellow had opened her closet and was staring at her clothes. Just standing there, staring. Spencer breathed a little easier. The old man seemed to be harmless enough. He'd deal with him later.

"Stace, are you all right?" Spencer stepped into the room.

She turned then, blinking as if she'd just realized he was there. For a moment he saw her wavering between relief and resentment.

"Yes, I'm fine." She lifted her chin. "No thanks to you."

Spencer sighed. Resentment had won out. It usually did these days.

"I was calling you out my window, but you had that stupid tiller going."

A knot of emotions—guilt and anger and sadness—tightened in his gut. He loosened it with a reminder not to take her bait. "We'll talk about that later, Stace."

"I won't hold my breath."

He counted to ten. With two intruders in the house, the last thing he needed was to get sidetracked. Besides, arguing would only be counterproductive. He was trying to move Stacy past this stage she was in. Whitman Prep wasn't likely to put up with her surliness too long.

With a start he realized the old man was now rifling through Stacy's clothes. He was obviously no burglar, but Spencer still chafed at the idea of his rooting around in there.

"Hey, what are you doing?" he called, and when the old man still didn't turn, Spencer started toward him.

"Wait, Dad," Stacy warned, momentarily overlooking her resentment. "I think there's something wrong with him." She lifted her right hand to her temple and made a circling motion with her index finger.

Just then the woman Spencer had caught prowling downstairs burst into the room. He heard a choked "Oh, thank God" as she rushed past. A moment later she had the old man wrapped in a warm embrace.

"Hi, Dad. It's me, Gina. What are you doing here?" Her voice was soft and soothing, murmurs imparted as affectionately as the small kisses she dropped on his gray head. "Who's that?" Stacy asked in an undertone. Her color was coming back, curiosity replacing the fright Spencer had seen in her eyes just a moment ago.

"She says she's his daughter."

"I *am* his daughter," the woman responded, her syllables clipped. With a little coaxing, she got her father to turn around. Stacy flinched. The old man's cheeks were wet with tears.

Unlike Stacy, Spencer studied the man with clinical dispassion, noting not the tears but the cataracts in those old brown eyes...and the red spot on his lower lip that ought to be biopsied...and the nicotine stains on his fingers that accounted for his wheeze. At a glance, he could easily identify half a dozen things wrong with the old guy. From the general disorientation he manifested, Spencer had no reason to doubt the woman's claim of arteriosclerosis, either.

He watched her with mounting curiosity. She continued to stand close by her father, murmuring, cajoling, rubbing his rounded back as she talked. All the while, a delicate blue vein throbbed at her temple, betraying her anxiety.

"There, that's better," she said when a weak smile tipped the old man's lips. "God, you're a handsome devil when you do that." His smile broke into a shy, wheezy chuckle.

Supporting him with an encircling arm, she guided him forward. She looked at Spencer and with calm dignity said, "I'm sorry we disturbed you. We'll be going now."

Spencer stepped aside, his entire demeanor telling her, *Fine, there's the door.* He was still too angry to say anything that might ease her discomfort. She and her father had trespassed. They'd violated his and Stacy's privacy.

Even in the city no one had ever done that. The old guy had terrified Stacy, too.

Suddenly the man balked, and the smile his daughter had coaxed vanished. "Margaret?" he said, turning and searching the room.

Spencer frowned. He could've sworn the woman had said her name was something else. Jeanne?

She gave her father's arm a gentle tug. "Come on, Dad. Let's go home."

The baffled look in the old man's eyes deepened. "But we are home, sweetheart." Yes, he was definitely disoriented. His words were slow and slurred, as well.

"Come on, Dad," the woman urged, pressing him forward, but he dug in his heels and refused to budge. "Dad, we've got to go." Still, he remained rooted, and her cheeks went from pink to red.

She didn't look like the sort of woman who blushed easily, Spencer thought. There was too much strength in her, a trait he'd picked up on within seconds of meeting her, a trait he found curious, because her big brown eyes and dark pixieish hair gave her a French gamine look he tended to associate with youth and vulnerability.

But she wasn't young; crow's-feet fanned from her eyes. She also seemed far from vulnerable. On her, those feathery wisps of short hair became as intentionally provocative as a little black dress with a slit up the side.

He noticed, too, that she wore a pleasant floral scent. And jewelry—long earrings, a silver belt and rings, lots of rings. He wasn't sure why he linked her scent and jewelry with strength. Those things had nothing whatsoever to do with strength. Maybe it was just that she seemed comfortable in her femininity; she knew who she was.

"Well," said this woman who was garnering far too much of his attention, "as long as we're parked here..." She stepped away from her father and extended her right hand. "I'm Gina Banning."

Spencer hesitated. He had no intention of becoming acquainted with anyone in Bingham. He'd chosen the farm primarily because of its peaceful isolation.

But he didn't know how *not* to take someone's hand when it was offered. So he took Gina's in his and gave it a shake.

He was surprised to find himself unusually aware of her grip: the firm pressure of her fingers, the mildly rough texture of her palm, the dry warmth, delicate bones, the warmth again, the warmth...

"And this is my father, Joe," she said, her hand still engulfed in Spencer's. She waited.

Oh, right. My turn. "Spencer Coburn," he said.

The Banning woman smiled cordially. If she held any grudge over the poor reception he'd given her downstairs, she certainly didn't show it.

Suddenly he remembered that his hands were dirty. He released her and said, "And this is my daughter, Stacy."

"Hi, Stacy. You're new to Bingham, right?"

"Yeah," Stacy drawled sullenly.

"How long have you been here?"

"Too long."

"A week," Spencer cut in. "Six days actually."

"Ah. And how do you like it so far?"

Spencer could see she was making an effort not to look below the neckline of Stacy's large black Metallica T-shirt. And why should she? There was plenty above the neckline to offend and keep her staring: the pierced eyebrow, the pierced nose, each violated body part adorned with several small hoops and studs. His insides broiled.

Just an hour ago he'd told Stacy to take those ridiculous things off.

He didn't mind her pierced ears quite as much. Wearing several earrings had become an accepted style. What did rile him, though, was that Stacy's earrings were on such blatant display. Her hair—her beautiful, honey brown, once waist-length hair—was growing out from a hideous buzz cut, and to control the uneven mess, she'd slicked it back with gel. He only hoped he could bring about a change in her looks before she set out for boarding school. He was afraid she'd be terribly embarrassed if he didn't.

Studying his daughter, Spencer was suddenly reminded of his most pressing reason for bringing her here to Bingham—Todd, the body-pierced punk who'd influenced her to change her appearance. While they'd still been living in Boston, Spencer had overheard her calling Todd late at night, begging him to come back to her.

With a start Spencer realized that Stacy and this woman, Gina, had been trading comments about Bingham for some time. He was amazed by his daughter's almost amiable tone. Where had that come from?

Apparently she'd complained about the lack of things to do.

"Yeah, Bingham's quiet, all right," Gina agreed with a fond smile. "But I was never bored growing up here, especially in the summer. There's a lake with a great little beach just up the road, and if you like to hike, the state forest is right there." She looked toward the window. "Literally. It abuts the farm."

Spencer frowned. His daughter wasn't exactly up for a summer of swimming and hiking.

"Then there's Hobbs Hollow Falls," Gina continued. "My friends and I used to spend whole days jumping off the bridge at Hobbs Hollow."

The last thing Stacy needed this summer was to go jumping off some damn bridge. Spencer was about to say as much too, when Gina added, "Though if I were you, I'd spend this particular summer just sitting on the bank and watching." Her smile was totally unselfconscious.

"Do you live nearby?" Stacy asked her.

"No, not really. My home's in Syracuse. My father lives nearby, though. In the village. I'm staying with him for the summer." Gina cast a smiling glance at the old man. "Well, we really should be going. Again, I apologize for intruding. I hope you weren't too upset."

Stacy let a shrug be her answer. "Is he gonna be all right?"

"Sure. We'll stop for some ice cream on the way home and he'll be happy as a clam at high tide."

The old man suddenly grew more alert. "Ice cream?"

"That's what I've been trying to tell you, Dad!"

"Mind if I ask you something?" Stacy fixed her gaze on the tips of her heavy black combat boots.

"Ask away."

"Who's Margaret? Your father seems really concerned about finding her. Is she missing or something?"

"No, nothing like that. It's..." The woman's smile faltered. "She was my mother. She passed away four years ago. Some days he really gets to missing her."

"Oh."

"Do you mind if I ask *you* something now?"

Stacy's defensiveness suddenly radiated like quills on a porcupine.

"Where did you get those little gold bumblebees?"

"Oh." Stacy touched the rim of her left ear. From the size of her eyes, Spencer guessed that was the last question she expected to be asked. "My... someone I knew gave them to me. I think he got them at a jewelry show. They're handmade."

"Yes. I can see. They're adorable." Gina smiled so brightly Spencer felt the heat all the way to the soles of his feet. "I'm a fool for jewelry. It's my biggest weakness."

Suddenly her father began to shuffle toward the door. "Hey, looks like we're finally moving." She took his arm. "Again, I apologize, but it was really nice meeting you. I hope we run into one another again sometime soon."

Spencer didn't return the pleasantry. He was too busy watching the old man.

"Ms. Banning? Has your father seen a doctor lately?"

She swung around at the doorway. Her brow lowered in a sudden frown. "Why do you ask?"

He noticed she hadn't answered his question. "He's dragging his left leg. From the way his left arm is hanging, I'd say that entire side is weak."

"He's eighty-three years old, Mr. Coburn." She smiled—defensively, Spencer thought. "If you were eighty-three I think you'd be drooping a little, too."

He hadn't made a good start with her, and what he was about to say might only aggravate the situation. Still, he had to say it. "Maybe. Especially if I'd had a stroke."

Her dark eyes sparked. "My father hasn't had a stroke."

Yes, definitely defensive.

"How do you know?"

"How do *you* know?" she fired back.

Spencer felt a pressure building inside. Stacy was looking at him expectantly. But he let it go and, with a shrug, said, "It was just a thought."

Gina Banning stared at him, her brow knit, her expression speculative. At last she glanced away and quietly said, "Thanks for being concerned."

Spencer wasn't sure where the tension had come from, but he was relieved it was gone. "Come on," he said, "I'll help you out to your car."

The old man was slower than molasses in January. Physical limitation wasn't his only problem. He continued to think he belonged here, that this was still his home. He kept stopping on the stairs, turning, trying to go back up, look for Margaret.

When they finally reached the driveway, Gina looked wrung out. "Thanks. I appreciate your help."

Spencer suddenly noticed there were two cars parked out front. One was half-buried in shrubbery.

"Sorry 'bout that." Gina wrinkled her short nose in an expression she probably thought was cute. It was, but that wouldn't get her off the hook.

"You mean, your father *drove* here?"

"Afraid so."

Spencer stared at her with open incredulity. "He's allowed to drive?"

"Well, no." She had an interesting jawline, delicately boned yet strong of shape. "He just sort of snuck by me."

"You really ought to watch him more carefully."

"I know." Her mouth tightened, creating dimples Spencer hadn't noticed before.

"Driving in his condition, he could get into an accident. He could hurt himself. He could hurt others."

"I *know*. Look, I've already apologized, and I really am sorry, but right now I have a more pressing problem on my hands. Namely, I have two cars here and can't very well drive both." Abruptly she sprang forward. "Dad, this way."

Joe had drifted up the driveway, and in his vague, wobbly gait, was headed for the orchard. Spencer heard him mumbling something about...ham? Ham being done? He closed his eyes, pinched the bridge of his nose and thought, *I don't need this.*

Gina caught up with her father and escorted him back. Trying to bank his exasperation, Spencer said, "Do you mind if I ask what sort of care your father is getting?"

"Well..." Outdoors, her eyes became a warm chocolate brown. They also shifted restlessly.

"He *is* getting professional care, isn't he?"

"Right now, no. As I said, I'm staying with him for the summer."

"And after that?"

She shrugged dismissively and opened her car door. "I'm not sure. I'm still investigating my options. Come on, Dad. In you go." She obviously preferred to drop the subject.

Spencer couldn't blame her. He'd been boxing with everything she said. "I didn't mean to lecture. If I offended you..."

She shook her head. "It's okay. Actually, I owe you an apology, too. For snapping at you when you suggested he'd had a stroke. My mother always said that was my worst habit, shooting from the lip."

Spencer wanted to smile. "It's understandable. Taking care of an aging parent can be a strain."

She buckled Joe into the passenger seat, then shrugged and said, "He's my father."

Spencer waited, but apparently that was all she had to say on the matter. She handed Joe a dog-eared seed catalog, rolled down the window, pressed the lock and shut the door.

"You were right. My father did have a stroke. I just hate admitting it." She began to walk toward her father's body-rotted Chevy.

Spencer followed her. "When?"

"Sometime in January. Nothing that incapacitated him. I just noticed a new difficulty in his speech and a slight loss of strength on his left side. His doctor called it a ministroke. Said he'd probably had them before." They paused by the old car.

In spite of himself, Spencer was curious. "Your father's been on his own since January?"

"Well, of course not. He's had help," she said defensively. "He's had help for almost a year—Meals on Wheels, a home health aide, a retired woman who did his laundry. Neighbors have been checking on him for me, too. Before that he was able to get by with just my help on weekends. But then—"

"You traveled from Syracuse, New York, to Bingham, Massachusetts, on weekends?"

"Yes. It's only a three-hour drive. I'd leave on Friday evening and return Sunday afternoon. Unfortunately my father's come to the point where he needs help full-time. His problem is further complicated by the fact that his landlord would like him to move out. He's afraid of the liability."

"So you've come home to work all this out?"

"Yes."

Spencer shoved his hands in his pockets and stared at the branches draped over the hood of the Chevy. He didn't understand how he'd gotten so deep in conversation with this woman. He had no desire to get to know her or her problems. Yet the next words out of his mouth were, "Is your father on any sort of medication?"

"Oh, sure. For his blood pressure."

"Anything else?"

"I try to slip him an aspirin a day. I've also cut salt and caffeine from his diet."

"Cigarettes?"

She shook her head. "I know his doctor wants him to quit, and I've restricted his daily consumption, but I don't have the heart to take his cigarettes away entirely. In my opinion, making him quit now isn't going to do much for his health, anyway. Addicted as he is, it would only add unnecessary anguish, right?"

Spencer burned to argue the point, but reminded himself it wasn't his business. "Did his doctor hospitalize him, have any tests done to see what was wrong?"

"No. He wanted to, but I refused. My father hates hospitals, hates doctors, and quite frankly, I don't see the point. What would they prove with their tests? That his arteries are clogged?" She snorted. "No kidding."

"Maybe they were hoping to operate."

"They were. But for heaven's sake, he's eighty-three. All his systems are shot. The anesthesia alone would probably kill him." She shook her head. "Honestly, sometimes doctors can be so dumb it scares you, doesn't it?"

Spencer opened his mouth, then abruptly shut it. Better just to end the conversation there. "Well, best of luck to you."

She looked suddenly confused.

"In your search for a facility for him," Spencer clarified.

"A facility?"

Why did he feel he'd stepped in something he should've avoided?

"You mean a nursing home?"

He shrugged uncertainly. "Well, nursing homes do provide a good solution for someone with your father's needs. I just assumed that was one of the options you were investigating. If it is, I have a directory you could—"

She shot him a glance that cut him off in midsentence. "No. I won't put my father in one of those places."

"There are some excellent facilities—"

"I'm sure. But my father would be miserable, and if he's miserable, the best facility in the world would be no better than a jail."

"Can't argue with that," Spencer said, although he wanted to.

"Besides, I promised him I'd never put him in one."

"What are you going to do, then?"

She sighed and most of her prickliness fell away. "Seems there's only one thing I *can* do. Take him back to Syracuse and have him live with me." She sighed again.

"It isn't easy, is it?" Spencer commiserated.

"No, it isn't." With a smile that was too brief, she pushed away from the Chevy and opened the door. "I'll just move my father's car out of the way for now and come back for it later—this evening, tomorrow the latest. Are you okay with that?"

Spencer climbed onto the porch steps, just in case she drove like her father. "Sure."

He considered offering to drive the car himself. That way he'd get it off the property immediately. But if he drove her father's car to wherever they lived, Gina would have to drive him back. That was a lot of riding around together and talking and getting further acquainted.

Maybe that was why he added, "Come by anytime. Just drive in, feel free to go about your business. I might not be here, or I might be out back." *Just understand I don't intend to come out and talk to you again.*

"Thanks." If she caught his implication, she wasn't offended.

She eased the old car out of the bridal wreath, and when she went past, Spencer stepped off the stairs and followed her.

She drove around the corner of the house where the driveway lost its definition and became a wide dirt yard, a sort of courtyard bounded by the house, the barn attached to the house and a two-car garage.

She parked near the colonial-blue door of the barn, but oddly, Spencer noticed, she didn't get out right away. She just sat there, draped over the steering wheel, staring at the barn. What was she looking at? What did she see? An old blue door adorned with a grapevine wreath? Windows with closed blinds? An empty bird feeder below the bathroom window?

His approaching footsteps seemed to finally get her to stir. She opened the door and, sliding out, asked, "Will the car be in anyone's way here?"

Before Spencer could answer, Stacy piped up with, "No, nobody's living there." He hadn't realized she'd followed them outside.

Gina's gaze zoomed back to the barn. "There?"

"Yeah." Stacy's heavy boots scuffed the hard-packed dirt. "The apartment."

"Ah!" Gina exclaimed as if puzzle pieces had just fallen into place. "An apartment!"

Stacy came forward, hands slung casually into the pockets of her denim maternity shorts, rucking up the offensive black T-shirt. "You didn't know?"

"No. It was just a lowly barn when I lived here." Moving to close the car door, Gina suddenly went still. The next moment she pressed her face into her hands. Spencer's pulse picked up. Something was wrong.

Before he could ask, she lowered her hands and he saw she was laughing. "You're a doctor?" she exclaimed.

The doors of the garage were open, and he realized she'd noticed the small "MD" designation in the corner of the license plate on his car.

"Why didn't you say something? Why did you let me run off at the mouth like that?"

He lifted his shoulders in a helpless shrug.

"Now I'm really embarrassed."

Just then the old man, left sitting in her car, called out the window for her to hurry.

"Coming, Dad." Her incredulous eyes swept over Spencer one more time. "Well, I'd better go. Catch up with you later."

Spencer glanced at his daughter and was surprised to see she was smiling. But then, so was he.

CHAPTER FOUR

GINA AWOKE the next morning to a rustle of small sounds coming from her father's kitchen. Her heart sank. The thin gray light that seeped around the edges of the window shades told her it wasn't much past dawn.

She leaned up on one elbow. "Dad?"

Her father, fully dressed in a plaid flannel shirt and green work pants, stood at the sink pouring coffee from a large glass measuring cup into a red thermos bottle. His grip wobbled, sending much of the coffee spilling over the sides. On his head sat a blue corduroy cap with a quilted lining, earflaps down and chin strap snapped.

Gina fell back onto her warm pillow, chuckling in spite of the ungodly hour. She was so tired there was nothing to do *but* laugh.

Yesterday afternoon, after returning from the farm, her father had slept for three full hours, an unusually long and peaceful nap, which had allowed her to put away the groceries, wash lunch dishes and fold some laundry.

She should've napped too. Joe had stayed awake until nearly two in the morning, and she didn't dare go to sleep while he was awake. Too often when he made instant coffee he neglected to turn off the gas burner under the kettle. Too often when he smoked he forgot where he'd laid his cigarette.

Yawning, she sat up. "Dad, what are you doing?"

"Oh." He turned stiffly. "I didn't mean to wake you, sweetheart." Using his left arm, he held the thermos to his chest while he screwed the cap on with his stronger right hand.

"What are you doing?" she asked again.

"Today? Oh, I thought I'd try and put in the peppers."

Her eyes widened. "Peppers?"

"Yup. Ground's finally warmed up enough and the moon's right."

Gina wiggled her feet into her slippers and reached for her robe. "Dad, you don't have to plant any peppers today." She crossed the room and took hold of the thermos before it dropped.

"Well, sure I do. John Macomber planted his two weeks ago."

Quite a feat, Gina thought, since John Macomber had been dead for more than a decade.

Noticing an unusual lumpiness to her father's shirt, she undid the top two buttons and discovered he was still wearing his pajamas. "Have you had breakfast yet, Dad?"

"Why, naturally. Margaret made me my oatmeal hours ago."

She sighed, removing the corduroy hat from his head. "How about having a bite with me, anyway?"

Joe fixed a vague, protracted look toward the door.

"A quick bite. Keep me company. Applesauce muffins?"

"Well, I suppose it won't do no harm."

She led him to the table and helped him sit, then set about warming yesterday's muffins in the microwave. Meanwhile, Joe launched into a slow, rambling tale about a blizzard that hit one April. Gina smiled and nodded appropriately, but her mind was elsewhere. She'd heard the story before, dozens of times. Just yesterday, in fact.

Besides, she had something more pressing to think about. Today she had to retrieve her father's car from the farm, and she wasn't sure how she was going to get there.

She took the warm muffins out of the oven, set them on the table and sat down opposite her father.

She could probably call her old friend, Barbara. Barbara kept telling her to call any time she needed help. But Barbara had a home, a husband and five kids to tend to. Gina hated disturbing her for so trivial a matter.

What she'd probably do was just call a cab. *The* cab. Bingham only had the one. Sure, the cab was the simplest way to get to the farm.

Her spirits lifted at the thought. Being there yesterday had brought back torrents of warm memories. The next thought that popped into her mind was that it would be nice seeing the new people who lived there again, Spencer Coburn and his daughter, Stacy.

Doctor Spencer Coburn. Gina was still choking on that surprising fact. Worn denim jeans and an economy car with a rusted tailgate didn't exactly fit her notion of doctor.

Neither did having a teenaged daughter who was pregnant. Things that unpleasant just didn't happen in doctors' lives. They were different from ordinary people, at least according to the stereotype. They were too smart, too meticulous.

Apparently Spencer Coburn wasn't your stereotypical doctor.

But what he was exactly, Gina didn't know. Stacy had mentioned they came from Boston and were just staying for the summer. That was the only solid nugget of information she had. Squishy intimations, however, she had a bucket of.

Like, he was probably divorced—badly so. He wore his wariness like a suit of armor.

A pity, too. He was a good-looking man. He had a wonderful face, excellent bone structure, and a mouth with a sensuous bottom lip that remained full, almost pouty, even when he was angry. Then there were those intense blue eyes. And that solid build. And those attractive feathers of gray in his hair.

But those were stupid reasons for thinking a man would make a good mate. If anyone should know, it was Gina.

Not that she thought Spencer Coburn would make a bad mate. She just didn't think looks could decide the issue. And, anyway, she really didn't care. While it might be nice to get to know a man like Spencer Coburn, she simply didn't have the time. Too many other obligations to meet this summer.

She glanced at her father—he was still rambling on about that April blizzard—and tamped down a lump of unexpected resentment. It wasn't his fault. It wasn't. She'd had obligations long before his health began to fail.

But that only reminded her of the years she'd spent taking care of her mother.

Good Lord, grow up, she reprimanded herself. So what if she'd spent almost every weekend for the past five years on the road between Syracuse and Bingham? She still had a full life, didn't she? Good friends? A valuable and rewarding career? What did she have to complain about? The fact that she wasn't married? Didn't have children? Was looking down the barrel of her fortieth birthday? Forty wasn't old. Many fine marriages were made in midlife. Lots of children were born then, too.

So why couldn't she shake this nagging sense of time racing, this feeling that the best years for raising kids and enjoying marital relations were already gone?

Maybe it had something to do with meeting Stacy yesterday, pregnant so young—although Gina was sure she hadn't resented Stacy. She'd only felt bad for her.

Being a high-school teacher, Gina was no stranger to teenage pregnancy. Still, it always shook her when she came upon a new case. And Stacy especially shook her. Five foot nothing and all contradictions.

The girl was obviously into black grunge and body piercing. Yet the cute-as-a-button sweetness of her face totally undercut whatever offensiveness she was trying to evoke.

Gina had noticed, too, that Stacy had tried to act too cool for Bingham. And maybe she was. But Gina had also seen a wealth of loneliness under that veneer of disdain.

And her eyes. Such sad, serious eyes. Eyes so like her father's. She seemed to be such an ordinary teenager, too—posters of Keanu Reeves and Brad Pitt on her walls, the smell of Noxema in the air. Replace the current stars with the Beatles, Gina thought, and it could've been her room twenty-five years ago. It *had* been her room twenty-five years ago.

Gina couldn't quite figure out Spencer's attitude toward his daughter. He'd seemed concerned enough, the way he'd raced up the stairs to save Stacy from whatever harm he thought Joe might be inflicting on her. But Gina had felt a lot of tension there, too.

Well, he couldn't be pleased by his daughter's pregnancy. Probably didn't think much of her appearance, either.

Joe's coffee mug hit the table, sloshing some of its contents. Gina came out of her reverie with a start. Her father was staring at the spill with a look of little-boy guilt.

"That's okay, Dad. Don't worry." She mopped up the spill with a paper napkin, gave him a reassuring smile and concentrated on eating something herself. It might be a long morning.

But she didn't have much of an appetite. It was too early.

And she was suddenly too troubled to eat.

Her father's mind had been deteriorating for a couple of years. There were times, like today, when his long, rambling narratives contained an internal logic that almost made her forget he'd lost touch with reality. Other days his ramblings contained nothing but disjointed fragments, flotsam and jetsam of life experiences floating around in his damaged brain. She hated the term "senile dementia," but on those days the term applied only too well.

Suddenly Gina was choking back tears. Her father's condition, both physical and mental, was worse than she'd imagined before moving in with him. In fact, she had a strong intimation he wasn't going to live to see another summer. When she took him away from Bingham, he wouldn't be coming back.

The idea of moving him bothered her. Her place would be strange to him and was sure to add to his confusion. He might feel lonely and isolated, too, knowing no one there but her. On top of that, it was a condo. He was unhappy with apartment living in a two-story house, never mind on the sixth floor of a sixty-unit building. But worst of all, he was going to miss Bingham. It was all he'd ever known of the world.

But what choice did she have? She had to move him; she'd promised to take care of him herself during his last days. Furthermore, she had to move him soon. The landlord was hoping to have this apartment rented out to new tenants by month's end.

The clock in the living room began to chime. Five a.m.

"Oh." Joe became agitated. "Look at the time."

Yes, look, Gina thought with a sinking heart. Was he up for the day? She needed more sleep. Three hours wasn't going to do it.

"I should've been out in the field hours ago." He struggled to his feet.

Gina sighed. "Dad, listen. Sit down. Sit."

He frowned. "What is it, sweetheart?"

"Dad, you don't have to go plant peppers today. You don't farm the land anymore, remember? You haven't for years."

His agitated expression froze, then slowly began to cloud with confusion.

"You live in an apartment on Elm Street now. Second floor of the Toomeys' house."

"That's crazy, Gina. What are you saying?" he asked, but she could tell that wisps of understanding were blowing across his thoughts.

"Dad, remember yesterday? We went to the farm and there were other people living there?"

"Other people?"

"Yes. A man. A teenage girl."

"I don't remember."

No, he wouldn't. His short-term memory was gone. "Just take my word for it, Dad. The farm isn't ours anymore. But hey, you ought to be relieved. No more back-breaking work, right? Just time to read and take walks and sleep late."

"Gina, what...? I don't..." He stared at her, fear in his eyes, and she realized he did understand something. He understood that he didn't understand.

Joe got up from the table and hobbled to the window. He said nothing, just stood there, looking down on the street as if he was wondering what had become of his world.

Gina swiped at her eyes. Damn, she couldn't take him away just yet. And maybe she didn't have to. Ever since yesterday, the apartment at the farm had been on her mind. If she could rent that apartment, move Joe there until September, that would be perfect. He'd regressed to a stage where he was always at the farm in his mind. She could think of no greater pleasure than to actually make living there a reality, not just a fading memory.

Resolving to check into the possibility as soon as the local real-estate office opened that morning, Gina rose from the table, came up behind her father and lightly laid her arm across his shoulders. "Sun's coming up."

He said nothing.

"Looks like it's gonna be a nice day."

Still nothing.

Gina blinked away the stinging in her eyes and said, "I love you, Dad," so softly she didn't think he heard.

Another few moments of silence passed. She was already pulling back, her thoughts on the long day ahead, when he whispered, "I love you too, sweetheart."

SPENCER FELT increasingly restless. He sat on the living-room couch and tried to read. The book was supposed to be a page turner, but after twenty minutes he chucked it aside.

He paced the length of the room, from the oak-manteled fireplace to the two long front windows. He pushed back the lace curtain at one of those windows and leaned on the sill, staring at the sturdy ash rocker on the porch. Should he read outside?

With a slight shake of his head, he straightened. No, the book would be no better on the porch. Besides, sitting on the porch might look as if he was waiting for Gina Banning to show up, which certainly he wasn't.

He crossed to the old upright piano and ran the back of his thumb along the keys. He'd always enjoyed playing piano—although, to be honest, he couldn't remember the last time he'd sat down at one. He wouldn't do it now, either. His playing left a lot to be desired, and the tutor was still upstairs with Stacy.

He walked through the archway connecting the living room to the dining room, circled the mahogany table twice, then exited by the door to the kitchen where he looked in the refrigerator and poked at some Jell-O before exiting by the door to the hall. A few steps down the hall he opened the cellar door and listened. Halleluja! The dryer had stopped.

Upstairs, putting away his just-folded clothes, Spencer wondered what he normally did to relax. He came up with nothing. During the past few years he'd pretty much let his hobbies slide. Life had come to revolve around only two elements, his work and Stacy. No wonder he'd burned out.

Even here—what had he brought with him? He glanced around the bedroom. Adoption materials. Brochures from Whitman Prep. A stack of wholesome young-adult novels he hoped to interest Stacy in.

Opening the closet to hang up a shirt, he noticed his medicine bag resting on the floor. He squatted and ran his fingertips over the smooth black leather—a gift from his father when he'd graduated from med school. Doug had suggested he not bring anything medical with him to the farm, but he hadn't been able to leave his bag behind. Even though all inclination to use it had deserted him, it was too much a part of him.

With a sigh, he got to his feet and shut the closet door. He put away the rest of his clothes, then, restless beyond all comprehension, he brought the hall phone into the room and gave Doug a call.

"What's the problem, Spence?"

"Me. I'm not cut out to take it easy for an entire summer."

Doug laughed. "Give yourself a few more days. You're just going through work withdrawal."

"Maybe. But I doubt it. There's got to be something I can do around here, mowing the grass, stuff like that."

"You want to mow the grass?"

"Yeah."

"We already have somebody who mows the grass."

"I know. He was here two days ago. So fire him. I'll do it for nothing."

By then, Doug must've figured out he was serious. "Well, okay, if you really want to."

"Thanks. Now, how about the toilet in the upstairs bathroom?"

"What about it?"

"The flush mechanism is shot. Can I fix it?"

"If it makes you happy. Just keep the receipts from anything you buy and give them to the realtor. He'll reimburse you."

Spencer's shoulders loosened a bit. "If you can think of anything else . . ."

"I'll call my folks and get back to you. How's it going otherwise?"

Spencer hesitated. He wished he could report that everything was great, that he was eager to get back to the clinic and that Stacy had returned to being her old sweet self. But he couldn't. Things seemed discouragingly the same. Just that morning, in fact, he and Stacy had had another run-in.

He'd been about to tap on her door, wanting to ask if she had any laundry that needed doing, when he'd heard her inside talking on the phone.

"Dammit, Stacy!" He'd burst into the room, thinking she was crawling to Todd again. It had been Maureen on the other end of the line, calling to tell Stacy she was getting married in August.

Stacy had been outraged by his assumption she'd been up to no good. But she'd been even more upset about her mother's news, although it couldn't have been a surprise. Spencer hoped she wasn't still clinging to the idea that he and Maureen might reconcile someday.

He decided Doug didn't need to hear it, though. "Things've been fine. I found a tiller in one of the barns. I hope nobody minds, but I've been using it. I noticed there used to be a kitchen garden out behind the house. The fencing is gone, but the posts are still standing."

"You're planting a garden?"

Spencer began to regret his admission. He knew Stacy thought he was crazy, and now Doug would, too. Maybe he was.

He grunted, a reply Doug could interpret any way he wished. Truth was, Spencer had no intention of planting anything. All he was interested in was working the dirt. He was drawn by the simplicity of it, the mindlessness of it. It defused his anger and it tired him out. He couldn't exactly claim to be sleeping well yet. He still awoke two or three times a night. But he was sleeping better.

"I envy you," Doug said. "I wish I was there. I bet the dogwoods are in full bloom."

Dogwoods? Spencer frowned. What dogwoods? He peered out the side window and scanned the farm and the green hills beyond. On an objective level, he knew the land around him was breathtaking. Subjectively, though, he still derived no joy from it. The blue sky, the myriad greens, the sunlight playing off the hills—those things were just there, outside himself.

He consoled himself with the thought that he'd only been here a week. He'd break out of this malaise eventually. He would. He had to. There would be no going back to his practice unless he did.

"Hey, Spence, I'd like to talk longer, but patients are backing up here."

"No problem. Take care, Doug."

Spencer hung up the phone. What now? Fix the toilet? He'd have to drive to the hardware store first.

So, do it, he told himself.

I will, he replied. *Tomorrow.*

He walked to the front window and looked toward the road. It was senseless to stay inside trying to guess what time Gina Banning intended to come get her father's car. She hadn't come yesterday and she might not come today.

He gave his clean shirt and jeans a rueful glance, then put himself out of his misery and went outside to the garden.

Spencer yanked the tiller's starter cord, and the engine turned over. He adjusted the throttle, took hold of the hand grips and squeezed the attached levers. The tines began to rotate, the powerful machine pulling him forward, bouncing and bucking and churning the dirt.

The soil was a pleasure to turn. A few days ago he'd thought the tiller might break, the soil had been so hard and weed-choked. Now it turned like butter.

He arrived at the edge of the garden, easing up on the levers. As he did, a flash of chrome on the road caught his attention. A car was slowing down. Before he had a chance to check his reaction, a small bright zing of electricity seemed to shoot through him.

He'd told himself he wouldn't go out to greet her. He preferred to remain a nonentity in this town, and he certainly didn't want to get to know a woman whose father had so many medical needs. But even while he was reminding himself, he shut down the tiller, pulled off his work gloves and fit them over the hand grips.

Spencer rounded the barn just as Gina was helping her father out of a black sedan. He paused by the rosebush that grew beside the blue door, watching her.

Today she was wearing a peach-colored T-shirt dress that showed a lot of leg. He approved the style. She had nice legs, shapely and well-toned. His gaze moved upward, following the clingy fabric over the curve of her hips, to her breasts, approving all the way. He moved on to her face, with its large, expressive eyes and impertinent chin. It wasn't a drop-dead gorgeous face, but it was certainly one a man could linger over and explore.

The late-morning sun was just coming over the house and spilling fire into her dark, dark hair. That urchin's cap of layered wisps still struck him as a most unlikely style for the provocative effect it created. But then, she was a most unlikely woman to be giving off such an effect. Hovering over her father, she was familial warmth personified. Spencer whistled softly through his teeth. Why, he wasn't certain.

He plucked a rose off the bush, held it to his nose and took a sniff of the mild fragrance. Only then did he become aware of the person who'd driven Gina. He tossed the rose aside and frowned.

What the hell was the real-estate agent doing here?

CHAPTER FIVE

GINA GRIPPED her father's ankles and lifted his legs out of the car. "Look where we are, Dad."

Joe gazed at the white frame house for one blank moment before his gaunt face brightened. Gina smiled, pleased beyond measure.

There were only two realtors in town, and she'd called them both as soon as they were open. The second office carried the listing, and Bob Johnson was the agent.

She remembered Bob sketchily. A pleasant guy, who'd been a couple of years behind her in school. When she'd called and explained her business, he'd seemed genuinely pleased and eager to help. And, of course, he wouldn't mind driving, he'd said.

The only discouraging note was that he'd said Spencer Coburn had voiced the desire to keep the barn unoccupied. They could talk to him, though, Bob told her, see if they could change his mind.

"Say, Dr. Coburn." Bob walked toward Spencer, hand outstretched. Ridiculously, *Gina's* palms began to perspire. Concentrating to keep her expression set, she lifted her eyes. But mental preparation did little good. When her gaze met Spencer Coburn's, she felt as if she'd collided with a comet. Since yesterday she'd been telling herself he was just a good-looking man. She'd been wrong. As her students would say, he was awesome.

At the moment, though, Spencer Coburn didn't look too happy. "What's up?" he asked without preamble. There was no question what he meant, no question he wanted a direct answer.

Bob chuckled. "Gina called me this morning and told me about what happened yesterday, Joe coming to visit you and all." He chuckled again, and Gina realized the poor man was nervous. "That must've been quite an experience, not knowing who he was."

Spencer hooked his hands on his hips and frowned. Gina understood. She was rather a fan of directness herself.

"I'm here for two reasons, Dr. Coburn," she said, stepping in. "First, as you already know, I've come to get my father's car. And second, I'd like to look at the apartment. I'm thinking of renting it for me and my father from now till the end of August."

Spencer's eyes flicked over her. He didn't respond right away, and in the interim she thought she sensed a push-pull strain in his attitude.

She decided she must've been wrong, though, because his answer was quite unequivocal. "Sorry. The apartment isn't available."

She nodded agreeably. "Bob told me you'd prefer not to have any other people here." Actually, she'd had serious second thoughts about living here herself, next door to a physician. He was sure to criticize her for the way she was caring for her father—on her own, with minimal professional input. "I just thought you might've changed your mind."

"I haven't." He turned his gaze on the realtor. "The day I signed my agreement, I told you I'd be willing to pay the rent on the apartment if anyone ever came along who wanted it, and you said fine.'' Spencer's look sharpened. ''My word still holds. Does yours?''

Bob almost chuckled again but changed his response to a cough. ''It seems a terrible waste of money.''

''I'll be the judge of that.'' As Spencer spoke, Gina noticed Stacy at a downstairs window, eavesdropping. She was so pale, Gina wondered if she ever went outside.

But now wasn't the time to get sidetracked. This issue was too important. Chances were Joe wouldn't be with her next summer, so there was only this summer, these two precious months, to make a dream a reality.

''Please, Dr. Coburn. I'm sure we'd be good neighbors. My father and I are quiet, and it would mean so much to him, more than you can possibly imagine. Won't you please reconsider?''

Joe stood at her side, fumbling in his pants pockets, coming out with lint and bits of silver foil, studying them the way a toddler studies minutiae.

''I'm sorry.'' Spencer folded his arms. ''I have my daughter to consider.''

''Your daughter? What exactly is your concern?''

''Isn't it obvious?''

''No. Seriously, I don't follow.''

''In her condition she shouldn't have to be exposed to someone like . . .'' His gaze flicked toward Joe.

Gina's blood began to simmer. Someone like? What was he implying—that her father was a freak?

She wouldn't argue, though. She was used to her father and she loved him. But a stranger might very well be disturbed by him.

To give herself a moment to rethink her approach, she walked Joe over to a garden bench under one of the huge maples that rimmed the front lawn and waited until he'd lit a cigarette and was contentedly puffing. She wanted him at a distance from the discussion, anyway, just in case bits of what they were saying penetrated his confusion.

Returning to the conversation, she said, "If you're concerned about my father wandering into your house again, let me assure you it won't happen."

"You can't promise that. And even if you could, he'd still be here, sitting outside, walking around the yard."

"Well, yes, of course. But—"

"Sorry. I don't want my daughter living in such an upsetting environment."

Again Gina reached for patience. "I hope I don't sound preachy, but the only thing that makes a situation upsetting is ignorance. Did you explain to her what's wrong with him?"

"She can see what's wrong, Ms. Banning."

From a short distance away, Stacy said, "That's not necessarily true."

Gina swiveled. The teenager was walking toward them, clad in black again, her gait stiff, her mouth tight. "What *is* wrong with him, Ms. Banning?"

Teacher that she was, Gina didn't hesitate. "Clogged arteries, Stacy. My father's blood flow is quite constricted, and not enough oxygen gets to his—"

"Leave my daughter out of this," Spencer interrupted.

"Excuse me?" Gina was thoroughly taken aback. "I was merely trying to explain there's a physical reason for his behavior. It's nothing to be afraid of." She found it absurd that she was explaining this to a physician, a person who should be a fan of reason, a proponent of demystifying what was frightening.

A light seemed to go on behind Stacy's eyes. "Oh, I get it." She glanced at Joe with new interest. "I studied that in biology this—"

"Stacy!" Spencer snapped.

Gina had tried to be patient, but if there was one thing she couldn't abide, it was stifling a young person's voice. "Why don't you let her speak for herself? Since she's the reason you object to my father living here, I think she has a right to add her two cents."

Stacy's eyes widened. A nervous grin twitched over her lips. Had no one ever spoken up to her father before? Or was she just unaccustomed to adults treating her like an individual?

"Is it true, Stacy? *Will* my father make you uncomfortable?"

Before the teenager could answer, Spencer interrupted again. "It doesn't matter what she says. The argument isn't open to debate." His gaze narrowed on the realtor. "Right?"

Bob pulled on his earlobe. "Well, I'm not so sure. Nothing you said to me was put in writing."

Gina watched Spencer's face darken with anger. It was a daunting sight.

"You're denying we had an agreement, then?"

"Well, no. I just don't think I have the right to refuse the apartment to Gina and then give it to you. If you'd been paying rent on it right along, that would be one thing. But to suddenly jump in with the sole purpose of freezing her out..." He shook his head. "That doesn't seem ethical to me."

Spencer gave an ironic laugh. "Ethical? You wouldn't know ethical if it bit you in the crotch."

Stacy's eyes popped to saucer size. Her face turned red with the effort to hold back a laugh. Gina was fairly stunned herself. Pleasantly so.

Spencer thrust his hand through his hair. "Oh, Stace. I forgot you were here. I'm sorry, baby."

Stacy shrugged. "Hey, I've heard worse. I've *said* worse."

Spencer sighed, still contrite. "How about leaving this discussion to us, Stace." He indicated Gina, the realtor and himself. "I'd feel better if you did. It isn't the sort of thing you should be involved in, anyway."

Stacy's smile vanished. Glancing pointedly at Gina, she muttered, "You wouldn't want to take a vote on that, would you?"

Gina suffered a pang of guilt. She hadn't meant to come between Spencer and his daughter.

Before she could find a way to redress the situation, though, Stacy sauntered off—not toward the house, but to the bench where Joe was nodding off in the shade. Gina watched, surprised, as the young girl gently removed the cigarette from his slack-fingered hand and crushed it under her boot.

So much for her being upset by Joe's presence, she thought. She cast Spencer a look that said as much, too.

But he didn't notice. He was too busy staring at his daughter, his eyes dark with the pain of betrayal.

AFTER SNUFFING OUT the cigarette, Stacy cast a glance at the three adults, who'd gone amazingly quiet. All three were staring at her. Her father was staring the hardest. She'd known he would be. Heck, she'd just pulled the rug out from under his feet.

Served him right, she thought, lifting her chin. Where did he get off telling people what she thought and felt?

He didn't know what she thought or felt. He didn't know anything about her.

With a fluttering of both hands and an insolently bright smile, she said, "Go on, continue. I'll just sit here and keep my old friend Joe company. Go on."

Slowly, the tongue-tied adults resumed their conversation. With careful nonchalance, Stacy sat back and linked her fingers under her protruding belly.

Joe began to snore. She shuddered.

Okay, so maybe sitting beside this old guy *did* give her the creeps, but seeing that kicked-in-the-ego look on her father's face had been worth it. It wasn't often she got such a rise out of him.

Joe began to slump toward her. She held her breath, didn't move. He slumped a little closer and, oh, ick, he was leaning right against her. She refused to show a reaction, though, because her father was still occasionally glancing her way. Instead, she plastered on a smile, concentrated on what he and the others were saying and tried not to think about that bony shoulder pressing into her arm.

"All right," her father said to the realtor. "I'll concede that my daughter *might* be able to handle having Joe Banning as a neighbor. But my point remains, we had an agreement. We didn't sign any documents, but we definitely understood one another."

Stacy watched the real-estate guy purse his lips to make himself look thoughtful. She was pulling for him. It would be nice to have somebody else living here this summer. And Ms. Banning seemed okay. Sure, she was old, but she didn't seem phony like most grown-ups, and she was gorgeous. What Stacy especially liked about her, though, was the way she looked after her father. It was obvious she was crazy about him, no matter how old and pathetic he was.

The realtor unpursed his lips. "I understand where you're coming from, Dr. Coburn. It's just that after I had a chance to think about it, I realized it was an arrangement I couldn't, in all conscience, live with."

"But you can live with going back on your word?"

Stacy watched the realtor's Adam's apple bob several times. What a wuss!

In his sleep, Joe gave a snort as if in agreement. Stacy fought back a laugh. She'd almost forgotten about the old guy resting against her. Maybe being around him wasn't as creepy as she'd thought.

Gina must've sensed the realtor's insecurity, because she came to his rescue with, "I think we ought to present the problem to the owners of the property."

"Do you really believe they'll care?" Spencer asked. "As long as they receive their rent, do you think it matters who it comes from?"

"As a matter of fact, yes," Gina said.

Definitely no wuss.

"Any place is better off with people living in it, keeping it up. I think they'll appreciate that fact."

"I don't buy it."

Gina's eyes narrowed. "What's really bothering you, Dr. Coburn? I can't help thinking there's something else, something we can surely work out if you'll just tell me."

Amazing. That was just what Stacy had been thinking.

Spencer scrubbed at his head. "Is it so hard for you to understand I like living in a one-family house? I like the privacy. I like not hearing other people's conversations. I like the freedom to have my morning coffee outside in my bathrobe if I choose. I took this house precisely because it gave me that privacy, and if you move in . . ." He paused and Stacy held her breath. "If you move in, I just might have to move out." He looked at the realtor, calling his bluff.

The realtor just shrugged. Stacy couldn't believe it. The wuss was calling her father's bluff in return.

As entertaining as the argument was, she didn't like the way it was going. She knew her father's stubborn pride; he'd cut off his nose if that meant keeping his integrity.

"Da-ad!" she called in an intentional two-note whine.

He cast an irritated glance her way. "What?"

"You don't really expect me to move now, do you?" She sat so that her belly stuck out even more than normal.

After a long, agonizing moment he looked away, but she'd already seen the answer in his eyes. Yes! She'd won! With just one puny whine, she'd won!

But at that moment the oddest thing happened. The woman, Gina, began to back off. She looked at the house, looked at Spencer, and then shook her head. "I'm not interested anymore, Bob. It's obvious that being the sole tenant is important to Dr. Coburn."

The realtor looked perplexed. He'd obviously sensed Spencer changing his mind, too. "But this place belonged to your father, and as you said, this'll probably be his last chance to—"

"Why don't you go, Bob. I know you have a client to meet in twenty minutes, and I can manage from here. I do appreciate your driving me, and I'm sorry it didn't work out, but I think it's best this way."

The realtor sighed heavily. "Well, if you're sure . . ."

Stacy was dumbfounded. Just like that, the tide had turned.

With a disconsolate sigh, she gave Joe's arm a gentle pat of farewell, got off the bench and returned to the house.

SPENCER HEARD the front door slam and told himself to ignore it. Stacy got mad at everything he did these days, even when he was doing what was best for her. He turned his attention, instead, on Gina. She was trying to rouse her father from his nap.

Spencer told himself he'd gotten what he wanted and he ought to be pleased. Dammit, he *was* pleased. So why did he have this knot of guilt in his chest? Why this weight of disappointment?

Don't think about it, he advised himself. *She isn't your responsibility.*

Gina leaned forward to get a grip on her father's arm, and her soft knit dress lifted to reveal the backs of her thighs.

Don't think about that, either.

With her father on his feet, Gina turned and met Spencer's gaze. He suddenly felt awkward. What did you say to someone whose hopes you'd just crushed?

"Will you be able to handle your father alone?"

"Sure. Thanks," she said with a conciliatory smile, as she guided her father toward the old Chevy.

"Well, in that case . . ." The awkwardness had became painful. Not knowing what else to say, Spencer simply nodded clumsily, turned and fled back to the garden.

He didn't like what had just happened. He wasn't sure why exactly. He just felt bad, especially in light of how decent Gina had been toward the end. As he gripped the handlebars of the tiller, the sound of an engine straining to turn over drifted to him from the other side of the house. He lifted his head, realizing that fate was step-

ping in. Fate was giving him a second chance to say what
should've been said before he'd left her. A simple "I'm
sorry."

He and Gina met at the rosebush at the corner of the
barn. "Oh. I was just coming to look for you," she said.
Spots of color bloomed on her cheeks.

Spencer understood. He felt a little embarrassed too.
Less than ten minutes earlier they'd been standing in this
very spot arguing.

"It's the car, right?"

She nodded. "The battery's dead." She looked back
over her shoulder. Her father gave a regal wave from the
passenger seat.

"Dead or just low?"

"Maybe just low."

Spencer was reluctant to move. They were standing so
close he could almost count the few faint freckles on her
cheeks, so close he was able to pick up her fragrance—old
roses and sunshine. Or was that just the scent of the air?

Shaking off his stupor, he said, "Well, let's go take a
look."

"Oh, no, please. That's not why I was coming to look
for you. I just wanted to ask if I could use your phone to
call a garage."

Spencer took her by the arm. "Let me have a crack at
it first. I'm not a mechanic, but I'm no dummy around
cars, either." Inwardly, he grimaced at the macho swag-
ger that had slipped into his voice.

"Stay with your father. I'll get my car and jumper cables."

He went into the garage, backed out his car and parked
it near Joe's. By then, Gina already had the hood up and
was leaning over the fender, braced on her forearms,
looking into the engine. The V-neckline of her dress was

pulled slightly off center, and Spencer noticed a quarter-inch of undergarment lace in the same shade of peach as her dress. He tried not to be fascinated by that small disclosure, but he'd never known anyone who dressed so carefully.

With an effort, he cleared his thoughts and opened the hood of his car.

He'd already clipped one of the positive ends onto his battery and was moving over to Joe's car with the other end when Gina said, "Make sure you clamp those things on correctly. If you do it wrong, you can blow out your battery."

From under the hood Spencer cast her a look of mock forebearance that, even as he denied it, teased and flirted.

Her left eyebrow lifted, just enough to betray that she'd caught his message. Oh, hell. What was he doing? The only reason he'd come out front was to help her with the car and maybe apologize.

"Sorry," she said. "I'm sure you know what you're doing."

He did, but just as he was about to clip the cable to Joe's battery, his teasing mood returned. Instead of positive to positive, he moved as if to affix positive to negative. Gina, still leaning on the fender, went still, except for her huge, expressive eyes, which lifted to his, lowered to the cables, lifted, lowered.

"This is a test, right?" she asked, her delivery so dry he was laughing before he knew it.

"Yes, and I guess you just passed."

He finished attaching the clamps, then slipped inside the old car and switched on the ignition. The battery fired and the engine turned over. He got out, unhooked the cables and tossed them into his trunk. "Let the car run for a while," he said, reaching inside his own car and turning it off.

Spencer could've gone back to the garden then, but somehow it didn't seem polite to just leave her. Besides, only half his business with her was done.

"How's your father doing?"

"I think the heat's getting to him."

"Would you like me to bring him something to drink? We've got lemonade."

"No thanks. We'll be home soon enough."

But we're home already.

Spencer scuffed his tennis shoe in the dirt. "It's no trouble. I'll be right back."

By the time Joe had drunk the lemonade, Spencer figured the battery was charged. He made no mention of it, though. "Did Joe live here long?" he asked over the rumbling of the still-running engine. "You said he was born and raised here, but..."

"Yes." Gina lifted her eyes, making him aware of lashes like brooms, lashes that could do a guy some serious damage. "He lived here all his life, except for the past thirteen years."

"I guess that means you lived here, too."

She nodded. "Until I moved out on my own. It was home."

Spencer's gaze roamed over the farm with new interest. Gina had grown up here? She'd occupied the rooms he occupied now? Unexpectedly, a landscape that had been dull and flat came vividly alive with depth and color.

"I was even born here," she said, "and I mean that literally. My mother's doctor came to the house to deliver me. Same room my father was born in, the one next to Stacy's."

Spencer gazed up at the house in deepening fascination. "It must've been hard for your parents to sell the place."

"It was. It had been in the family since the mid 1800s. But my father had turned seventy and my mother thought it was time he quit farming." Spencer watched a small V deepen between her downcast eyes. "They'd also finally accepted the fact that my life was in Syracuse and I wasn't interested in taking over here. They had expenses, too, college bills of mine they were still trying to pay off. I only found out about them recently, when I took over my father's finances."

Spencer wondered if she regretted her decision not to settle in Bingham, if her attempt to rent the apartment for Joe was her way of easing her guilt for disappointing him.

His interest in the inner tickings of Gina Banning's life suddenly made him nervous. "How'd you end up in Syracuse?" he asked safely.

"I went to the university there. After graduating, I was offered a position at the school where I'd done my student teaching. That's why I stayed on."

"Oh, so you're a teacher?" In the same breath Spencer drawled, "Brilliant deduction, Coburn."

She shed her seriousness and laughed, and he felt sixteen again and clever as hell for making a pretty girl laugh.

"Yes, I'm a teacher. High-school English."

He winced, and she pretended to be offended. "What's the matter with English?"

"Nothing," he said halfheartedly. "I guess I didn't mind grammar."

"I don't do much grammar, Dr. Coburn. My goal is to teach kids how to think, and they do that through reading and open discussion and lots of writing."

Gina paused, suddenly pensive. "I didn't mean to come between you and Stacy earlier. I'm sorry. It was just an automatic reflex. I spend my days trying to get kids to open up and express their opinions, not..." She let the rest of her thought slide.

"Seems to me," Spencer said carefully, "kids express too many opinions. If they listened more, they'd probably be better off."

Gina's eyebrows lifted and disappeared under her long bangs. Spencer wasn't sure he wanted to continue this particular conversation.

Besides, he still had a bit of business to take care of. "I, uh, I'm sorry about the way things turned out around here."

She blinked. "Renting the barn? Yeah. It would've been nice for my father. The years he spent on this farm were the best of his life. Very happy. Very productive. My hope was that, being here again, he'd rediscover that happiness and satisfaction, at least for a couple of months before... before I moved him to Syracuse." Her smile was sorrowful and reached inside Spencer where he didn't want to be touched.

He dragged a hand down his face. "Where am I supposed to go with that?"

"Nowhere." She shook her head. "Nowhere. I'm sorry, I'm not trying to make you feel guilty. Honestly, I do understand your position, and I agree you have every right to expect to be the sole tenant here."

Spencer sighed. He wished he hadn't gotten so confrontational with this woman. He really liked her. Admittedly, what he felt was mostly just a physical attraction, but there was a lot to be said for physical attraction, especially when it had been missing from one's life for so long.

"It isn't you personally I object to," he explained. "I just foresaw this as a summer to be with my daughter."

"You don't have to explain."

"I feel I do. As I said, it isn't you. Other people just never figured into my picture."

He swallowed, wondering if she understood. What he'd said was the truth. But not the whole truth.

Before he could frame another sentence, however, Gina swung her legs into the car and said, "Well, I should be getting my father home."

Maybe it was better he didn't get into the rest of his motives. Frankly, he didn't understand them himself.

"Thanks for the jump, Dr. Coburn." She shifted into reverse.

"My pleasure."

With a wave out her open window, she added, "Enjoy your summer."

Spencer felt a strange, all-over sinking sensation. Guilt again? No, not just guilt. Disappointment, too. For when she'd said, "Enjoy your summer," what he'd heard was, "Goodbye, I won't be seeing you again."

But there was nothing to be done about the situation. And so he just waved and said, "You, too."

THAT NIGHT Gina awoke from a sound sleep and squinted across her father's living room. The phone in the kitchen was ringing. She threw back the sheet and rolled off the couch.

"H'lo," she mumbled, almost dropping the receiver.

"Ms. Banning? Gina?"

Her jaw fell. The caller hadn't identified himself, but there was no mistaking that deep, dark voice. She came fully awake. "Spencer?"

"Were you asleep already?"

"Mmm." She squinted at the clock on the stove. Ten minutes to ten. "I sacked out early. I only got a few hours' sleep last night."

"Sorry. I can call another time."

"No. It's okay." It was far from okay, but not because he'd disturbed her sleep. During her last visit to the farm, she'd thought Spencer had periodically crossed the line from cordiality into...into what? He certainly hadn't been coming on to her. But she'd definitely felt *something*, some thin, bright, occasional connecting.

"What's up?" she asked cautiously. She didn't have time for anything so frivolous as a summer romance. Didn't have the inclination, either.

And because she was so preoccupied with wondering how she ought to handle this call, she felt totally foolish when Spencer replied, "I've changed my mind."

CHAPTER SIX

"CHANGED YOUR MIND?" Gina sounded confused. "About what?"

"The apartment." Spencer carried the phone to his bed, placed it on the nightstand and sat. "I did a lot of thinking after you left, weighed all the pros and cons of having you and your father living next door, and I've decided it wouldn't be so bad, after all."

"Spencer, it's okay."

"I mean it, Gina." He said her name again, tasting something in the syllables he hadn't enjoyed in years—the excitement of simply uttering a woman's name. "I'd really be pleased to have you and Joe for neighbors."

"What made you change your mind?"

Spencer lifted his feet up onto the bed and lay back, tucking one arm under his head. *You*, he thought. *Your legs. Your sexy hair. Your lethal eyes.*

"It's a noble gesture, moving your father here, and maybe I want to get in on it. Hell, everybody can use a little more nobility."

"You're sure?" she asked, giving him one last chance to back out.

And for a moment he considered it. But then she went and yawned, and fool that he was, he wondered what she looked like tousled and sleepy. He'd been doing a lot of that since waving her off today—wondering about her, conjuring up her image. "Yes," he said. "I'm positive."

His doubts returned within seconds, but it was too late. He'd already committed himself, and now the best he could do was control the damage. "I'm sure we'll respect each other's right to privacy."

"Of course." She yawned again.

He suddenly realized she was speaking in a hush. "I hope this call hasn't disturbed your father."

"No, he's still asleep. But I don't want to talk too loudly."

"Me, neither. Stacy's just across the hall. So, what do you think?"

"About what?"

"Moving in."

"I think it's a good idea. I think I'll do it."

Spencer placed a hand over his stomach. Why wouldn't it stop jumping? "Just like that? Without even seeing the place?"

"Oh, right." She laughed softly. "Spencer, you've got me thinking in circles. Yes, no."

He sort of liked the idea of causing her to think in circles. He punched up the pillow under his head and settled more comfortably—a man adjusting himself to fit a woman closer.

"So tell me what it's like," she whispered.

"Downstairs, there's an open kitchen/living-room area with a combination bathroom and laundry. Upstairs, two bedrooms and another bath."

"Sounds great."

"Mmm. I think you'll like it." Their hushed tones were infusing their ordinary conversation with an intimacy that heated him in places he didn't want to be warm. Or maybe he did. Of course he did. Wasn't that really why he was calling her tonight, instead of tomorrow?

But that was okay. He was all right. He could control this sort of thing. It was only sex.

"I should warn you, the place doesn't have much furniture."

"No problem. My father has his own stuff." She breathed a soft laugh. "Ironic. His stuff came from the farm to begin with."

"That right?"

"Mmm."

"When do you think you'll be moving?"

"Soon. I already have a lot of his things sorted and packed."

"Good. I'm looking forward to it." He heard his voice. It was low and dark, trying to start something.

The line hummed with silence for a long moment.

Wise woman. He was making an ass of himself.

Spencer got up, crossed the room and looked at a piece of paper on the dresser on which he'd written a list of points he wanted to make during this call: (1) make offer, (2) assert right to privacy, (3) establish not available for medical services. Nowhere did it say: get something started.

So what the hell was he doing? A relationship between him and Gina Banning had absolutely nowhere to go. They lived in different cities, hundreds of miles apart. And although a relationship might be enjoyable while it lasted, what would Stacy think?

She'd think he was crud, that's what, involving himself with a woman he knew he'd have to say goodbye to at the end of the summer. After the way Todd had broken up with her, she'd probably believe *all* men were crud. Spencer refused to do that to her.

In addition, a matter of morality was involved. If Stacy needed anything at this stage in her life, it was a good example, someone to say abstinence was right, casual sex wrong, someone she could look up to and trust to be consistent in his integrity.

Getting something started wasn't an option this summer. He knew that perfectly well. Trouble was, talking to Gina, he kept forgetting.

"Before you do move in," he said in his most objective doctor voice, "there's one other thing I need to say. Your father is obviously in poor health, but this summer I'm not seeing any patients. I'm not available for medical services."

"Oh? How come?" Abruptly her tone dropped. "Oh, gosh, you haven't lost your license, have you?"

Smiling, he said, "No, nothing like that."

"Oh." She hesitated, and he could almost hear her thoughts turning and clicking. "Spencer, I hope you don't think I'm moving next door to you because I expect you to dish out free medical services to my father."

"No. Free has nothing to do with it. I'm just taking a break from medicine." He paused, realizing he didn't want the conversation to go in that direction. "My concern is that I'm just a general practitioner, not a stroke specialist. I wouldn't feel comfortable taking responsibility for him."

"Oh. Oh, well, don't worry. My father has his own doctor. I wouldn't think of imposing on you."

"Well, I just thought I'd lay my cards on the table."

"No problem."

His shoulders relaxed.

GINA RUBBED at the furrow between her eyes. Her father's physician was a general practitioner, too, but he'd never voiced doubts about treating Joe. Was Spencer throwing up excuses? Not that it mattered. She had no intention whatsoever of bothering Spencer. The thought had never crossed her mind.

Preferring to move on, she said, "Spencer, you shouldn't say *just* a general practitioner. Family practice is the wave of the future. Haven't you heard?"

He laughed. "You don't know my practice."

"No, I don't. What's it like?"

"I run an inner-city walk-in clinic."

"Oh. Now *that's* interesting." Gina was beginning to think she'd find anything he said interesting. "Now I see how you're able to take the summer off. You run the place."

She paced the warped linoleum of her father's kitchen, teeming with questions. "Have you always worked there?"

"Yes. Well, no. I opened the clinic eleven years ago. It only feels like always. Before that, I spent a couple of years working emergency at Boston City."

Gina stopped pacing and stood at the window that looked down on the street, trying to imagine him in his life away from Bingham. She only saw a man in jeans, shirtsleeves rolled, with sweat on his brow.

"I'm having a hard time picturing you," she said, and then hastily added, "as a doctor." She hoped he didn't think she made a habit of fantasizing about him.

She cleared her throat and assumed a more serious tone. "What made you want to become a doctor?"

"My father was a doctor. So was my grandfather."

She stepped away from the window. "Good God, Spencer. You couldn't've gone into another profession even if you'd wanted to."

"I never wanted to. Medicine was all I ever dreamed of."

"Then you're blessed," she replied.

He said nothing.

"Is your father's practice in Boston, too?"

"Uh . . . no. He practiced in Illinois, a suburb of Chicago. That's where I'm from, where I grew up."

"Oh!" Her perceptions of him took an abrupt shift. "Am I right in thinking your father's passed on?"

"Mmm. He died last February."

"I'm sorry."

"Yeah, me too. Me too."

Too much melancholy was creeping into the night. "How did you ever end up here, this part of the country?"

"No mystery really. I went to college in Boston, married a Boston girl, we settled near her family."

Gina stood motionless, not knowing how to ask.

"We're divorced," he said, answering her silent question.

It shouldn't make any difference, she told herself. Spencer was just a man passing through one summer of her life, one short, displaced summer, and she'd already guessed that he was divorced. Yet she slumped against the wall in relief and kept on slumping until she was sitting on the floor.

Her voice was all breath when she said, "I figured as much."

"That right?" She heard a smile warm his words—a teasing, flirting smile. "How'd you do that?"

"You don't wear a ring." Closing her eyes, she waited.

"Neither do you."

Gina picked up the dustpan and fanned herself. "That's because I'm divorced, too." She heard him swallow.

She recognized this conversation, this circling and measuring. *But it can't happen,* she thought. Spencer Coburn lived five hours away from her by car. He was a blind alley. She didn't have any more time for blind alleys. She couldn't afford the emotional investment, and she certainly couldn't take any more of the heartache. In a few weeks, she would be turning forty. From now on, the only men she intended to take chances on would have to be sure bets.

Should she say something, then, tell Spencer outright she wasn't interested in starting anything? That was a tricky step, one that could backfire. He could say he hadn't been implying anything of the sort, and she'd end up with egg on her face.

And maybe he really *wasn't* implying anything. Maybe it was just the late hour and the way they were whispering in the dark that made her think they were circling each other.

"Was the split recent?" he asked.

"No. Almost ten years ago."

He whistled softly. "And no one's been able to catch you since?"

She waved the dustpan faster. No, it wasn't just the hour or the way they were whispering. He was circling, all right.

"Not for long," she tried to answer lightly. "I've been involved in a couple of relationships that didn't work out. How about you?"

"It's been four years."

"Ah. Long enough."

"For what?"

Gina inhaled, her back pressing against the wall. She'd been thinking, *Long enough to heal and get out there again.* She laughed nervously. "I have absolutely no idea. Spencer, I think I should say good-night. My mind has gone to mush."

"Mmm. It is getting late. Sorry for keeping you up."

"It's okay. Thanks for calling." Why *had* he called? Oh, yes. "And thanks especially for changing your mind about the apartment."

"My pleasure."

His pleasure? She hung up the phone, thinking, *That's what I'm afraid of.*

FOUR DAYS LATER, Gina and Joe moved to the farm.

When they arrived, the place was quiet as a church-yard, the garage open and empty. "Just as well," she murmured, gazing at the spot where Spencer usually parked his car. She didn't need any distractions today, and after that call a few nights ago, Spencer would definitely be a distraction.

She parked her car on the lawn alongside the garage. That gave the movers, who'd followed her, room to back the van up to the door. One of the men was driving her father's car. She waved to him to park on the lawn beside her.

Joe, who'd ridden with her, waved, too. He'd been trying to help all morning, wanting to be part of the exciting, happy activity.

"Okay, come on, Dad. Let's go see our new home."

While the movers were readying the unloading ramp at the rear of the van, she unlocked the colonial-blue door and stepped inside. Her father followed as quickly as his unsteady gait would allow. Once over the threshold, though, he gazed about in confusion. He seemed to know the place from the outside, but inside was all new.

"Like it, Dad?"

Joe smiled his shy, childlike smile, a smile that broke her heart every time.

"This used to be the woodshed, remember? This is where we're going to live," she explained for about the twenty-fifth time. "The people who bought the farm from you did all this. Isn't it great?"

"Yes, very nice," he said, not understanding, but amenable, anyway.

It *was* nice, Gina realized. Golden oak kitchen cabinets lined the front wall, immediately setting a warm country tone, while smooth, white walls lent an airy, contemporary feel. A long, green-tiled cooking island divided the kitchen from the living area where buttery sunlight spilled through a row of windows onto shiny oak flooring. A spiral staircase to one side wound artfully up to the bedrooms. The place wasn't just nice, Gina thought, it was beautiful.

She strolled around the island, her sneakers squeaking on the bare oak floor, and headed for the bath and laundry. Straight ahead was the access door to the main house. She noticed it had a lock and remembered a matching one on the other side.

After checking out the washer and dryer, she meandered across the living room again, coming to pause at one of the south-facing windows.

Her gaze moved over the farm's back acreage, the patchwork of yards, sheds, stone walls and fields that was her heritage. Although the surroundings hills looked unchanged by time, time had certainly brought change to the farm. The greenhouse had lost several panes of glass, and the fields beyond it had gone wild. Where her father had cultivated corn and tomatoes, peppers and squash, there now grew buttercups, daisies, thistle and tall saplings. If the fields weren't plowed soon, the saplings were bound to take over. Within a few years, there would be trees, and soon after that, there would be woods.

She opened the back door and breathed in the scent of June through the outer screen door: sweet rhododendrons, azaleas, newly cut grass and the unmistakable spice of dianthus. Her throat tightened with the ache of remembrance. After all these years, her mother's "pinks" were still blooming along the back foundation! And the garden was turned, she noticed in surprise. That was what Spencer had been working on each time she'd visited. He'd done a thorough job of it, too. Not a weed in sight.

The movers worked quickly. Within an hour they'd unloaded the van and Gina was writing out a check at the kitchen counter. That was when Spencer's car turned in off the road. She glanced out the window and saw that Stacy was with him. She went back to her task, trying to get her new neighbors out of her thoughts.

But apparently her new neighbors had sunk deeper than thought. Her very handwriting was different. Instead of her usual neat flow, her penmanship looked crabbed and shaky.

She handed the check to one of the movers. "Thanks a lot. You did a great job," she said, but her mind was on the car pulling into the yard and heading for the garage. Her eyes were on its driver, who tooted and gave a casual wave in her general direction.

The movers left the house and a moment later had driven away. From inside the garage, doors slammed, feet scuffed on concrete, and presently Spencer and his daughter emerged into sunlight.

Gina stepped back from the window, but not before he'd glanced over and seen her watching. *Why is my face turning red?* she chided herself. *Why is my heart in my throat?* She hadn't reacted to a man with such girly stupidity since . . . since she couldn't remember when.

Moaning in self-disgust, she marched off to the bathroom, turned on the tap and splashed her face with cold water. *This can't happen. It can't. It can't,* she told herself with each splash.

From the front door, Stacy's clear, young voice carried easily. "Hey, Joe! Is Ms. Banning here?"

Joe had turned on the TV and made himself comfortable in his brown vinyl recliner. Since the TV hadn't been connected to the antenna yet, he sat watching a screen of fuzz. "Who?" he asked.

"Gina."

"No," he said. "She went to school."

Laughing, Gina replied, "In here, Stacy." She patted her face dry with a paper towel, then hurried out of the bathroom.

Stacy was standing on the threshold, wearing a blue-flowered maternity dress. Her boots had been replaced by classic white flats.

Stacy looked at her dress and grimaced. "I know. El puko, right?"

"Actually, no. It's very nice."

Stacy grimaced. "My father bought it, so I figured I'd wear it at least once." She gave the flouncy bow at the collar an insolent flip. "This is his idea of how a proper young lady dresses when she goes to see her obstetrician."

Gina noticed that Stacy's nose was unadorned today. In fact, the tiny hoop on her left eyebrow was the only unusual jewelry she wore. Also Spencer's influence?

"Is that where you were, the obstetrician's?"

"Yes. My first visit." Stacy's eyes clouded and Gina's radar went up. Dear God, she hoped nothing was wrong.

"Would you like to come in, Stacy?" Perhaps the girl could do with a little female companionship.

"I'd love to, but my father said not to be a haunt." She rolled her eyes. "I just wanted to say hi."

Though she was concerned, Gina didn't press the issue. "Well, hi. And thanks. I appreciate the welcome."

Stacy could've gone then, but she didn't. She continued to stand on the doorsill, her gaze curious and roaming. When it encountered Joe's old depression-era bed, set up by the stairs, her eyes widened.

Gina smiled. "What, you don't like my living-room decor?" The teenager looked at her uncertainly. Gina laughed, explaining, "My father can't climb stairs very well. That's one of the reasons I was so eager to get him out of his old apartment."

"So he's going to sleep there?"

"Yes. He'll have a bathroom close by, and I'll be right at the top of the stairs to hear him if he stirs."

"Cool," Stacy said with typical youthful delight in anything unorthodox.

"Mind if I start unpacking?"

"No, don't let me stop you."

Gina walked along the row of cartons stacked against the wall. When she found the picnic cooler, she dragged it over to the refrigerator and took off the cover.

Stacy, still on the threshold, inched forward and let the door click shut at her heels. Glancing up from the cooler, Gina noticed the girl's face had become quite solemn.

"I guess you've been wondering what the story is with me, huh?"

Keeping her expression neutral and her eyes on her unpacking, Gina said, "I've been curious, yes."

"I'm not married, if that's what you've been wondering."

Gina suppressed a smile. "Somehow I didn't think you were."

"I'm not even going out with my boyfriend anymore." Stacy paused as if expecting a negative reaction. Gina continued to transfer food. "And I'm only fifteen. Does that gross you out?"

"Not really. I'm a high-school teacher, Stacy." Into the refrigerator went orange juice, margarine, a container of leftover peas. "I see young women in your situation all the time."

From the corner of her eye, she saw Stacy stand a little taller. "You do?"

"Sure. The faculty lounge is in the same wing where the pregnant girls and new mothers meet." Gina put a bag of plums into the crisper. After a while she became aware of the lengthening silence. She glanced toward the doorway. Stacy looked thoroughly perplexed.

"For classes," Gina tacked on. But the teenager's perplexity only deepened. Gina sat back on her heels. "Doesn't your school have a program for teenage mothers and mothers-to-be?"

"No." Stacy wore the expression of someone who's just discovered she's been seriously deprived. But then she let it go with a shrug. "It isn't a very big school. Not enough pregnant girls to fill a special program, I guess."

"Well, that's good. Unfortunate for you, though. I know our girls really appreciate being able to continue their education in a setting that's geared to their special needs. Besides academic subjects, they learn practical things like infant care and child development. There's job counseling, too, and we even have a day-care center for their babies.'' Gina finished emptying the cooler and set it aside.

''They take their babies to school?''

''Sure.'' Gina opened a carton marked ''canned goods'' and lifted out two cans of creamed corn. ''Most of the time they have to. They don't have anyone to baby-sit for them. Usually, if they're still living at home, their parents work or they're too angry to help out. Sometimes they've even made their daughters leave home.''

Stacy gave a huff of scorn that didn't quite mask the pain in her eyes. ''I can relate to that. My mother kicked me out, too. That's why I'm with my father.''

Gina's busy hands stilled. ''Oh, Stacy.'' Her heart ached for the girl. The thought that Stacy might be with Spencer because her mother didn't want her had never crossed Gina's mind. She'd simply assumed Spencer had custody.

''Maybe my school should look into getting a program like that. It sounds great.''

Still somewhat shaken, Gina went back to unpacking groceries. ''Well, yes, but it isn't easy. I see the girls coming into the building in the morning, lugging books and babies and diaper bags, looking exhausted from homework and 2 a.m. feedings, and I say to myself, 'How on earth do they do it?' ''

She was putting cans and boxes on shelves helter-skelter now, her mind too full of Stacy.

''Ah, well. Doesn't matter, anyway.'' The teenager shrugged and looked aside. ''I'm giving my baby up for adoption as soon as it's born, so I don't need a program like that. Besides, in September I'll be changing schools. My father's sending me to a boarding school in Pennsylvania.''

Again Gina stopped unpacking. She gazed at Stacy and frowned. "When's your baby due?"

"The middle of August."

Gina's frown became almost painful. How could Spencer do that? How could he ship his daughter off to a strange school so soon after such a traumatic experience? Would she be feeling well enough physically? And how about emotionally?

"What's the matter?" Stacy crossed her arms. "Don't you approve of me giving up my baby?"

"Oh, no. That's not it. Personally I agree with you. I think adoption's the best way to go—for you, for the baby, everyone concerned."

Gina immediately felt uneasy voicing her opinion on so personal an issue, even if that opinion did coincide with Stacy's. "But of course, what I think doesn't matter. The important thing is that *you've* made the decision that adoption is the best solution. If I looked surprised, it was only because of your mentioning boarding school."

"Oh." Stacy uncrossed her arms and inched farther into the kitchen, coming to rest against the end of the counter. "I'm not too crazy about the idea myself. The funny part is, I don't even know why. It makes perfect sense up here." She tapped her temple. "Like my father says, I'll be making a completely fresh start. Nobody'll know anything about me, so I'll be able to continue my life as if none of this ever happened."

"You say it makes sense in your head." Gina spoke hesitantly, knowing she was poking into a matter that wasn't her business. "But what does your heart say?"

"Well, that's the thing!" Stacy waved her arms emphatically. "I don't *want* to go away to school, but I don't exactly fit into my father's life, either, so what choice do I have?''

Did she think nobody wanted her? Gina wondered sadly. Was it true?

"I think you're selling your father short. Just look at the two of you, spending the summer together here. You seem to fit into his life just fine."

"Yeah, maybe," Stacy conceded but with so little conviction Gina sensed she was only trying to get off the subject.

Before Gina noticed what Stacy was doing, she'd picked up a carton marked "kitchen" and carried it over. "Hey, be careful, Stacy. You shouldn't be lifting heavy things like that."

"I'm okay. Healthy as a horse, the doctor said."

Gina was relieved to hear it, but she'd still detected a note of reservation in Stacy's voice.

"And the baby?"

"Fine, too, as far as I know."

They worked alongside each other in taut silence, one putting away silverware, the other, china. Finally Gina's curiosity got the best of her. "Did something happen at the doctor's today to upset you?"

"No! Nothing happened! That's exactly why I'm so P.O.'ed." The vehemence of Stacy's reply set Gina back on her heels. "I was hoping he'd do a sonogram so I could see the baby. I'm six and a half months along, so there'd be plenty to see, but he said his equipment was down. I think he was lying." Her words poured forth hotly, angrily.

"I didn't even get to hear the baby's heartbeat. Hearing the baby like that, he said, I might get too attached." Stacy placed her hands on her stomach, flattening the poufy blue dress. "I *might?*" she squeaked in exasperation. "I wanted to ask him how much more attached he thought I could get."

Gina let out an unexpected laugh. She was beginning to find this fifteen-year-old a genuine delight.

"Stace, if you're not satisfied with the quality of care you're getting, you ought to tell your father. I'm sure he'll help you switch to someone else."

"I doubt that. He handpicked the guy himself. Thinks he's great." She spoke with a drawling sarcasm that left no doubt as to what her opinion was.

"But if he didn't do a sonogram and didn't—"

"I think my father talked to him before we went there."

Gina stared at the girl's angry mouth and hurt eyes. It was clear she'd come here bearing a grudge against her father. But Gina continued to give Spencer the benefit of the doubt. Grudges against parents came automatically with being a teenager.

"I still think you ought to talk to him. Sounds like he's unaware of how you feel."

"He and I don't communicate too well these days." Again, that drawling sarcasm. "He didn't even talk to me about choosing a doctor, just said here he is, here's the guy who's going to take you through the most important event in your life."

"He didn't discuss it with you?"

"Nope."

"Oh, Stacy. You've got to talk to him. When it comes to matters this important, a woman has to speak her mind. Otherwise, she gets bulldozed into situations that just get more and more painful."

Gina lowered her eyes, realizing she'd gotten up on a soapbox, one constructed from personal experience. Her parents had had her relatively late in life, so by the time she was born, they'd formed a firm notion of who she ought to be. Growing up, Gina had occasionally felt a vague lack of control, but mostly she didn't consider it a problem. Did it really matter that her mother bought all her clothes, or that those clothes were consistently out of style? Along with the clothes and everything else her parents did for her came a love and a sense of security that she wouldn't have traded for all the Calvin Kleins in the world.

It was only later, when she was on her own, that she came to understand the problem. They'd been too protective, and she wasn't used to making decisions. Instead, she'd let life happen to her: Syracuse University, because guidance counselors had steered her there; her job, because it was offered before she'd even applied anywhere else; her condo in Syracuse, because of her job; Jeff, because *he'd* thought marriage a good idea. Jeff, who'd bulldozed her into marriage—and then left her because he said she was wishy-washy.

Gina had learned to be her own person the hard way, through experience. Still, she considered herself lucky. Some women never grew up.

She looked at Stacy, not quite a woman yet but certainly no child. "It's awfully important to know yourself, Stacy—what you want, what you need. Even more important is to then be true to yourself."

Stacy folded her hands on the counter and frowned at them. Gina took a carton of orange juice from the refrigerator. Her father had fallen asleep, so she poured out only two glasses.

"Who would you have chosen for an obstetrician?"

Stacy took the glass Gina offered. "I'm not sure. Probably not a man." She paused thoughtfully. "No, definitely not a man."

"Did you have to get into those awful stirrups during your examination?"

"Yes!" Stacy's eyes lit. "How did you know that's what I was thinking about?"

"I've been there myself, many, many times."

"Oh, Ms. Banning! It was so embarrassing. I mean, I know he wasn't looking at anything he hasn't seen a million times before, but still!"

"There are lots of female obstetricians around. There's got to be one that'll please both you and your father."

Stacy finished her juice and rinsed out the glass. "I doubt it."

If there was one thing Gina had learned from working with teenagers, it was to listen. What she'd been hearing throughout this visit was a voice saying, *I'm facing this ordeal alone.* Gina wondered if she shouldn't speak to Spencer herself.

Trying to move on to a more upbeat subject, Gina asked, "Have you given any thought to the birth itself?"

"Have I! I think about it all the time. I mean, I've seen movies. I've seen women giving birth on TV."

It wasn't the reaction Gina expected. She'd been thinking about the numerous options available these days: birth-preparation classes, special birthing rooms, natural delivery versus all the various forms of anesthesia, even videotaping the event. Stacy was only thinking pain.

"Sometimes," Stacy said with an audible tremor, "I doubt I'll even be able to do it."

Gina could make excuses for Spencer no longer. He was a doctor, for heaven's sake. If anyone was able to answer Stacy's questions or allay her fears, it would be him. Where the hell was he in his daughter's life?

"Try not to worry, Stacy. Giving birth is a perfectly natural experience. If that doesn't reassure you, just keep thinking of all the billions of women who've given birth before you. Think of my cousin Carol."

"Who?" Stacy's nose wrinkled.

"Carol. Biggest wimp on earth. Weighed only about ninety pounds all her life, always had the sniffles or a headache, yet she gave birth to four healthy kids. I always said, if I ever got pregnant, thinking about wimpy Carol would get me through."

"Thanks. I'll remember that." Stacy smiled, but Gina could see her doubts were still with her.

"You know, there's another option I just thought of, Stace." Gina gave up unpacking altogether and sat on one of the bar stools at the cooking island.

Stacy joined her. "What's that?"

"A midwife."

The teenager's eyes rounded. "A midwife?"

"Yes. They're coming back into fashion big-time, and I think it's because they give their patients so much personal attention."

"Are they safe?"

"Sure. They're certified nurses who've gone on to get lots of special training. The ones I'm familiar with usually deliver in the hospital in case there's an emergency."

Stacy didn't react with half the curiosity that Gina had expected. In fact, she didn't react at all. Her features simply froze, her eyes fixed on a point behind Gina.

Gina turned. She started to smile, then changed her mind. Spencer Coburn was standing at the back door, and he didn't look happy.

"Stacy, don't you think it's time you gave Ms. Banning a break?"

"I don't mind," Gina said. How long had he been there? "We've been having a great chat."

"Yes." The one word was so cold Gina was surprised frost didn't form on the windows. "Still, she should come home. It's lunchtime, and she has some schoolwork to do."

"Oh, I didn't realize..." Gina looked at Stacy. The teenager was flushed with anger and embarrassment. "Thanks for stopping by, Stacy. Come visit anytime."

Stacy said nothing. She just nodded and left by the front door.

Gina turned, expecting Spencer to still be at the back door, *wanting* him to be there so she could give him a piece of her mind. But he, too, had vanished, leaving only his disturbing image in her heart.

CHAPTER SEVEN

STACY SLAMMED the front door of the farmhouse and strode toward the stairs. Spencer headed her off. "Come have some lunch."

He knew she was angry. He'd eavesdropped on her conversation. He'd fetched her home for lunch as if she were a six-year-old. He'd embarrassed her.

Tough. He was angry, too.

Stacy looked aside at a rectangle of sunlight dancing on the hallway floor. "I'm not hungry."

"You're almost seven months pregnant. You need to eat."

"I'll eat later." She elbowed her way around him and got halfway up the stairs.

"Stacy!"

"What!" Her thin shoulder blades lifted, tensed.

"It might be a good idea if you stayed on our side of the property this summer."

She turned slowly, pinning him with her incredulity. "What are you saying? You don't want me talking to Gina anymore?"

"I didn't say that. And it's Ms. Banning to you. Of course, I expect you to be cordial, but there's no reason for you to get into personal discussions with her. Your pregnancy is none of her business."

She gripped the banister, her breathing quickened. "I don't see the harm."

"I do." He made an effort to soften his face, his voice, his stance. He wasn't really mad at Stacy. It was Gina who had him so riled. Nobody messed with his daughter. Nobody. "It sounded to me like she was giving you some advice about doctors and delivery, and I thought we'd already decided all that."

Stacy's mouth hardened. *"We?"*

Spencer pushed his hand through his hair in frustration. "Baby, don't you think I would've taken you to a midwife if I thought that was the best care available?"

"I have no idea." She flicked her head, and although she no longer had long hair to toss, the gesture still managed to evoke enough insolence to sting. "This isn't about doctors or midwives, anyway. It's about you talking to me, telling me what my options are, letting me share in some of the decision-making around here."

"Options." Sighing, Spencer dragged a hand down his face. He'd only caught the tail end of Stacy's conversation with Gina, and that alone had gotten him upset. "What other options did Ms. Banning talk to you about?"

"I don't know," Stacy snapped. "Just...stuff."

"Like?"

She huffed and crossed her arms over her stomach. Her eyes gleamed with belligerence. "Did you know that some schools have special programs for pregnant teenagers? Gina said if I was in a school like that, I could learn all sorts of things besides academics. I could even take my baby to school with me. They have day-care."

Spencer stopped breathing. He stood frozen, one foot on the bottom step, his hands hanging uselessly at his sides, utterly unable to move.

Quickly Stacy added, "If I was going to keep the baby, I mean." She looked aside at the wall. "Which I'm not, of course."

Spencer exhaled a held breath. His knee cracked as he straightened. "Baby, listen to me. Ms. Banning seems to be a nice person, and she probably means well, but the more opinions you hear, the more confused and upset you'll get."

He watched his daughter's color deepen, her lips working over some unspoken frustration. "Don't you trust me to be able to judge for myself? Gina says it's important for a woman to make her own decisions."

Gina says. Gina says. Spencer was almost choking on *Gina says.* Of course he agreed it was important for women to make their own decisions, but Stacy wasn't a woman, and Gina had no right to agitate her with the notion that she was. Maureen had given Stacy all the freedom in the world, and look where that had landed her.

"There's nothing wrong with parental guidance, Stace."

She laughed abruptly. "Is that what you think you're doing, guiding me?"

"I'm trying."

She sneered, her gaze sliding off to the side again. "You just don't want me talking to anyone, do you?"

"What?" Where had that come from?

"You're ashamed of me."

If she'd hit him with a bat between the eyes, he wouldn't have been more stunned. "That's not true, Stacy."

"Oh, yeah? Then how come we're spending the summer here? How come we're not in Boston? You want to hide me until this is over, that's why, then pretend it didn't happen.''

"I've told you why we're here. Do you want me to go over the reasons again?"

"Don't waste my time."

"Stace, everything I've done has been with your best interests in mind."

"Yeah, right." Suddenly her anger drained out of her, and she just looked sad. "If I thought you cared, I wouldn't mind. But you don't. When you look at me, all you see is a great big problem that needs to be taken care of. All you're interested in is making it go away, like I was the flu or something."

"Baby, of course, I care. How can you possibly think I don't? You're the most important thing in the world to me. I love you."

Stacy shook her head, her eyes overly bright. "What you love is a memory of me, not me as I am now."

He started to say something, but then just closed his mouth.

After a moment Stacy turned and continued up the stairs. This time he let her go.

GINA DIDN'T BELIEVE for a minute that she'd heard the last of Spencer Coburn—and she hadn't. Half an hour later, he was back.

She'd given up on unpacking for a while, deciding, instead, to take Joe outside to reacquaint him with his farm. She was getting ready to do just that—on her hands and knees, looking for his poplin cap under his chair—when Spencer rapped on her back door.

She'd had thirty minutes to stew over Stacy's grievances, so when she sat back on her heels and said, "Yes?" her tone was cool and crisp.

Spencer shaded his eyes and squinted through the screen. Finding her, he gave a start.

She didn't explain what she was doing on the floor, just went back to doing it. When she found the cap, she got to her feet. By then Spencer was staring at Joe's bed. She didn't explain that, either.

"Gina, we need to talk."

Joe had drifted over to the door and stood smiling through the screen. "Don't I know you?" he said.

Spencer sighed. "Sure, Joe. We met a few days ago."

"That's right, that's right. Over at the Agway on Miller Road."

Gina placed the cap on her father's head, kissed his cheek and looked at Spencer. "What's on your mind?" She kept the screen door between them.

She wished it was made of something sturdier, because the screen did nothing to obscure his good looks or blunt their impact on her.

"I really have to object to your filling my daughter's head with your... your ideas," he said.

"Can't help it. That's my job."

He didn't seem amused. "Look," he said.

And she did. He really did have the most remarkable eyes. Peering into them was like diving into the deepest, darkest part of the ocean.

"Stacy doesn't need to be confused right now."

And his hair. Although it was neatly cut, it remained just long enough to curl over his collar and become sexily tousled.

"She and I have already mapped out a path, and I don't appreciate your leading her off that path."

With a mental reprimand to quit ogling, Gina focused on the argument at hand. "And how, pray tell, am I leading your daughter off her path?" She opened the door, forcing Spencer to back off the wide granite slab that served as a step. She took Joe by the arm and helped him over the threshold.

"For starters, by telling her about midwives and how great they are."

"Your daughter is unhappy with her obstetrician, and we were simply discussing alternatives. In fact, I repeatedly encouraged her to talk to *you* about them."

Still holding Joe's arm, she began to walk. Spencer joined her. He was frowning. After a while he said, "I wouldn't have included a midwife as a choice."

"Why not?"

"Why would I, when I know of a dozen excellent M.D.'s in the area?"

"Are any of them female?"

"I'm not sure. Maybe."

"Well, maybe you ought to check."

"Why?"

Gina exhaled irritably. "Because Stacy happens to feel awkward being seen by a male doctor, that's why."

They paused by the freestanding gate opening into the tilled garden. Spencer seemed to be pondering her comment. His brows were knit so intensely they almost met. Obviously this was news to him. Obviously he and Stacy hadn't talked.

"You know, you really ought to discuss this with Stacy, not me. She's the one who's unhappy. I just happen to be the person she opened up to."

"Yes," Spencer said, none too pleased, and they resumed walking. "You also happen to be the person who told her she could go to a school where there's a special program for pregnant teenagers. You told her she could even take her baby with her. What I want to know is why, why you'd do such a thing? What's your agenda?"

"My agenda?" Gina mocked. She stared at him, stunned and dismayed. Had she dreamed up that phone call four nights ago? Dreamed up the man who'd seemed interested in her? "I didn't tell her she could go to any such school. I merely mentioned there was a program at the school where I teach. What are you getting at, that I encouraged her to consider keeping her baby?"

Spencer's hard-set jaw was her answer.

"I did no such thing!" A hot ball of anger lodged in her chest.

"Glad to hear it, because no way in hell am I going to let my daughter ruin her life."

He still didn't believe her! She could hear it in his tone!

Before Gina could say another word in her defense, however, he added forcefully, "Do you realize she scored the equivalent of 1400 on her PSATs?"

"PSATs aren't given to freshmen."

"Right. They were given to Stacy in eighth grade."

The implication of his remark hit hard, yet Gina kept her reaction in check. She refused to give him the satisfaction of even one little *Oh, my.* Instead, she said, "You think keeping a baby means a girl's life is ruined?"

He looked at her aghast. She'd known he would and she didn't care.

"Don't *you?*" he said.

"No. It isn't an easy life, but it's a possible one. Lots of young women do it."

Spencer shook his head. "Adoption is the only solution."

"Really? And what if Stacy decides she wants to keep her baby? What about her rights as the birth mother?"

They squared off, face-to-face. Spencer's eyes grew stormy. "She's fifteen years old, Ms. Banning. She has no rights. She's a baby herself."

"Take another look, Dr. Coburn."

"No, *you* take a look. My daughter is not one of your students, and I'll thank you to butt out of her life."

"And I'll thank you to stop telling me what to do."

"When it comes to my daughter, I'll tell you and the devil himself what to do."

"You want to play hardball? Fine." Gina met his anger, chin first. "I think you stink as a parent."

"Oh, I'm quaking in my boots."

"You should be, with your plans of sending her off to a strange school so soon after giving birth. Where's your common sense?"

Spencer seemed offended. He probably thought he was the quintessence of common sense. Being offended didn't slow him down, though. He seemed about to fire back another retort when a harsh gasp wrenched Gina's attention. She glanced aside, and the world suddenly reeled. While she and Spencer had been engrossed in their arguing, Joe had drifted into the garden and fallen.

Gina took off, cursing her negligence.

"Dad, are you all right?"

Joe levered his torso off the ground, pushing with his hands. He'd toppled to his left, his weak side. "I'm fine." He smiled his shy, heartbreaking smile. "Fine."

"Don't try to move too quickly. Just sit for a while. Here, let me help you. Lean against me."

A shadow crossed Joe's chest. "Do you need help?"

Gina fumed. If Spencer really wanted to help, he wouldn't ask. He'd just pitch in.

"Go away. I don't have time for any more of your nonsense. Just leave us alone."

Spencer knelt beside her, anyway, and did the fastest check for injuries she'd ever seen, fingers pressing into brittle hipbones and ribs, hands running the length of arms and legs.

Ambivalence tore at her. She wanted to thank him; she wanted to shove him aside. She did neither. She was too lost in the fact that Spencer Coburn was not an easy man to know.

Spencer said nothing, not to her or to Joe, just gave a nod when he was done and stepped back.

With her heart still racing, Gina brushed the dirt from Joe's shirt, reset his cap on his head and carefully helped him to his feet. By then, Spencer was gone.

STEPPING BACK from the window, Stacy whispered, "Damn! Double damn!" She hadn't meant for *that* to happen.

What was she going to do now? She liked Gina. Gina saw the bright side of things. Because of Gina, she'd begun to look forward to the summer. After eavesdropping on that argument, she realized Gina was a friend. And yet she'd managed to land poor Gina plumb on her father's manure list. Now he'd never let them talk or visit or anything.

Cradling her stomach with one arm, Stacy carefully lowered herself to her bed, lifted her feet and lay back.

He was being so unfair, too. So pompous and bossy. So *wrong*. She really couldn't stand him. He made her want to stay in this room forever, never speak to him, never listen, never even look at him again.

Gina's voice rose from below the window. "Dad, did you see these flowers? Remember these?" Stacy could picture her and Joe as clearly as if they were standing right in front of her: Joe smiling pathetically, Gina kissing him, anyway. A tear ran from the corner of her eye into her hair.

Maybe she'd give Todd a call tonight, if her father would only go to sleep. On second thought, she didn't dare. The long-distance call would show up on the phone bill.

Another tear left her eye. *Might as well face it,* she told herself. *You're in this mess alone.*

SPENCER SPENT the rest of that day avoiding Gina. Before going outside, even for the briefest of errands, like taking out the trash or walking to the mailbox, he went from window to window, making sure he wouldn't run into her. When he did see her out there, he waited until she went indoors.

He was mad. Nobody interfered with his daughter, not even a woman who'd made her way into his dreams. Hell, women were everywhere, but he only had one Stacy.

He didn't go out to the garden that day. Although he missed the exercise, he knew he'd feel foolish if he got behind that tiller again. The garden was obviously tilled. There was nothing left to do.

He spent some time at the piano. His playing was rusty, but after a few five-minute passes through "The Minute Waltz," he thought he sounded better. He took a crack at "Great Balls of Fire," but his rendition lacked the necessary verve.

So he read for a while, and after enough time had passed, he busied himself in the kitchen, making meatballs and spaghetti sauce. Spaghetti was Stacy's favorite. Not that he was feeling guilty or anything.

What you love is a memory of me, not me as I am now. Now where did a fifteen-year-old get a notion like that? And why did it hurt so much? Was it true? Did he not love her as she was now? Of course he did. Of course. He just felt she'd changed, and he wasn't too pleased with the changes. Nothing wrong with that.

Spencer sliced open a green pepper, scraped out the seeds and ran it under the faucet. Spaghetti. He didn't know why he was bothering. She was probably going to say she wasn't hungry, and he certainly wasn't deriving much joy from his efforts.

He paused, his hands lowering to the cutting board. Joy. What a foreign concept. He gazed out the window toward the hazy green hills in the distance. He remembered joy. Feeding a baby strained peas. Hitting a clean jump shot. Driving to work. *Being* at work. That first bite of pizza. Christmas lights reflected in a certain woman's eyes.

Like so many candles being snuffed, all the joys of his life seemed to have disappeared one by one. Nothing moved him anymore. Nothing filled him. But he remembered, and he wished he didn't.

AFTER SEQUESTERING herself in her room for six hours, Stacy came downstairs. She sidled into the kitchen and casually went through the mail sitting on the end of the counter.

"Would you like to eat in the dining room?" Spencer asked just as casually, pouring the steaming sauce and meatballs into a bowl.

She shrugged, eyes still averted. "Makes no difference."

"We'll eat in the dining room, then." Spencer had, in fact, already set their places. He carried the bowl past her and bit back a chuckle as she followed it with her nose.

They sat and served themselves and began to eat in silence. But the air throbbed with things yearning to be said.

Spencer broke through the tension first, but only after Stacy had blunted her hunger sufficiently to listen. "Stace, I've got to ask you something. Are you dissatisfied with the obstetrician you saw this morning?"

Stacy poked and nudged the pasta on her plate, her brows knit.

"It's okay if you are. I won't be disappointed."

Apparently that was the right thing to say. She finally looked up at him. "Yeah."

"Would you rather be seeing a woman?"

"Yeah!" she repeated, but with a lot more exuberance.

"Consider it done."

Her brow went smooth. Sighing, she sank about four inches into her seat. She twirled a forkful of spaghetti, lifted it halfway to her mouth, then lowered it again. "Dad, Ms. Banning didn't try to push a midwife on me. We were just talking. And she certainly didn't try to get me to change my mind about giving the baby up for adoption. In fact, she said she thought adoption was best. She really did."

Spencer grimaced. "You overheard our argument?"

She looked at her plate again. "You weren't exactly whispering out there."

He felt like a jackass. His volatile temperament was one of the reasons he was taking a break from the clinic. He'd been putting his staff on edge and jeopardizing his patients. So now he was going to start in on the population of Bingham?

Obviously he'd overreacted and jumped to false conclusions. How unreasonable of him. How unscientific. If he diagnosed patients' ailments the way he'd judged Gina, he would've lost his license to practice years ago.

I don't have time for your nonsense, she'd told him, and she was right. His arguing with her *was* nonsense. It seemed doubly foolish when he thought of the burden she had caring for her father.

"I'm glad you told me, Stace."

"Well, I had to say something. I couldn't let you go on thinking she'd done something she hadn't. She's really a cool person, Dad. You ought to give her another chance."

Spencer almost dropped his fork. How perceptive was his daughter, anyway? "Another chance?"

"Mmm. You know, letting me go over there to see her."

"Oh." Maybe he'd been wrong about that, too. Stacy had come to trust Gina in a remarkably short time, and Gina *had* found out about the obstetrician. If she hadn't, he might've continued taking Stacy to someone she hated seeing, causing untold anxiety in her life.

"I don't mind," he said. "Sure, you can go over. Just remember, she's an outsider. She can't possibly want to look after you the way I do. Understand?"

Stacy smiled, just a little—just enough. "Okay."

"She has a lot on her hands with her father, too, so don't be underfoot."

"I won't. Do you need help with the dishes?"

"No, I have a dishwasher for that. You go study. Your tutor will be here first thing in the morning."

Stacy's smile began to fade. Spencer couldn't imagine why. What possible disappointment could she be suffering from getting out of doing the dishes?

"One more exam," he said encouragingly, "and your freshman year'll be over."

"Good riddance," she drawled.

"With any luck your grades will be transferred to Whitman by the end of next week, and by mid-July we should know whether you've been accepted or not."

"Oh, boy. Can't wait."

Spencer had admitted to being wrong first about the obstetrician and then about Gina, but he refused to back down on the boarding-school issue, even if Gina did think he stank as a parent because of it. He would *not* take Stacy back to Boston, *not* subject her to the cruelty other teenagers were capable of inflicting, *not* place her in proximity to Todd.

Stacy had changed, but with time and the right environment he was sure she could change back. For now, Bingham was the right environment. In September Whitman Prep would be. He was sure of it.

Whitman would be a clean slate. She'd just be a transfer student as far as anyone knew. From there she could go on to college, and from college on to a career where she could use her gifted mind, just as if none of this had ever happened.

"No, I can't wait, either," he replied, deliberately disregarding her sarcasm. "Hey, I found some jigsaw puzzles under the sofa in the living room." He and Stacy used to spend hours when she was younger putting puzzles together. "Care to tackle one?"

She shook her head, her eyes downcast. "Nah. No point in doing puzzles. When you're done, you just have to take them apart."

Spencer hid his disappointment behind a sip of wine. What else might she enjoy doing? he wondered.

But before he could come up with another suggestion, Stacy scraped back her chair and levered herself to her feet. "As you said, I have to study."

Left alone, Spencer carried their dishes into the kitchen and placed them on the counter. What happened? It had seemed as if they were getting along and then, wham, her petulance was back.

He returned to the dining room and gathered up the rest of their dinner things. Evidently his daughter wasn't going to bend on this boarding-school issue, either. She would remain opposed and petulant.

He hated it, hated the tension that filled this house. He wished he could defuse it, but he only seemed to make things worse when he tried.

He was rinsing out a bowl at the sink and frowning over that depressing notion when he thought he heard a voice. Gina's voice. He peered out the window toward the area outside her back door. He saw no one. At the same time, the muscles across his shoulders tightened. More tension, different direction. He'd been thinking of going outside after the dishes were done, but if *she* was out there, he'd have to do something else.

He muttered under his breath. This wouldn't have happened if he'd stuck to his guns and not invited her to move in next door.

But it was too late for regrets, and now he was facing a mighty long summer.

Pouring detergent into the dishwasher, he noticed the hard pulse at his wrist and laughed nervously. In spite of their differences, he couldn't get Gina off his mind—her face, her hair, her scent, her smile. Just thinking about her made his blood stir.

It was nuts. He hadn't been this drawn to a woman in months. No, years. Why now? Why her?

The sound of her voice came again, soft as water over stone. He leaned toward the window again, just as she emerged from the apartment. As usual her father was at her side.

Spencer watched Joe lean on her arm as they began their evening walk, his steps slow, small, unsure. He imagined that at one time Joe had been quite tall. Now he was bowed over, reduced to a height less than his daughter's.

Spencer shook his head. He didn't like Joe's living so near. He'd come here to get away from sick people. He needed a break. Had every right to take a rest. He was suffering from burnout.

But hints of deeper motives were beginning to nibble at his conscience, formless shadows he couldn't grasp. All he knew was, calling himself burned out was looking more and more like a handy excuse.

He watched Gina reach toward a mock orange bush that grew alongside the garden shed. Low, slanting sunlight bathed her raised arm and seeped through her blouse, gauzily silhouetting the contour of her breasts. She broke off a stem and held it to her nose.

Maybe it wasn't necessary to worry about his attitude toward Joe tonight. He had an entire summer to do that. In the meantime, he'd stand here a while longer, watching Gina and the evening sunlight, and wonder what to do about this stirring in his blood.

THAT NIGHT, to Gina's undying relief, Joe went to sleep at nine o'clock. She considered doing the same. She'd worked hard that day, moving them in and getting them settled.

But in spite of her physical weariness, she knew she wouldn't sleep. She was too wired. Being at the farm excited her too much. She wanted to keep looking around, making sure she was really here.

She adjusted a folding screen near the foot of her father's bed to give him more privacy, then pried off her sandals and tiptoed to the refrigerator.

Moving by the light cast from the low-wattage bulb over the sink, she found the zinfandel, poured herself a glass, added some ginger ale and a couple of ice cubes, and called it a wine cooler.

Glass in hand, she padded to the front door she'd opened for a cross breeze. Even at nine-fifteen the sky was still luminescent, objects below palely visible—the heads of faded irises growing by the garage, the mailbox at the top of the driveway, the stone wall along the road.

Such long days, these in mid-June. She took a sip of wine and listened to the chorus of crickets. She tilted her head, bemused. Along with the crickets she could hear a piano being played somewhere. Or maybe "tortured" was a better word. A smile eased its way over her lips and into her eyes. Anyone who played piano that poorly yet persisted couldn't be all bad.

She took another cool sip. She'd gone through the afternoon telling herself that her argument with Spencer had been fortuitous. She'd been a little too eager to move in here, and not all the reasons involved her father. Best to nip this thing in the bud before she did something she'd regret.And she would regret Spencer Coburn.

Only problem was, she didn't want to stay mad at him. Unless they started speaking again, the summer was going to be pure misery. Stacy and Joe would suffer for it, too.

The piano sounds faded into the night, leaving only the chorus of crickets and bullfrogs and bugs dive-bombing the window screens.

Maybe she ought to apologize.

Maybe she ought to have her head examined. Spencer was going to tell her to get lost.

Her musing was interrupted by a particularly insistent bug tapping at one of the back windows. Or was that the door? She frowned. Couldn't be a bug. The tapping was too rhythmic.

Gina's heart was instantly racing. She spun around, her gaze zooming to the back door. "Spencer." She thought she spoke his name, but maybe she only thought it. He was leaning against the door frame, arms crossed, the lantern above throwing light and shadows over his handsome face and rugged body.

When her unsteady legs finally got her across the room, she saw he was holding something in one hand. She leaned closer to the screen, squinting, uncertain she was seeing right. A shoehorn?

"Hi. I thought I'd bring you this," he said in that quiet, reserved way of his that appealed to her so much.

She frowned. "Why? What would I ever do with that?"

The corners of Spencer's mouth lifted. "Help a jackass get his foot out of his mouth?"

CHAPTER EIGHT

GINA MELTED. From the tip of her head to the soles of her feet. Pure mush. She opened the screen door, looked at the shoehorn and forgave every sin it represented, although at the moment she couldn't think of a single one.

She held out her hand. "Thanks. I've been looking for mine. Must've lost it."

Spencer placed the shoehorn in her hand and smiled a tender half smile that seemed to say "Thanks" and "I'm sorry" and "Can we be friends again?" It struck her as unfairly seductive.

Slipping the shoehorn into her trouser pocket, she said, "I'd ask you in, but my father's asleep."

"Oh, I didn't realize . . . It's so early."

She nodded. "Being here seems to agree with him."

"Would you consider sitting outside, then?" His dark eyebrows lifted in invitation.

"Sure." Gina was about to step outside when she remembered she still had a wineglass in her hand. "Would you care for some wine?"

"That'd be great."

She padded off to the refrigerator, pausing only to slip on her sandals again. Her breath was so shallow she almost couldn't catch it. She'd known they'd have to confront each other sometime, but she hadn't expected the confrontation quite so soon.

By the time she stepped outside, Spencer had set up two chaise longues. "Where'd these come from?" she asked.

"The garden shed." He aligned them and waited.

She handed him his glass, then set the wine bottle, which she'd also brought along, on the grass between their chairs. Why was he still standing? Was he planning to make a toast or something? She sat, then he sat, and she hoped the night hid her chagrin. Had it been that long since she'd run into a man with manners?

"How are you doing?" he asked.

She swallowed. "Better. You?"

"Better." His eyes met hers and held, and on their linked gaze suddenly rode all the apologies that needed to be made. They smiled softly, hearing the unspoken words, accepting them.

"Mind if I ask what got you to come over here?" In the pale summer-night light she studied the planes and contours of his face. He was a man who was going to age well, she thought unexpectedly. Ten years from now, twenty, he was still going to turn heads.

"Stacy straightened me out about the conversation you two had."

"Ah." Gina felt pleasantly vindicated.

"My reaction was irrational and inexcusable." As he raised one knee, his denim jeans rasped, and even such a small sound as that heightened her awareness of him.

"It's perfectly understandable, Spencer." She became aware, too, of his wonderful scent: soap and musk...and oregano? "She's your daughter, and you thought I was harming her in some way. More parents should be so concerned about their kids."

"Yes, well, I just wanted you to know I regret the things I said. Actually, I want to thank you for talking to her. I never would've found out she was dissatisfied with her obstetrician otherwise.''

Gina smiled up at the slowly emerging stars. They seemed to be spinning like sparkles from a mirrored globe. ''Did you discuss it with her?''

''Briefly. We agreed to see a different physician, a woman this time.''

''Great.'' Gina sipped her wine, then set the glass on the ground. ''Did she confide anything else to you?''

''Like?''

''How concerned she is about the birth.''

He scowled. ''No. She's concerned?''

''Mmm.'' Gina thought she detected a sadness in his eyes that hadn't been there a moment ago. Was it because here was something else his daughter had withheld from him?

He bristled in defense. ''I gave her a couple of books.''

''Books are great, but there are times when there's no substitute for a walking, talking human being.''

He looked aside, squinting at an overturned wheelbarrow by the garden. ''What's she concerned about?''

''The pain. I think she's seen too many melodramas. She says she's afraid she won't be able to do it.''

Spencer's frown intensified. ''Know something, Gina? Sometimes I worry about the same thing myself.'' He took a mouthful of wine and quickly swallowed it. ''She's such a tiny thing, probably not fully developed yet. I...I get a little crazy when I think about what's facing her.''

Gina swung her feet off the chair and stared at Spencer. ''For her sake, maybe you should keep those fears out of sight for a while.'' He gave a scant nod. ''What I was about to suggest was that you talk to her. Being a doctor, as well as her father, you'd have the best shot at reassuring her, answering her questions.''

Spencer took another gulp of wine. "She won't listen to me."

"Why not?"

He shrugged and glanced away. The sadness in his eyes intensified. "We weren't always this way."

Gina took a chance. "The divorce?"

He blinked rapidly. "Yes."

She nodded. In her line of work, she saw the effects of divorce every day, nuclear families suddenly exploded, the individual members spinning out and away from each other.

"When Maureen and I split, Stacy was only eleven, a little girl who used to run down the driveway and leap into my arms when I came home from work. Now I don't know her. In four years, she's become so hard and distant. And her appearance..." The grooves on the sides of his mouth deepened. "I don't recognize her, Gina, inside or out."

Gina wanted to reach over and smooth away the creases on his forehead. She folded her hands in her lap, instead. "Her attitude could be an act," she suggested. "A defense against her belief that everyone's abandoned her."

Spencer's eyes narrowed warily. "Who's abandoned her?"

"Her mother."

"Yeah." He nodded. "Who else?"

"Her boyfriend."

"Thank God."

"And you."

"Me?"

"I could be wrong, but I think she feels you don't care about her anymore."

Spencer swung his feet to the ground so that he was facing her, toe-to-toe. "Did she tell you that?"

"Not in so many words. What she said was, she didn't fit into your life."

Spencer leaned forward, resting his elbows on his knees, and sighed heavily.

"I can understand why you'd feel confused," Gina offered, trying to ignore how close his head was to hers, how intimate the space between them. "You've taken her under your wing, you've left your work for an entire summer to bring her here, you're making all sorts of arrangements to minimize the damage of this experience. However—" she paused to gather her courage "—I think you might've inadvertently forgotten to look at things from her side."

"How so?" His intense blue gaze drilled into her.

"Well, take this boarding-school idea, for example." She decided to avoid the primary reason she still objected to it, the speed with which Stacy would be shipped off after the birth. Spencer wasn't likely to listen if she went on the attack again. "I understand your reasoning, and I agree it would be great for her to make a fresh start. But I can't help thinking, if I were in her shoes, I'd feel you were trying to get rid of me."

"That's not true," he said with emotion.

"I know. But think about it from her perspective."

Elbows still on his knees, he tapped his fingertips together. Such beautiful hands. Long and strong, with wide knuckles and just the right dusting of dark hair. Hands she suddenly imagined touching and being touched by in return.

"What am I supposed to do, take her back to Boston where her friends are? They'll never forget what happened, and they'll never let *her* forget. Word'll spread.

Guys won't ask her out, or if they do it'll be for the wrong reasons. The stigma will be with her constantly. And then, of course, there's Todd, the son of a bitch who got her pregnant. She still has a crush on him. Did you know that?''

"No. I'd wondered.''

"If I take her back to Boston, she'll just have a harder time getting over him.''

"I see. And I assume he's somebody she should get over?''

Spencer cast her a glance so dismal she almost laughed.

"I met him last Christmas. Good thing I didn't know Stacy was already pregnant. I would've torn the kid limb from limb, starting with his greasy ponytail and ending with his spiked motorcycle boots. A senior, a street-hardened senior, dating a freshman right out of parochial school. Even then I wanted to send Stacy away.'' He sipped from his glass. "To a convent.'' Took another sip. "In Maine. An island in Maine.''

Gina laughed softly, happy to see Spencer smiling, too. His face changed so when he smiled. It fell into lines that fit him much more naturally.

"So that's why you brought her here? Todd?''

He shrugged. "Do you blame me?''

"No.'' And she really didn't.

"I wanted to get her away from her friends, too, the kids who probably peer-pressured her into experimenting with sex. I don't know how she got mixed up with them in the first place. She used to hang out with such a nice bunch. But that was back at St. Anthony's.''

Gina was at a loss as to why Spencer was confiding in her tonight. She supposed everyone needed to make human contact sometimes. Maybe this was just one of those times and she happened to be within reach.

"It happens. Kids get to high school and think they have to act wild or grown-up, so they start hanging out with the wrong crowd."

Spencer didn't agree. Nor did he disagree. He just tipped back his glass, drained it dry, then reached for the wine bottle. After filling his glass, he topped off Gina's and placed the bottle down again. Gina was feeling pretty light-headed and wondered if Spencer was, too, wondered if that was the reason he was opening up to her tonight.

"So what am I supposed to do, Gina? I refuse to take her back to Boston."

"It's a difficult situation, and I'm the first to admit I don't have any answers. I was just explaining how I think she sees this boarding-school issue. I was also hoping you'd talk to her more. I may be wrong, but I think she'd really appreciate being let in on some of the decision-making that's affecting her life."

Spencer sighed. "Are you suggesting I let *her* decide where she's going to attend school? Where she's going to live? She isn't capable of that right now."

Gina had to choose her words carefully. "I understand. You feel you know best, and you probably do, Spencer. But I think she'd still like to be included. Her life is galloping at such a frightening pace. Everything is changing. She's probably scared witless."

"I've never seen her scared. All she does is give me lip."

"Look more closely, Spencer. She's probably longing for a way to make things slow down so she can get some control over them. I think if you talked to her more, let her make some decisions, she'd feel she had that control."

"I don't know," Spencer grumbled.

"She'll probably surprise you. She's a pretty intelligent kid. Even the not-so-intelligent ones will surprise you when you're honest with them and explain your reasons for wanting them to do certain things."

Gina got the feeling he still didn't care much for her advice. Maybe it was best to let it lie for a while.

"Now, as far as her appearance goes, she looks fine, Spencer. It's the style. Among her peers, she's probably considered quite a knockout. Believe me, I see a lot worse. And this time next year, she'll probably look totally different, anyway."

"Yeah, I know. In my practice I see a lot worse, too. Usually I don't care. Usually I don't even notice how my patients look. But Stacy... she's my daughter." Spencer hung his head. "I guess I just worry about her too much."

"That's because you love her."

His voice was suspiciously thin when he replied, "Yes."

Gina reached across the shadows and placed her hand on his forearm, patting it with all the sympathy in her heart. His skin was warm, the tendons like oak, and the dark hair prickled her palm.

Softly she said, "It must be difficult seeing her this way, pregnant so young."

"Difficult?" Spencer breathed out a shaky laugh. "There should be a special term for what I'm feeling. As far as I know, the word doesn't exist."

How about heartache? Gina thought, for heartache certainly darkled his eyes. *How about frustration and despair?* They were there, too.

"This pregnancy... it's just... not what I wanted for her. It's such a sad... disappointment."

Gina stroked his arm and murmured, "I know."

"No, you can't know."

Gina's hand stilled. She felt rebuffed in a most personal way. She'd never had a child of her own.

"When Stacy was born, my entire life changed. I didn't think it was possible to love anyone as much as I loved her. She became my reason for being. She was so tiny, so vulnerable. And I was her father."

Gina stared into the deepening night. Father. The word, coming from Spencer, carried a weight that said "protector."

"Do you know what I miss most about her, Gina? Her enthusiasm. That kid was so damn enthusiastic no matter what she was doing, and she was always doing something. She didn't just put on puppet shows. She made her own puppets, made her own stage." He smiled, his eyes focused on a past that Gina wished she could see.

"Pompon people." He laughed. "She used to buy these colored pompons and glue plastic eyes on them. Made refrigerator magnets out of them. Once she learned how to do it, she made millions of them. I've still got a drawerful."

"She was into crafts?"

"Into everything—crafts, theater, science. We once did this science project—you know, a volcano using baking soda? I can still see her dancing around the kitchen as we set it up. Dancing, twirling, so full of life." He paused, and Gina could only wonder what other bright memories were tumbling through his mind. "This wasn't supposed to happen to her. It just...shouldn't have happened."

Gina's grip on his arm tightened. "Hang in, Spencer." Her voice barely rose above a whisper. "She needs you now more than she's ever needed anyone in her life."

He placed his hand over hers and gave it a squeeze. Then they both pulled away and sat back. Night had deepened, and the stars had emerged.

Spencer wondered if he shouldn't go inside now. He'd only meant to come over and apologize. He hadn't intended to stay, and he certainly hadn't intended to talk so much.

But Gina was easy to talk to, and she was more than easy to look at. After a few minutes, he'd forgotten all about what he'd intended to do.

He tipped back his head and gazed at the stars. They seemed to be spinning tonight. Or maybe that was just his head. He fought back a grin.

"So, when are you going to plant your garden, Spencer?"

He brought his gaze down from the sky and looked at her. The stars seemed to have come down with him, settling like sequins on her dark sexy hair, sinking into her dark, sexy eyes. "I..." He paused, coming out of his stupor. Oh, hell. She was asking about the garden. What could he say? "I'm not. I've decided it's too late in the season. I'll already be gone when most of the harvest matures."

"It isn't that late, only a couple of weeks by local standards. Plus, you could always come back some weekend in September. I'm sure nobody would mind."

"Well..." He went searching for another save. He'd thought the last one was brilliant. "Maybe I've just lost interest."

"Oh, what a pity. All that work."

He shrugged. "I enjoyed the exercise."

"Do you mind if I use it, then?"

"Be my guest."

"You're sure?"

"Positive."

"Great. I haven't had a garden in ages. That one there used to belong to me and my mother. We planted cutting flowers and vegetables my father didn't grow in the fields."

Spencer closed his eyes, trying to imagine it—the flowers, the fields, the girl Gina had once been.

"It's a nice night," she said now.

"Mmm. Soft. Summery."

"Brings back memories of when I was a child."

Spencer smiled. "Listening to White Sox games on the radio."

"Catching fireflies in mayonnaise jars."

"Bruises from falling out of trees."

"Making hats out of paper plates and wildflowers."

They both fell quiet again, and he thought, *It feels good to talk with someone your own age at the end of a long day.*

A mosquito buzzed his cheek. He slapped at it, but too late. He'd already felt a sting.

"Mmm, I know," Gina droned. "They've found us."

"I'll have to put citronella candles on my shopping list."

Gina slapped at her ankle. "Aw, darn. I think we've got to call it a night."

Her disappointment cheered him. He got to his feet, bringing the empty wine bottle and glass with him. Together they walked toward her door.

"I have a favor to ask," he said.

"Fire away."

"Stacy seems to really like you, and I was wondering if you'd mind her coming over to visit occasionally."

"No, I'd love it. But are you sure *you* don't mind?"

Her large, upturned eyes made him kind of dizzy. Maybe that was why he said, "I like you, too."

She swallowed, hearing an innuendo he'd meant to hide. He placed the glass and wine bottle he was carrying down on the granite step, noticing that she held her glass to her chest with two hands. She glanced at him briefly, looked away, glanced back. He'd undoubtedly made her nervous with that remark.

She wet her lips. "I've been thinking about how concerned Stacy is about the birth, and I was wondering... I still say you should talk to her yourself, but I also have a friend here in Bingham, Barbara Woods, who's had five children, and I was thinking Stacy might benefit from talking to her."

Spencer wasn't sure he liked the idea of one more person butting in, but tried not to show it.

"Well, think about it," she said as if reading his thoughts.

He nodded, loath to say good-night. He'd reasoned through all the pros and cons of starting something with Gina this summer, and the cons had won, hands down. But reason had little to do with raw hormonal attraction, and right now every cell in his body was sitting up and taking notice of her. He wasn't sure he could fight it anymore. He wasn't even sure he wanted to try.

Gina stood with her back pressed against the screen door, head tilted upward, gazing into Spencer's mysterious, sea-deep eyes. They were locked on hers so steadfastly she felt physically strapped to him. It wasn't a good feeling. She very nearly couldn't breathe.

"Well," she said, sliding her hand into her pocket and coming out with the plastic shoehorn. "Thanks for letting me borrow this."

He moved to take it from her, but, afraid to touch him, she let it go too soon. "Sorry," she murmured as it hit the step.

Spencer bent to retrieve it and came up slowly, too near, his shoulder grazing her hip, his breath fanning her arm. A shiver of danger raced through her, a river of delight.

She dared a look into his eyes. Heat burned in their depths. He placed the shoehorn in her hand and, in a move that turned her inside out, closed his fingers over it. His thumb stroked her knuckles, while his palm met hers in a touch that seemed indecently intimate. With the touch, pretense fell away. He knew what she was feeling; she knew the feeling was reciprocated, and neither of them tried to hide it.

Slowly he pulled her to him. Her breath seized up on her. All her senses quickened. And then she was there, kissing him.

It was a kiss that said, "At last," a kiss that said, "Not yet." It was light, yet it lingered. It was constrained yet fierce in its powers of arousal.

When he eventually lifted his head, Gina was a mass of physical need. Feeling liquid and dizzy, she slid her hands up over his hard chest and wound her arms around his neck.

"Gina." Her name came out a plea. He seemed to want her and not want her, both at the same time.

"I know," she whispered. "I understand."

He shuddered and his hands spread wide across her back, pulling her closer, fitting her to him as he lowered his head once again. This time there was nothing tentative about their kiss. Angling his mouth, he took her deeply. She crumpled, curling around him like a sheet of paper around a flame.

When the kiss finally ended, they looked at each other through surprised, glazed eyes. *That wasn't what I expected,* she thought. He released her, took a breath, released that, too, and raised his eyes to a moth beating at the lantern bulb. "Good night, Gina. See you tomorrow."

She sagged with disappointment. She soared with relief. "Yes. Sleep well, Spencer."

He tilted his head as if her remark surprised him. Then he gave her a provocative half smile and said, "You, too."

Still wearing that smile, he took a couple of backward steps. She lifted a hand. He lifted his. Another backward step, and finally he turned and strode off.

Gina went inside, closed the door and fell against it. "What in heaven's name have we started?" she groaned.

CHAPTER NINE

SPENCER LIFTED the sponge from the pail of soapy water, slathered it over the roof of his car and wondered how Gina was going to react to what he had to tell her. His head ached. He'd been wondering all night.

She was probably going to be hurt. Or angry. Or both. Whatever her reaction, there would be a scene, and after that, tension, tension so thick the rest of the summer might be hell.

But he had to tell her, had to explain he wasn't looking for a relationship this summer. Before they got any deeper, he'd have to make it clear to her that nothing could happen.

But it had happened already, he thought as he dunked the sponge again. It was too late.

Lifting the dripping sponge, he thought, no, it wasn't. He and Gina had only kissed.

Only kissed? There was nothing "only" about what they'd done last night. He still got achy just thinking about it.

Against his better judgment, he started thinking about it, and as he relived each touch, each shared breath, each slide of hand or tongue, a smile eased its way across his face. Drugged with remembrance, his movements slowed until eventually he was barely moving the sponge at all.

With a snap of his head, he reapplied himself to his task. Oddly, despite his restless night, this morning he felt good. Energized. He thought he understood how these big old maple trees felt in March when their sap began to rise.

Damn. It wasn't fair that he had to end something so sweet so soon after it started.

Just then the blue door opened, and Gina stepped out of the apartment. As usual, her father was close behind. Upon seeing her, Spencer's heart kicked into a faster rhythm.

"Good morning," she said, coming toward him. Despite smudges of tiredness under her eyes, she looked great. She always looked great. Today she was wearing a short-sleeved knit shirt and matching shorts in a color that made him think of ripe strawberries.

He cleared his throat, gave the car a few busy swirls, then returned his gaze to Gina. She was squeezing and twisting the handle of her purse. "Going somewhere?" he asked.

"Yes. We're off to buy some plants and seeds for the garden." She cast a sideways glance at her father. Joe was hobbling about the yard, talking to the flowers that bloomed in the bordering beds. "But I need to talk to you first."

Spencer frowned. "About what?"

Her long, black lashes swept upward, and when her eyes met his, he saw a familiar agony in them and comprehension dawned. "Oh. Well, I'll be damned."

Her purse strap got another twist. "What's the matter?"

"Nothing, except that I agree we need to talk, and apparently we both wasted a lot of time worrying about it."

She breathed out a shaky sigh and smiled. "What a relief."

Spencer grinned. They understood each other. He was off the hook. Still he felt they ought to spell things out. "It isn't that I wouldn't love to follow up on what happened last night. You know that, right?"

The wistful look she gave him said she understood, perfectly. It also gave his ego an unexpected boost.

"But it wouldn't be fair to either of us. Once the summer's over—"

"My reasoning exactly," she cut in.

"We could tell ourselves that we'd continue to see each other, but three hundred miles is a lot of miles."

"Three hundred and thirty," she corrected him.

"Especially in winter with all these mountains between us."

"Precisely. We'd be hurt. I know we're not talking love here," Gina said, not meeting his eyes, "but we'd still be hurt."

"And then there's my daughter."

"True. I bet she wouldn't like the idea of sharing you."

Spencer had his doubts about that but only shrugged. "What I was thinking was, she's only recently given up the idea that I should try to reconcile with her mother." He rinsed the sponge and squeezed it out, dripping water on his shoes. "I wouldn't want her resenting you."

"Oh. I hadn't thought of that."

"Another thing—what sort of example would I be setting for her?"

"I hadn't thought of that, either. But you're right." Gina frowned pensively. "You're right." Spencer went back to washing his car, and after a long while she added, "Ah, well. It wouldn't've been much of a relationship, anyway."

His ego, so recently pumped up, deflated. "Thanks a lot."

"What I mean is, I'm caught in a situation that most men find burdensome." She cast a meaningful glance toward her father. He was still hobbling along the flower borders, three pink peonies flopping in one hand. "The time and attention I can give to others is limited. I'm sure you would've eventually gotten tired of it, too."

Too? Spencer frowned. "Is that what happened to those other relationships you were involved in?"

Reluctantly Gina nodded.

Spencer made a deprecating grunt. She heard it and took umbrage.

"No. It was understandable. Gary hung in for almost two years, and believe me, they weren't easy years. My mother had cancer. I was here in Bingham more often than I was home. I don't blame him for breaking up with me."

Spencer rubbed his hand over his hardened mouth, feeling tides of emotion shifting inside him. "It was serious between you and this Gary?"

Gina tipped her head. "We . . . were engaged."

"And the other guy?"

"Steve? He came along later, after my mother died, after my life had returned to normal. Only problem was, it didn't stay normal for long." Gina shrugged, smiling wanly.

Spencer gazed at her, a vibrant, attractive woman in the prime of her life, then shifted his gaze to Joe. Earlier he'd been railing against the unfairness of not being able to follow his pleasure this summer. Seems he hadn't even scratched the surface of unfair.

Why didn't she just put her father in a nursing home? Not only for her own sake, but for Joe's, as well. With a trained staff to watch over him, he'd be safer than he was here. A lot more comfortable, too.

Or maybe, Spencer realized, he was just thinking about himself. *He* would feel safer and more comfortable with Joe gone.

Gina fitted her purse strap over her shoulder. "Well, I'm glad we got that over with."

"Yeah. Me, too."

"I trust we can go forward with the summer, then?"

"Sure. No problem." For the moment Spencer believed it. No problem. Just neighbors. Gina walked off to collect her father, and Spencer returned to washing his car.

"Spencer?"

He looked up, sure he'd gotten his feelings under control, and suddenly there it was again. One smile from her and a small earthquake was roaring in his chest.

"Can I get you anything while I'm in town?"

"No, thanks." He dunked the sponge in the pail of water, wishing he could dunk his head.

SPENCER WAS in the shower, lathering away the sweat of his morning labors, when Gina returned. After washing his car, he'd mowed the lawn and taken a weed trimmer to the area up by the wall.

Under the running water, he didn't hear her car, but he did hear Stacy thump on the bathroom door and holler she was going outside to see what Gina was doing. He assumed the tutor had left.

"Sure, go on," he called, then grunted. His daughter wasn't asking his permission. She was already on the stairs.

Spencer was drying himself off when the phone rang. He wrapped the towel around his waist and stepped out into the hall. "Spence?"

"Hey, Doug. How're you doing?" Water trickled from his hair down his back. Through the phone came noises that were as familiar to him as the sound of his own breathing. He even knew what phone Doug was using; the squawk of tight metal gave it away. That would be the bottom file drawer in the billing office.

"Great. Listen, I talked to my folks yesterday, and they do have a couple of jobs that need doing at the farm. I have to warn you, though, they're not small."

"What are they? If I can't handle them, I'll tell you. I'm not shy."

"Glad to hear it because . . . you know the old barn up by the road?"

"Yeah."

"They want to knock it down. They think the place'll be more salable without it. They've already contacted a demolition company and gotten a price, but if you want to do it, instead . . ."

"Whew! I've never knocked down a barn before. Sounds like fun, but I'll have to take a look at it first, see what we're talking about."

"Sure, and as I said, they've got that demolition company as backup. I'm just mentioning it because you sounded sort of desperate for something to do when you called the other day."

"Still am, my friend." More so than ever, now that he'd had a taste of Gina. "So what's the other job?"

"Painting the house."

"That I know I can do."

"It's a big house, Spence."

"It's a long summer. What brand of paint should I get and what color?"

Doug laughed. "Any good-quality brand, and keep it white. Black for the shutters. Oh, and they want to pay you."

"That isn't necessary."

"That's what I told them you'd say, so they've decided not to take any rent from you."

"We'll see," Spencer said noncommittally. From his viewpoint, they were doing *him* the favor.

"Okay, well, I gotta bolt. Seems our favorite housing project's running a sale on stomach virus this week."

"Oh, boy. Have fun. And thanks for calling, Doug."

Spencer hung up the phone, but stayed where he was, trickling water. Stomach virus, he thought. And the guy sounded like a kid at Christmas. Like he himself had probably sounded once upon a time. Now all he could think was, thank God he wasn't involved.

In his room, he opened the top drawer of his dresser and picked out a pair of socks and some underwear. Maybe his father had been right. He should've joined his practice. If he had, maybe he wouldn't be so emotionally depleted right now. His father had kept sensible hours, reserving plenty of time for his family and his passion, golf. The practice had been lucrative, too. Spencer lived a comfortable life, but it certainly wasn't like his father's.

Spencer let the towel fall, stepped into his underwear, then pulled on a clean shirt. Maureen would have been happier, too, that was for sure.

As usually when he thought of the demise of his marriage, he suffered a pang of guilt. Gina had excused that toad Gary by saying he'd hung in for two years. Maureen had hung in for thirteen.

They probably shouldn't have gotten married so young. Medical school, his internship, his residency—

those had not been easy years, especially after Stacy came along. Then, just when he and Maureen could've gotten on their feet financially, he'd opened the clinic—his idea, his dream.

She'd resented it from the start. Resented its location, its welfare-class clientele and the enormous amount of time he spent there with only a modest payback. She even used Stacy as a point of argument, and maybe she'd been right. If he'd lived the typical doctor's life—the upper-class house, the upper-class friends—maybe Stacy would've turned out differently.

In retrospect, Spencer felt he should've known the depth of Maureen's discontent years before they'd split. He should've at least had a suspicion when she'd refused to have another baby. But he hadn't. He'd been too happy, too blindly, foolishly content. Sure, he and Maureen had argued, but everybody argued. He'd never dreamed she was so fed up she'd go out and have an affair.

Spencer reached for his jeans. He didn't like thinking about that time in his life, a time when he'd ricocheted from stunned disbelief to anger, from guilt to pain.

In the four years since, he'd gotten over all the disbelief—Maureen had gone on to have three more serious relationships—and a lot of the anger. But he hadn't quite overcome the pain. Not once in that time had he opened himself to intimacy or to the possibility of being hurt again.

He hadn't lost the guilt, either. He'd put his career first, what *he'd* wanted, not what was best for his family. As a result, his wife had left him. As a result, Stacy had suffered. She'd passed those critical years from childhood to adolescence without a father's influence. She'd passed them with a mother who, though she loved

Stacy, had been too absorbed with her own postponed gratification to take the time to raise her child properly. Nor had she heeded Stacy's cries for attention after the current boyfriend moved in.

But although he was angry at Maureen, he was even angrier at himself. He'd failed his daughter, too. He'd noticed the changes in her attitude and appearance last fall. He'd worried about them and argued with Maureen about doing something. The only thing he hadn't done was help his daughter. He'd failed her.

He wouldn't do that again.

Throughout Spencer's getting dressed, voices had been drifting to him from the backyard. Even though his room faced the road, he could still hear them. He could hear *her,* Gina. Her voice poured into the house like warm honey.

He tied his left shoe and, reaching for the right, thought about going into town and buying paint. But hearing laughter, he gazed at his empty doorway and wondered what Gina was doing, what was making her laugh.

Spencer shook off his curiosity with a grunt. He knew what she was doing. She was planting a garden, and he had no interest in gardening whatsoever.

But his curiosity was a stubborn thing, and before he knew it, he'd crossed the hall to the spare bedroom. It wouldn't hurt to see what his daughter was up to. In her condition, she shouldn't be overexerting herself.

Standing to the side of the window, he looked down on the broad expanse of dark, tilled dirt. His gaze zeroed in on Gina immediately, an arrow finding its mark. She was kneeling on an old chair pad, troweling a hole for a tomato plant. Her strawberry-colored shorts molded her shapely bottom. Her shirt rode up her back, exposing a crescent of skin. Sweat sleeked her arms.

Several minutes passed before Spencer remembered he'd come to this window to check on his daughter. He did. She was fine.

She was sitting, knees splayed, on a low milking stool that Spencer had seen in one of the sheds. A denim hat with a floppy pink rose on its brim protected her head from the sun. In her hands were two plants whose roots had grown together. Gently she pulled them apart, handed them to Gina, then heaved her bulky body over to another flat and carefully tapped out six more plants. She'd been talking nonstop since he'd come to the window.

Spencer's gaze shifted. On the lawn at the edge of the garden, between an open bag of fertilizer and a fizzing hose, Joe sat on a lawn chair with an attached green-and-white umbrella. The chair looked new. Despite the fact that Stacy and Gina weren't listening to him, he continued to direct their activity, mumbling advice, gesturing shakily.

Spencer didn't want to smile, but he did.

Gina sat back on her heels, pulled a handkerchief from her shorts pocket and pressed it to her upper lip. Then, ever so slowly, she wiped the cloth across her brow, down her cheek, under her chin and, lower still, into the V of her shirt.

Spencer didn't want to ache with desire, either, but he did that, too.

He reminded himself they had agreed to a platonic summer. Well, fine. He could be platonic and still join them for a few minutes. He'd take them something to drink, say he was concerned about Stacy, the heat, dehydration, that sort of thing. Sure. Then he'd go buy that paint.

"Stace?" he called, striding across the lawn a few minutes later.

She was pouring water around the base of a plant Gina had just set. She looked up and smiled. "Hey, Dad."

His breath caught, for at that moment he saw the Stacy of the past, his Stacy, the little girl with clear, untroubled eyes and love in her giggle, the daughter who used to race down the driveway and leap into his arms after work.

"What's the matter?" she asked, her smile growing uncertain.

He shook off his stupefaction. "I brought you some lemonade." He set the insulated jug on the picnic table, along with a sleeve of paper cups and, looking up, met Gina's eyes.

"Thanks," she said with a polite, restrained smile.

He poured out three cups. "How's the garden coming?"

"Pretty well." She came over, got two of the cups and took them to Stacy and Joe. Then she returned for her own and drank thirstily. He was standing too near, Spencer thought, watching her backhand her mouth. He could see the fine grains of dirt that streaked her cheek, could imagine the flavor of her lips—they'd be salty-sweet right now.

"We've put in four hills of cucumbers," she said, "some zucchini, a dozen pepper plants, and we're just finishing the tomatoes. But there's lots more to do. Want to join us?"

"No, thanks." Assuming an ironic tone, he added, "I wouldn't want to deprive you of any of your fun."

"Your loss."

Spencer looked at her hot, dirt-streaked face, looked at Stacy's. They did seem to be enjoying themselves. The worry lines that usually marred Gina's brow were gone, and Stacy was humming.

She'd finished her drink, gone to the edge of the garden and was rummaging through a plastic bag printed with the logo of a local garden shop. "I'm going to plant the sunflowers," she announced, pulling a seed packet out of the bag. She crossed the garden, stepping carefully between two planted rows, and when she got to Spencer, handed him the packet. "See? They're the giant variety. Gina says they come up real fast, and I should see them in bloom by the time the baby's born."

Spencer studied the illustration on the packet, several large sunflowers blooming against a sky almost as blue as the one above. Unfortunately his mind had stuck on the phrase "by the time the baby's born," and he wasn't thinking of sunflowers but rather the ordeal awaiting his daughter.

The packet trembled slightly as he handed it back and said, "Well, just don't overdo it."

"Oh, Dad."

Spencer became aware that Joe was waving to him, calling him over, a cigarette pinched between his fingertips. Relieved to be diverted, Spencer went. "Hey, Joe, whaddaya know?" he said.

Joe chuckled in his dry, raspy way, exhaling puffs of smoke with each chuckle. "Help me up, son," he said, gripping Spencer's right arm.

Spencer stifled a sigh. Foolishly, he'd been drawn outside by the curve of a woman's back, the promise in her smile. He hadn't thought he'd have to deal with the old man. He'd forgotten the two came as a pair.

"Where do you want to go?"

Joe didn't answer. He merely shuffled toward some garden tools on the grass, leaned over creakily and picked up a rake. Spencer shot Gina a glance, knowing she'd be watching. She answered with a nod.

Spencer walked Joe into the tilled garden where gradually the old man let go of his arm and began to rake the clumped soil. Spencer stayed close by. Joe worked slowly but methodically, grading a long row that seemed at cross purposes to everything Gina was doing. Her rows ran north to south; his, east to west.

He paused at the end of the row and leaned on his rake. When he'd caught his breath, he called, "Hey, sunflower girl."

Gina looked up, a sparkle in her eyes like that of a child awakening to the sudden realization that today was her birthday. But then she saw he was speaking to Stacy, and the sparkle faded.

"Me?" Stacy asked.

"Go on," Gina urged with a soft smile. "He wants you to plant your sunflowers."

"There?"

"Yes. That's where . . . we always planted them, at the back of the garden."

Spencer didn't like seeing Gina grieving over what was happening to her father. Her pain bothered him in ways he didn't fully understand and certainly didn't want to examine. All he knew was, a face that pretty ought not to be sad so often.

Conscious of her sorrow, Spencer endured the planting of the sunflower seeds the way a patient endures the cauterizing of a lesion or the stitching of a wound. He walked behind Joe and Stacy, making sure Joe didn't fall and Stacy didn't bury the seeds too deeply, but his mind was on Gina all the while. Quite often, so were his eyes.

Spencer had every intention of retreating as soon as the job of planting the sunflower seeds was done, but by then Gina had laid out lunch on the redwood picnic table—tuna-salad sandwiches, potato chips and watermelon.

Spencer protested. She shouldn't have gone to so much trouble, he said. But in the end he stayed, which was what he'd wanted to do all along.

While they ate, Gina told stories about growing up on the farm. Stacy couldn't get enough. Spencer rather liked them himself. Afterward, they took a walk—a very slow walk because of Joe—down to the greenhouse, along the edge of the fields, around the old smokehouse to the blueberry bushes and through the orchard. They would've continued on up the hill to the sugar maples—Gina said the view would bring them to their knees—but Joe was clearly not up to any more walking, and so they decided to head back to the house.

"I'll take him," Stacy offered. "You guys can keep walking."

Gina argued against the suggestion for several minutes, but in the end conceded. Spencer had been hoping she would.

They climbed through the orchard, between the rows of old gnarled trees, up a gently rising meadow toward an outbuilding Gina explained was a sugar shack. Spencer strolled along by her side with his hands in his pockets, listening to her recall those cold spring days after school when she'd trek through the snow to join her father, who'd be up here making maple syrup. Because Gina's words were so vivid, he could almost see the clouds of steam billowing from the boiling sap and spreading through the shack. He could almost smell its sweet fragrance and feel the heat of the burning wood.

She led him past the shack, farther up the hill, and showed him some of the huge old trees that her father used to tap.

"Turn around," she said unexpectedly. And because his mind was on trees and buckets and spigots, he was caught unprepared. He gasped. From where they stood the entire valley was visible, with the farm at its heart. They could see the lake and Emerson Brook and the spire of the Congregational Church in town. They could see everything, all the way to the hazy Green Mountains in Vermont.

With another gasp, purely for Gina's enjoyment, Spencer sank to his knees. Laughing, she joined him. They sat side by side, arms looped around their knees, saying little, just enjoying a view that seemed to reach into forever.

Spencer lay back, cushioning his head on an arm, and gazed at the sky through maple leaves the size of his hand. Beside him Gina launched into another remembrance, this one about sledding on a certain hill. Riding her soothing voice, he closed his eyes and soon drifted off to sleep.

He awoke late in the afternoon. He climbed down the hill, through the orchard, back to the garden. It was deserted, but he noticed several more rows had been planted. He wondered how he could have slept so long. For that matter, how could they have left him out in the open like that, so unaware, so vulnerable?

But he did feel rested, and he was grateful to them for that.

Voices drew him into the house.

"Hey, sleepyhead," Stacy greeted him from the living room sofa, her arm linked through Joe's.

Standing by the fireplace, Gina gave him a sheepish smile. "We were talking about the house, how it looked when I was young, and Stacy offered me a tour. I hope you don't mind."

Spencer scratched his head, feeling muzzy and rumpled and perfectly pleased to find Gina Banning in his house. He smiled. "No, of course not. What do you think? Has it changed?"

"Some. Not much. Most of the changes are surface ones—paint, wallpaper." She gave the room one more fond sweep, then said, "Well, I was just about to get back to my own place. Mind walking with me, Spencer?" And turning to Stacy, she said in an undertone, "Medical advice."

Spencer assumed she was referring to Joe. Apparently that was the impression she'd meant to convey, but once they were outside, she said, "While we were in the garden this afternoon, Stacy and I got to talking again about her delivery. Maybe I should've cleared this with you before I said anything, but you were sleeping so soundly and I hated to disturb you."

Spencer prickled with wariness. "What did you do now?"

"I suggested she attend birth-preparation classes. She was asking me questions I didn't feel qualified to handle. Are you okay with that idea?"

"Yes, of course. But I'm not sure we'll be able to find birth-prep classes around here. Even to get to an obstetrician, we had to drive over to Kingfield."

Gina looked at him encouragingly. "Kingfield isn't far. Will you look into it?"

"Yeah, sure."

"What's the matter? You still look doubtful."

He sighed. "Stacy will need someone to go with her." They turned to each other at her door, while Joe wandered over to the fragrant bed of pinks.

"I assumed that would be you, Spencer."

He shook his head. "Classes are one thing, but then I'd be expected to be her birth partner. I can't do that."

"Oh. I hadn't considered..." She frowned. "I suppose that would be awkward. Shoot! It seemed like such a good idea, too."

"Well, thanks for talking to her, anyway."

She was about to go inside when she added, "Oh, incidentally, you did very well today."

Even though he had no idea what she was talking about, he smiled foolishly.

"Coming outside and spending time with Stacy, doing stuff with her. That's exactly what you need to do to get to know her again."

Spencer nodded. "It *was* nice."

Gina's eyes lit. "Tomorrow I'm going back to the garden center. Stacy asked if she could go along with me. Want to come, too?"

He shrugged. "What would be my excuse?"

"You need an excuse to enjoy yourself?"

He said nothing. Seems he did.

"Well, you could buy some hanging plants for your front porch."

He felt a smile moving through him. "I could." Clear out of nowhere another idea struck him. "Let's leave early and have breakfast at the Sugar Shack down the road. All that talk about maple syrup's gotten to me."

Gina broke into a smile. "Stacy'll go nuts."

Before he could check himself, Spencer reached forward and fingered a lock of hair curling toward her cheek. Her entire face was ringed with wispy curls, and suddenly he wanted to touch them all.

She coughed and took a step back. He shoved his hands in his pockets and shrugged. Couldn't blame a guy for dreaming.

Dreaming? Suddenly he realized he *had* been dreaming. During his nap. About her. About making love to her. With a grunt of unadulterated frustration, he nodded goodbye and trudged back to his own side of the property, where he belonged.

GINA WAS DREAMING. She knew she was even while she was doing it. She also knew she wanted to continue dreaming. She was with Spencer. Dancing. Dancing something slow and wicked. At a faculty party in the gym. No, no. What were those other teachers doing there? She didn't need those teachers.

She awoke with a start, hot and sweaty and tangled in her sheets. Apparently she'd been dancing all night.

Four days had passed since she and Spencer had agreed to not become involved. But for two people who were determined to stay uninvolved, they'd certainly been spending a lot of time together.

The morning they'd planned to go to breakfast, it rained. Dauntless, they went, anyway. They went to the garden center afterward, as well. Gina got marigolds for the garden, while Spencer bought four hanging baskets of impatiens for the porch. While they were making their choices, Stacy drifted into the crafts section and gathered a basketful of supplies to make wreaths for their doors. And Joe, following in her wake, just smiled.

Gina had thought that was as good as the day was going to get, but in the afternoon they'd sat on the deep front porch of the farmhouse, talking and watching the rain sheet down, and the day had gotten better still.

The following day was just as pleasant. So was the day after that. They took walks in the woods, they gardened, they even paid a visit to Buffington Antiques. And through it all, Spencer and Gina remained uninvolved.

But the nights, oh, the nights. That was the time Gina paid for her days, and it was beginning to get on her nerves. She threw back the sheet and swung her feet to the floor, cursing Spencer Coburn to hell—or at least to a similarly dissatisfied awakening.

She tugged on her robe, stepped into her slippers and started for the spiral staircase, her mind on coffee and the morning paper.

Halfway down the stairs, she paused, overcome by an unexpected intimation that something wasn't right about this bright new morning. She cocked her head and listened, then leaned over the rail and glanced toward her father's bed.

"Dear God," she whispered as she flew down the rest of the stairs.

CHAPTER TEN

HER FATHER'S BED was empty, the covers pulled sharply to one side. "Dad?" she called, leaping the last two stairs.

She found him on the floor next to the bed. Her blood was pounding so hard it stole her breath. Lying on his side, Joe gazed up at her, blank-eyed, frightened and helpless.

"Dad, what happened?" She helped him to a sitting position. The coolness of his arms made her wonder how long he'd been lying there, waiting for her.

"F-fell." Though he spoke with difficulty, Gina was encouraged. He still understood her, still was able to speak.

Staggering under his deceptive weight, she got him to his feet and sat him on the bed. His left arm hung motionless from shoulder to fingertips. Using his right hand, he lifted his left and laid it on his thigh.

Gina's throat tightened. She sat beside him and wrapped him in her arms. "It's okay, Dad. You're all right." Inwardly she wondered if she was just trying to convince herself. "Would you like some coffee?" she asked, not knowing what else to do. Joe nodded. "Okay, you sit here and take it easy. I'll get us both a cup."

A few minutes later she returned. She'd filled his mug only half-full, yet he could barely carry it to his lips. She

braced his hand with hers and tried to keep the tears in
her eyes from spilling.

After he'd swallowed a few sips, she said, "How about
some cereal?" Again he nodded. "Stay here. I'll bring it
to you."

With her help, Joe managed to eat a small bowl of
oatmeal, but for the most part his appetite was gone. She
sat next to him on the bed, wondering what she should do
next, trying to ignore the tremors of fear still rippling
through her.

From beyond the door connecting her place and
Spencer's, she could hear activity. Breakfast sounds.
That relieved her somewhat, reminded her she wasn't
quite so alone. But she also suffered a moment of apprehension, the same apprehension that had made her reluctant to move next door to a doctor. Spencer was going
to criticize her for the way she was taking care of her father.

She reached for Joe's hand and squeezed it, a silent
reassurance that she wouldn't be swayed by criticism. A
promise was a promise. Besides, nothing major had
happened. What was to criticize? She could handle this.

"Dad, I'm going to go get Spencer, okay? You know
Spencer, right?" She searched his lost eyes but saw no
response. "Okay, sit still. I'll be right back." This was
nothing to worry about, she told herself again.

But as she started for the door, a voice at the back of
her thoughts whispered, *What would you be doing if
something major had happened? How would you be
coping then?* For one frightening moment, Gina didn't
have an answer.

With a snap of her head, she shook off her doubts. *I'd
cope just as I'm doing now.* She rapped on the connecting door and undid the lock on her side.

Footsteps approached. The lock on the other side turned, and the next moment she was facing Spencer. She squelched the urge to fall into his arms and bury herself in his strength.

He frowned, puzzled. "Gina, what's the matter?" Over his shoulder, Gina could see Stacy sitting at the counter in the kitchen.

"I'm sorry. I wouldn't knock on this door ordinarily, but..."

He stepped over the threshold and closed the door behind him.

"My father's taken a slight turn for the worse." She wrung her hands as Spencer's alert gaze darted past her. "Until now he's been able to dress himself with only a little help from me. But he's going to need more help today, and I was wondering..." Each word she spoke seemed to deepen Spencer's frown. Her hand-wringing intensified. "I'd do it myself, but I know he'd be embarrassed, and I was wondering, if you could just get him to the bathroom and into fresh underclothes, I'll manage from there."

She could feel disinclination coming off him in waves. "I'm s-sorry. This is a terrible imposition."

Sighing heavily, Spencer clutched the nape of his neck. "No, of course it isn't an imposition." But his body language said something quite different.

"Never mind." She was hurt. The past couple of days had led her to believe she and Spencer were friends. "Forget I asked."

She reached around him to reopen the connecting door, but he caught her wrist and said, "Bring me his clothes."

While Spencer was getting Joe dressed, Gina ran upstairs and tugged on a pair of culottes and a cotton sweater. When she came down, the TV was on and Joe was sitting in his recliner. Spencer stood at a window, looking out. His arms were folded, his profile grim. She approached with misgiving.

"Thank you. I really appreciate your help."

He turned, his stormy blue eyes clashing with hers. "He's had another ministroke. You realize that, don't you?"

"Yes."

"You told me he was *slightly* worse, but he can hardly use his left side. He almost fell as I was dressing him."

"Yes," she repeated, the word reduced to a mere sibilance.

"What are you planning to do about it?"

"Do?" She forced herself to think through the anxiety he was raising. "I plan...I plan to call his doctor, tell him what happened and get his advice."

"Good, because I don't want to take responsibility for him."

Gina stared at him, dumbstruck. "I know. You told me that before I moved in. When I asked you to help, I had no intention of getting you involved in my father's long-term care. I just needed a little assistance this morning."

Spencer leaned closer. "And what do you intend to do tomorrow and the next day and the day after that?"

"Well..." She tried to think of an answer, but the only thought in her head was, why was Spencer so hostile?

Into her silence he threw, "That man needs professional care, Gina."

Gina slumped against the windowsill, suddenly weary to the bone. She nodded. "I'll get a home-health aide to start coming in again."

Perhaps he heard the note of defeat in her voice, because his own voice softened. "I wasn't referring to a home-health aide, Gina. Joe needs continuous care. You'll be lucky if you can get an aide to come three hours a week.''

''What are you referring to, then? A nursing home?''

She wasn't surprised when Spencer nodded. He'd mentioned a nursing home the very first time they'd met.

She shook her head. ''I'm not putting him in a nursing home. I promised him I wouldn't, and even if I hadn't promised, I still wouldn't do it. First of all, I don't have the financial resources. Second, they have long waiting lists, and the paperwork . . .''

''I realize there are obstacles, but you can get around them. He has medical insurance, right?''

''Yes.''

''Well, then, what you should do right now is check Joe into a hospital. Given his condition, I'm sure his doctor will be more than amenable to that idea. His insurance will pick up most of the tab, and once he's in, the hospital will have to keep him. Legally their hands will be tied. In the meantime, they have social-services staff specially trained to help you negotiate the red tape of getting him placed in a home.'' He paused. ''What's the matter? You look as if you've swallowed a bug.''

Gina didn't smile. She almost didn't find her voice, she was that upset over Spencer's readiness to dump her father into a hospital where legally they'd ''have to keep him,'' as if he were a parcel nobody wanted.

''I'm sorry. I can't do that.''

''Why not?''

''My father dislikes hospitals.''

Spencer seemed about to laugh, then must've realized she was serious. ''But he probably wouldn't even realize where he was.''

"Don't count on it. He might not have much of a grip on reality anymore, but he still has an emotional memory. He remembers feelings, like the contentment he always felt living here at the farm, and I'm sure he'd remember he always feared hospitals."

"None of us likes hospitals, Gina. Even doctors."

She shook her head. "His fear goes beyond your common garden variety. I don't know where it came from, probably from the way he was raised, but it's there, deep and irrational, and it can't be ignored. He hid it well through most of his life, but now that he's regressing mentally..." She paused, remembering how her father trembled during even the most routine doctor's visits, how he clung to her and asked repeatedly, "What's he going to do to me?"

Spencer sighed irritably. "Well, that's just too bad. Children don't like to do certain things, either—eat the right foods, get enough sleep—but we don't let them get away with it."

Gina's vision jumped with red spots. Keeping a calm voice was a monumental effort when she said, "It isn't the same."

"Of course it is."

"No, it isn't. He's not a child, and this has nothing to do with stubbornness." Spencer seemed about to protest again. "Besides," she cut in, "he's getting continuous care already. From me. He doesn't need a hospital or a nursing home."

"Gina, you're an English teacher."

She suddenly wanted to ram his condescension down his throat.

"Though you may love him, giving love isn't the same as providing the right care."

"In other words, you're saying I'm being negligent."

Spencer dragged a hand down his face. "I think Joe should be in a place where he can be monitored by professionals round the clock."

"And I think I've chosen the best course for him."

"I'm sorry. I disagree."

She crossed her arms. "Well, I disagree with you." As angry as she was, she knew they sounded like children.

"Spencer, listen to me," she said, uncrossing her arms and seeking a more rational approach. "I know my father isn't going to last long, a year if he's lucky. His body is just...well, shot. And I don't want him spending his last days in a place that's strange and frightening to him."

Spencer was about to protest again. Gina raised her fingertips to his lips, not quite touching them.

"I'm not some crackpot who's capriciously opposed to hospitals. Good Lord, my mother spent nine weeks in one before she died, and I wouldn't have had it any other way. But she was a different person altogether. She was sharp as a tack. She understood why she was there and *wanted* to be there.

"But my father would only be confused and scared, and he'd be terribly embarrassed. I'm sure of it." She laced her fingers and pressed her knuckles to her mouth. How could she make Spencer understand? To most people her position would sound odd. To a doctor, untenable.

She lowered her hands, still linked. "My father has always been a private person, Spencer, independent and self-sufficient to the bone. He hasn't left a living will, but I know what he wants. We talked about it a lot after my mother died. He wants to die the way he lived, privately and on his own. I promised him that he would."

Gina dared a look into Spencer's eyes, but couldn't tell what he was thinking.

"My father was also a highly intelligent person. He could grow anything, build anything, fix it when it broke, and he read voraciously, everything from Ovid to Beetle Bailey. In fact, it was from him that I acquired my love of literature. I think such a man should be able to go out with his dignity intact."

She thought she'd explained herself well, and for a moment she thought Spencer understood and agreed. But then he said, "There are so many things that can be done these days, but you're not giving him a chance."

"What I'm giving him," she said carefully, "is the chance to die with dignity, something he'll lose if I put him in the care of people who don't know him, people who see him only as he is now."

She might have been talking in Swahili. Spencer's entire mien communicated disapproval. "I can't believe you've surrendered without a fight to the idea of his dying."

"Without a fight?" Strangling on frustration, she cried, "Ooh! You're such a . . . a doctor!"

Spencer's dark brows puckered. "Do I dare ask what *that* means?"

She wasn't sure herself; the thought had simply poured off her tongue. It took a moment for her to examine the jumbled emotions and ideas that had given rise to it. "You see death as the enemy," she explained, "as something to fight right to the end, no matter what."

"Damn right!"

"That's what's wrong with Western medicine," she insisted, ignoring the inner voice that said she was far from an expert on anything Eastern. In fact, the only book she could recall reading that was even vaguely Eastern was *The Tao of Pooh*.

Still, she said, "Our culture can't accept the fact that death is just a natural part of life. As a consequence, we put our elderly through holy hell when their time comes, instead of helping them on their final passage."

Spencer looked at her calmly. "Would you prefer we didn't try so hard to save lives?"

She hesitated, blinking. "No, of course not. Not if someone should be saved."

"Should be? Where do you draw the line, Gina?"

"I don't know." Her head was beginning to hurt. "All I know is, I promised my father I wouldn't put him in a nursing home. Neither would I send him to a hospital. He wants to die at home, and I intend to see that he does."

Spencer said nothing, just lifted his eyebrows as if to say, *It's your decision.* But she knew he disapproved.

That saddened her. She never would've taken Spencer for a man who'd advocate such a stand. Which only went to prove that, despite several pleasant days spent in his company, she really didn't know him. What saddened her more was, she didn't think she liked him, either.

Gina walked with Spencer back to the connecting door. When he opened it, Stacy was hurrying away, trying to pretend she hadn't been eavesdropping.

"I'm sorry I bothered you," Gina said politely. "It won't happen again."

Any other person would've said it was no bother, she could count on him anytime. Not Spencer. He looked at her a moment, looked straight into her eyes and nodded. In that moment she felt the ties of their friendship slip apart, and that was the saddest cut of all.

THAT AFTERNOON Gina took her father to see his physician, Dr. Abrams, who agreed Joe had suffered another ministroke. To determine the cause and to measure the damage, he persuaded Gina to take Joe to the hospital in Kingfield the next day for an MRI. The test was painless, but her father trembled throughout.

That fueled Gina's conviction. When Dr. Abrams called later in the day and recommended that Joe be admitted to the hospital for therapy, she pleaded her case. To her surprise and relief, the doctor agreed that as long as she was able and willing to care for her father, Joe could stay at home.

Dr. Abrams changed Joe's medication, and his nurse arranged for an aide to start coming by every morning to help wash and dress him. She also got Joe a walker to help him get around. That was all the help immediately available, however, unless she wanted to hire someone out-of-pocket. Gina chose to put that off. Not because of the expense—she'd find the money somewhere—but because she was sure she could manage.

And she did, cheerfully, for a couple of days. But on the third morning, she awoke with a vague sense of dread. By that evening it had grown to a weight that constricted her breathing. The next day, melancholy was so pervasive it was all she could do to put one foot in front of the other.

Her father's health had declined more than she'd thought. He couldn't even eat on his own anymore. Left to himself, he dropped more food than he got to his mouth. The rest, he played with. He sculpted mashed potatoes into hills and blanketed his peas with salt, forgetting its purpose, fascinated only by the sight of the tiny grains falling. Sometimes he even became delusional.

Thank heaven for Stacy and her frequent visits during those last difficult days of June. She seemed to get a real kick out of Joe, which kept Gina afloat on many a discouraging occasion. Her youthful laughter and cries of

"Joe! What are you *doing?*" often made him laugh, which got Gina to laughing in turn. She was sure he didn't understand why he was laughing. He only knew that someone was teasing him, and on some obscure emotional level, he remembered to associate teasing and laughter.

It wasn't long before Gina realized Stacy was a remarkable young woman, generous and resourceful beyond her years. It was Stacy who suggested she buy a nursery monitor to keep tabs on Joe's sleeping and waking, Stacy who sat chatting with him while Gina prepared dinner, Stacy who got the laundry done. Gina not only looked forward to her lively company, she came to depend on her help, as well.

Gina couldn't say that Spencer didn't help, too. He came over at least once a day and inquired after Joe. He also made a point of asking if she needed anything from town. Sometimes he didn't ask; he just returned with groceries he thought she could use. But aside from the cordial remarks they exchanged if they happened to meet in the yard or on the way to the mailbox, that was the extent of his involvement with her and Joe. There was no mistaking that their relationship had changed, that he'd withdrawn—they'd *both* withdrawn—and a chill had settled into the distance between them.

He'd begun painting the house, farthest side first. Some days, the only proof he was still around was the occasional clank of the aluminum ladder as he moved it. When he wasn't painting, he was cutting the grass, and when he wasn't doing that, Stacy said he was inside reading or tending to household chores. He didn't join them on their evening walks, which had shortened to trips up the driveway, and he declined invitations to accompany them to the Creamery. In fact, he didn't even come outside to see Stacy's sunflowers, which, to Stacy's delight, had sprouted within days of their planting, thick of stem and sturdy of leaf.

"Look at them, Gina!" she exclaimed joyfully. "I can't believe it! They're growing!"

Joe, nodding off in the shade, smiled dreamily, remembering joy.

Increasingly, Gina missed Spencer. She didn't know why. The man was overbearing in his opinions. His views regarding Joe's care were at loggerheads with hers. And she didn't much like the way he related to his daughter. He'd taken Stacy to see the new obstetrician, but had he *talked* to her about her fears? Had he done anything about birth-preparation classes? Stacy told her she thought her father was trying to pretend the pregnancy didn't exist. Gina was beginning to think she was right.

Still, she missed him. Missed him in the garden. Missed his lopsided smile. And, God, she missed the talking.

A woodchuck got to the broccoli, and she had to buy more plants. Stacy stayed with Joe while she zipped across town to the garden center. While she was there, she also bought a roll of chicken wire.

But a day passed, and another. A few more plants disappeared, yet the roll of wire remained propped against the garden shed. Gina simply had too much else to do and too little inclination.

"What's the point, anyway?" She sighed despondently as she flopped into bed a week after her father's setback. "The woodchuck can take it all." And she meant it. She didn't care. Her strength and enthusiasm were utterly gone. She didn't understand why. Although her father's condition had worsened, it hadn't created *that* much extra work or stress.

Gina sank into her pillows and closed her eyes tight. Tears squeezed through her lashes. Who was she trying to kid? Of course she understood. Today was her birthday. She'd turned forty today. She'd left behind a decade that could still be considered young, and entered unequivocally into middle age. Moreover, she'd been thinking of turning forty all week. That was probably the reason she'd been so down. No *probably* about it. She'd dreaded the approaching birthday so much she hadn't told a soul about it, hadn't even called her friends back in Syracuse to drop hints.

Forty! *And where am I?* she asked the darkness muffling her room. Certainly not where she'd expected to be at this age. Oh sure, her career was enjoyable and worthwhile. But a career wasn't everything in life. She'd expected to be married by now, to have a husband she adored, a house full of lively children. Instead, here she lay, alone, unfulfilled, an old-maid schoolteacher, growing older with each breath.

She swiped at her damp eyes, angry at herself for becoming so self-absorbed. Normally she wasn't in the least concerned about aging. Normally she thought people who were concerned, vain and silly. But here she lay, railing against the march of time, as vain and silly as any fool ever got.

She supposed her reaction to the big four-o had a lot to do with being with her father this summer, with seeing him decline. He was her last immediate relative, and a parent besides. Until now he'd stood between her and death. But once he was gone, she'd have to move up to the front line.

Her eyes filled and she swiped at them again, angry at time and fate. Hell, she had a right to be mad. Her dream hadn't been grandiose. All she'd ever wanted was an ordinary home life, a husband, a couple of kids. Other people had those blessings. Why couldn't she? Who had decided that Gina Marie Banning ought to be deprived?

She wanted to experience life before she died. She longed for it, pined for it with the hunger of the starved. And, oh, how she craved romance, intense romance, romance that blinded and dizzied. And sex. Not the kind she'd had with her husband. Earth-moving sex, teeth-rattling sex—at least once before time hurled her completely beyond its possibility.

But it wasn't going to happen. She knew that as certainly as she'd ever known anything. She was a single woman who'd turned forty today. She'd received only two cards, no gifts, no cake, proving the old adage: Out of sight, out of mind. But worst of all, oh, the worst, her father hadn't even known what day it was.

So let the woodchuck take her broccoli. Let him ravage her garden right to the very last leaf. It didn't matter anymore. It just didn't matter.

THE NEXT MORNING Gina awoke to a fine gray rain trickling down the skylight over her bed. She got up, crossed the room and started to lower the window. At the same time she gave the garden below a cursory glance.

Suddenly her breath hitched. Sometime during the night, as if some hovering angel had heard her despair, the garden had been fenced.

BECAUSE OF THE RAIN, Spencer was forced to forgo painting the house that morning. He walked from window to window, restless as a caged bear. Quite often the window he stopped at looked out on the garden. He wondered if Gina had noticed the fencing yet. He wondered what she thought.

He'd been concerned about her these past few days. She'd looked pale and drawn. She hadn't been taking her usual care with her appearance, either. He was all for people going natural and casual, but Gina's disregard for herself seemed to run deeper. Obviously, caring for her father was getting to her.

Spencer had feared that would happen. In his practice he'd seen the toll that caring for elderly parents often took on families. But that still didn't explain why he'd pushed the idea of a nursing home so hard on Gina.

He stood at his open kitchen door watching the muted hills in the distance, feeling the mist on his face. How many times had he himself argued to keep an elderly patient at home? How many times had he wrestled with bureaucracy to make arrangements?

The little insight he did have into his uncharacteristic behavior with Gina pointed to a fear he'd harbored since first laying eyes on Joe. Gina had once remarked that her father probably wouldn't last long, a year perhaps. Spencer knew it would be sooner, a lot sooner, and he realized he didn't want to be a part of it. If Joe was elsewhere, he wouldn't have to be.

He just wished Gina hadn't gotten caught in the middle. She had a right to care for her father at home. At another time, Spencer knew he'd even admire her for it.

Dammit, he *did* admire her. He'd never seen anyone more patient or devoted to a parent in his life. Her compassion moved him. It shifted things inside him: cells, emotions, perspectives. Left him feeling like a whining jackass. Made him want to help. Made him want to care.

He walked quietly across the kitchen and pressed his ear to the connecting door. All he heard from the other side were the bells and whistles of a TV game show.

He missed her, and he'd been missing her all week. That was why he'd fenced in her garden and why he stood here now in a state of unrelieved anticipation. His mother was fond of saying, "If you want a ship to come in, first you have to send one out." Well, he definitely had the feeling he'd sent out a ship.

Of course, if Gina didn't respond, he wouldn't blame her. He'd had no right to criticize the way she was caring for Joe. He'd been way out of line. But he sure hoped she would. He . . . missed her.

From the other side of the door, voices suddenly overrode the TV sounds. The home-health aide had arrived. Spencer hadn't heard the car pull up. He stepped back from the door with a sigh, deciding the best thing to do was get busy at something constructive. In his experience ships usually came in when you weren't watching.

The rain had stopped, but since the siding was still wet and unpaintable, Spencer decided to check out the old barn that was slated for demolition.

The barn stood up by the road. Daisies and lupines, profuse from years of reseeding themselves, bloomed against its splintered silvered shingles. Bird nests tufted from chinks in the eaves, and the center beam sagged like the spine of a tired, swaybacked horse.

It was with a measure of trepidation that he'd told Gina about the Fergusons' plan to demolish the barn. But her response had surprised him. She'd said the structure was so old and decrepit it hadn't been used since before her grandfather's time. "It doesn't even have the good grace to be picturesque," she'd said.

Spencer had brought along a toolbox and a long wrecking bar. When he reached the barn, he set them down, unhooked the rusted padlock and tugged open the broad wooden door. Birds flapped about in the dark rafters. The smell of must assailed him. Picking up his tools again, he strode in.

For a while, all he could see was white daylight beaming through pinholes in the east wall. When his vision adjusted, he looked about, trying to decide where to begin. When he found the ladder up to the loft, he hooked his wrecking bar to his belt and set off.

Once in the loft, Spencer stepped carefully to the haymow door and opened it. The sun had burned away the haze, and light came pouring in. He was just drawing back, about to start examining the aged boards and beams, when he spotted someone turning the corner of the house. He froze in place. It was Gina.

GINA APPROACHED the barn with her heart in her throat. She needed to thank Spencer for fencing in the garden. But she was also on her way to accept a peace offering, because a peace offering was the only interpretation she could place on his kindness. She hoped it also meant they would be returning to the easy friendship they'd shared before Joe's setback.

"Spencer?" she called into the cavernous gloom.

She heard movement from above, glanced to the loft and saw him step to the edge—tall, straight, magnificent. Her brain fizzed like a short-circuited wire. The next moment that same traitorous brain was flooding her with unwanted fantasies of haylofts and lovers coupling in beds of straw.

"Hello, Gina." His voice was low, dusky.

Suddenly unsure of herself, she looked aside, concentrating on a spiderweb strung across one of the old six-over-six windows. Sun shot, the web swayed in the slight air current like silver lace.

"I went to your door, but Stacy told me you were here," she said tentatively. "I hope I'm not disturbing anything."

"Nothing much. What's up?"

She laced her fingers and dug her right thumb into her left palm. "I just want to thank you for fencing in the garden."

He shifted his weight, one leg to the other, casual, almost aloof. "No problem. I couldn't sleep, and the moon was full. Plenty of light to work by. I figured it would tire me out."

"Oh. And did it?"

"Uh-huh. I came in around three, fell into bed and slept until seven."

"It served its purpose then." Disappointment slid through her. Maybe she'd mistaken his gesture. Maybe it hadn't signified anything at all.

But then she noticed Spencer's mouth soften into a wry smile. "I was also mad as hell at that damn woodchuck. You've put so much work into your garden he was lucky that stringing a fence was all I did."

She watched the warmth of his smile spread to his eyes and felt a matching warmth rise in her, filling her until she thought she might float right up to the rafters. Seconds passed and still they continued to gaze at each other, he from above, she below, wrapped in hazy light—and something more, she thought: the peace of reconciliation.

"Well, thanks again," she said. "I really appreciate it." She bit her lip, hesitating before she added, "It was my birthday yesterday."

He frowned.

"It was a wonderful present, Spencer, whether you were aware of it or not."

"My pleasure." But his frown remained.

"What are you doing here?" she asked quickly.

"Oh." He took a breath and scanned the beams overhead. "Just checking how the barn was built, seeing if I'm able to unbuild it."

"Mind if I come up and take a look?"

"Not at all. Be careful on the ladder. The first rung is missing and the third is ready to give."

Spencer watched Gina climb the ladder, each squeak of old wood shooting more adrenaline into his already overworked nervous system.

He still wasn't over the disappointment he'd felt when she'd told him about her birthday. Stacy hadn't mentioned anything about a birthday. Hadn't Gina told her? He hadn't seen any visitors, either. Had she spent the entire day alone, tending to her father? Her father, who didn't know Monday from Friday, this week from last century.

Spencer hovered above her as she crawled off the ladder into the the the loft. Still on all fours, she laughed. "That climb used to be a lot shorter when I was a kid."

He helped her to her feet. "And how long ago was that?"

She cast him a coy look. "Is that your way of asking what age I turned yesterday?"

He shrugged and tried to look sheepish. She answered him with a chuckle. Then, brushing at her knees, she scanned the roof beams. "Lots of dry rot."

"Mmm." He picked up the wrecking bar and poked at one of the beams, trying to do something, anything, that would take his mind off the woman standing next to him. It didn't work.

"Forty," she said, still looking at those beams.

He thought he hid his surprise well. "You look a lot younger."

"Good genes," she said casually before walking toward the haymow door. The sunlight met her and, as she stepped closer to the edge, wrapped around her like a lover's embrace.

"Why didn't you say something? We could've at least gotten together for a drink."

She cast him a wry over-the-shoulder glance. "I wasn't exactly in a mood to celebrate."

"What did you do?"

"Had a midlife crisis."

"Sweetheart, midlife *is* a crisis."

She turned, smiling. "Isn't it just? Look at the two of us, you with Stacy, me with my father."

He nodded. "A perfect generation sandwich."

The smile faded from her lips. "What did you do on your fortieth, Spencer?"

He ran a crooked index finger across his lips, trying to remember. "Stacy and I went to a video arcade, as I recall. We followed it up with dinner at Taco Bell." He chuckled. "It was great."

She smiled, her eyes sparkling. "I'm glad."

Suddenly Spencer noticed why her eyes were so bright. They were filled with tears.

"Spencer, let's not argue anymore," she said on a wavery breath.

Spencer lifted his arms. "Come here," he said, and with a small cry she ran to him.

"Oh, sweetheart," he murmured, holding her tight. "I don't want to argue, either." He pressed her closer, his hands spread wide across her back, trying to gather her closer still. A week ago, when he'd shut the connecting door on her, he'd thought it would be easy to get her out of his system, but he'd been wrong. Easy? It wasn't even remotely possible.

Gina tipped back her head, lifting her eyes to his in invitation. He tried to think logically. There were reasons they shouldn't be doing this. Lots of reasons. Unfortunately he didn't give a damn about a single one. The next moment he'd lowered his head and covered her mouth with his. Heat took hold of him immediately.

"I thought we weren't going to do this anymore," she murmured unsteadily against his lips.

"Bad idea. Very bad," he said as he kissed her again. It was impossible not to kiss her. He was drawn to Gina hormonally, and there was no arguing with hormones. Hormones didn't listen to reason. Hormones didn't care what was morally right for his daughter. Hormones took no heed of forecasts of heartache. After seven days of pure frustration, Spencer was too weak to argue, anyway.

He angled his mouth over hers more possessively and surrendered to his need. His only concern was that he was moving too fast and ought to be trying to hold back. He was afraid he'd scare her, maybe overwhelm her. But Gina opened to him eagerly, uninterested in holding back. With a moan, he sank deeper, helpless, stroking her tongue with his, learning its raspy texture, stroking the inside of her lips, discovering their sleekness. Then he plunged farther still, wanting to explore every dark mystery of her. She surprised him by exploring him, instead.

She ran her hands over his shoulders and up his neck, burying her fingers in his hair, pulling him to her. He ran his hands down her back to her hips. They swayed, dizzy with hunger. Without breaking the seal of their kiss, he lifted her, took a step and braced her against the rough board wall.

Gina moaned and nodded, which he took for gratitude for the support. Then their bodies melded, their shared desire burning through their clothing until they might have been wearing nothing. And through it all they kissed. Kisses that took on a rhythm and life all their own. Kisses that acquired an unselfconscious lushness that incited Spencer to explore other delights. Her breasts. Her thighs. The moist heat between her thighs.

She gasped as he cupped her, arched as he stroked. Impatient, she fumbled with the zipper on her shorts, then guided his hand inside. Still kissing her, Spencer opened one eye and scanned the loft. It was pitifully unaccommodating, nothing but hard, dusty floor.

"It's all right," she whispered huskily. "At least we're alone here."

Spencer marveled at the sudden force of his arousal. It almost knocked him off his feet. He wanted to pull her down to that pool of yellow sunlight on the floor and make love like she'd never known it before. And then when they were sated, he thought he might like to lie there for a while just watching the sunlight pouring over her, her face, her breasts, her feet. And when he'd had enough of that...

"Dad?"

Stacy's voice crashed over Spencer like ice water.

"Gina?" she called. "Are you in here?"

Spencer and Gina jumped apart. Had Stacy seen them? he wondered. Gina zippered her shorts. She looked terrified. Heat pulsed from her face. She tried to button her blouse. Her fingers trembled. Not sure he'd be any more effective, Spencer tried to help.

"Yeah, Stace. We're up in the loft," he replied as calmly as possibly.

"What are you doing up there?"

Spencer tucked in his shirt, combed back his hair with two hands and stepped to the edge of the loft, giving Gina time to gather her composure.

He was pretty sure they'd been standing too far back for Stacy to see them, but she wasn't stupid. Their silence alone must've spoken volumes to her.

Nevertheless, he gave her the explanation he'd given earlier to Gina, the one about checking on the barn's structure. By then, Gina had come to stand by his side. Her mouth and neck were blotched from the abrasiveness of his beard, and her bra strap hung over one arm. He almost laughed. He felt ridiculously like a teenager who'd been caught by his parents making out on the rumpus-room sofa.

But of course there was nothing funny about this situation. That was his daughter down there, a confused teenager who would never understand this liaison and certainly not be pleased by it.

"Did you want us for something?" he asked, picking up the wrecking bar and prodding a beam. Stacy was searching his face, searching Gina's. He could feel it.

"Yeah. The aide's ready to leave."

"I'll be along in a couple of minutes," Gina replied. "Will you tell him to wait for me?"

"Sure." Embarrassment pervaded the barn.

"Thanks."

Spencer and Gina watched Stacy return to the house from the haymow door.

"What do you think?" Spencer asked quietly.

"I think...I think you ought to go talk to her."

Spencer dragged a hand down his face. "I will."

"Now," she added, reminding him of all the other problems she'd encouraged him to discuss with his daughter and he'd postponed.

He gave the sunny loft a look of regret, then headed for the ladder.

CHAPTER ELEVEN

SPENCER STOOD on the threshold of Stacy's room, reluctant and uncertain. What to say to this daughter he couldn't talk to, this offspring he loved to distraction but didn't know? Where to even begin?

Stacy sat slouched in a chair, her swollen feet propped on the bed. She had to know he was there, yet she didn't look up, channeling all her attention to the music flowing through her earphones. Her right foot tapped out a jerky rhythm.

Spencer stepped into the room. She closed her eyes, kept the foot tapping. He walked over and removed the earphones.

"Hey!" she protested.

He set the earphones on the nightstand and sat on the bed, facing her. "We've got to talk."

"Maybe later. I'm sort of busy."

"I'd rather talk now," he said with soft insistence.

With a ponderous sigh, she subsided into the cushions of her chair.

"Stace, I'm not going to waste time lying to you. I'm sure you know what was going on between me and Gina up in the loft."

"It's none of my business." She gave her head an unconcerned toss, but her flushed cheeks betrayed her.

"Of course it's your business. Whatever happens to me happens to you, too."

Her mouth tightened and quite unexpectedly she asked, "Are you sleeping with her?"

Spencer jerked back. "What?"

Stacy's face was ablaze from hairline to neck. "You heard me."

"No, I'm not sleeping with her. We just met, for heaven's sake." Belatedly he wondered if he should've said, "No, we're not married." But Stacy would never buy that. Too much extramarital stuff on TV, in films. In her life.

"That isn't to say I *will* be sleeping with her later on," he added quickly. "It isn't a question of timing. She and I simply live too far apart to continue seeing each other after this summer. It wouldn't be right to start something serious now, and sex *is* serious."

For the first time since he'd entered her room, Stacy looked at him squarely. "Tell me about it," she said, placing a hand on her stomach. Then she utterly surprised him with a smile—just a little one, but it was enough. His tensed shoulders released.

"The reason I'm here," Spencer ventured, "is I thought you might be upset."

Stacy lowered her eyes.

"Are you?" he prodded.

"I was surprised. I knew you'd started dating—" her lips twitched over the word *dating* "—but I'd never actually seen you with anyone before. It threw me for a moment."

Spencer leaned forward, resting his elbows on his knees, and hoped he chose his words well. "Then it has nothing to do with your mother?"

"My mother?" Stacy's delicate face screwed up.

"Mmm. I thought you might've still been hoping she and I would reconcile someday. You did for a while. Remember the stunts you used to pull to get us together?"

"Like pretending I was deathly sick so you'd stay over?"

Spencer grinned. "Among other things."

Stacy swung her feet off the bed and sat straighter. "Those days are gone, Dad. I know it's never going to happen. Mom's life has moved on. Good grief, she's getting married in a couple of months."

"And what about me? Can you accept that my life has moved on, too?"

Stacy lowered her eyes and frowned. Spencer knew this wasn't easy for her. He wished he could hold her and rock her the way he used to when she was a toddler.

"As long as you don't leave me behind," she murmured.

His chest ached. "Oh, baby, never. You'll always be my first girl."

Her eyes filled. Shading them, she said, "Well, then, I guess it's okay, especially since we're talking about Gina."

Spencer felt as if he'd just emerged from a cave into warm sunlight. He sighed in relief.

They let some time pass in silence, enjoying the moment of accord, but eventually Stacy said, "I'm still confused."

"About what?"

"You and Gina not seeing each other after the summer."

"What's confusing about it?"

"Well, if you love her..."

"Who said I love her? I like Gina, I'm attracted to her..."

"And you care about her, right?"

He gave a reluctant yes.

"Well, then . . ."

"That still isn't love, Stacy." To get off the uncomfortable subject, Spencer quickly said, "Did you know yesterday was her birthday?"

Stacy's mouth dropped into a long oval. "No way!"

"Yes. Her fortieth."

"No way!" she said again.

He laughed, delighted by her animation. "I think we ought to get back at her for not telling us."

"I agree." Stacy's blue eyes gleamed. "A surprise party."

He nodded. "Yeah."

"When?"

"Tonight?"

"That's awfully short notice, Dad."

"Exactly. She'd never expect it."

"But can we pull it together so fast?"

"You and me together? Piece of cake."

"Great. Who will we invite?"

"Oh, wait. I don't think we should start thinking in terms of anybody but us. Joe isn't up to a lot of company."

"True. But Gina has this really close friend she's always talking about, Barbara. They've been friends since first grade."

Spencer ran his knuckles over his chin, considering. "If you can find her number, sure, we'll give her a call."

"Super."

"You think we should get her a gift?"

"Well, of course."

Spencer glanced at his watch. "Let me go next door and set this thing up first. Then we'll go shopping."

Stacy beamed. "I'll call Barbara while you're gone."

Spencer stood and, on a surge of affection, made a move to tousle her short, uneven hair. Thinking better of it, he shoved his hand into his pocket, instead.

Stacy looked up at him and smirked. "It's okay, Dad."

Marveling at how astute she was, Spencer lifted his hand again and scrubbed at her hair, ruffling it till it stood on end and both their hearts were eased.

AT TEN MINUTES TO SIX, Gina opened her refrigerator and took out a bottle of white wine. Half a bottle actually. But half was probably all they'd need. She glanced at a fuller bottle, but red wouldn't do. Spencer had said they'd be having fish tonight. Swordfish, to be exact. Her favorite.

Spencer had come over right after his talk with his daughter and said, "It's going to be okay. She doesn't mind us seeing each other. We just have to remember to make her feel included."

Which was just what Gina had been trying to tell him all along.

To prove to Stacy they weren't abandoning her, they'd agreed to get together for a casual, impromptu meal this evening. That was also the reason Spencer had invited his daughter to go shopping with him this afternoon. They'd been gone quite a long time, too, which Gina considered a great development in their relationship.

The only thing she didn't feel great about was her own relationship with Spencer. She didn't know what it was or where it was going or even *why* it was. They'd had no time to talk about it.

"Come on, Dad." Gina gently roused her father.

Slumped in his recliner, he came awake with a sudden, "Are they shootin' again? Them Carter boys, are they shootin'?"

"No, Dad, nobody's shooting. We've been invited to dinner next door. Come on." She helped her father to his feet, swung the walker in front of him and escorted him to the connecting door. It had begun to rain again, and although the rain was soft, her father walked so slowly they would've been soaked if they'd taken the outside route.

Stacy answered her knock. "Hi. Come on in." Her color was high, her shoulders stiff.

"I brought some wine." Gina waggled the bottle. She noticed Stacy was wearing a light blue maternity jumper with embroidered flowers on the bib. "Oh, you got dressed up," she said, glancing at her own shirt and jeans in dismay.

"This old thing?" Stacy quipped.

"Where's your dad?"

"In here," Spencer called from the dining room. "Why don't you come in and settle your father. The food's almost ready."

Gina was beginning to feel something odd in the atmosphere. Frowning suspiciously, she took her father by the arm, walked him through the kitchen and pushed open one of the swinging café doors. The next moment the air rang with "Surprise!"

Gina jumped. "What on earth? Barbara?" she gasped, noticing her old friend. For a moment she was totally disoriented, but then she gave the streamer-festooned room a scan and put two and two together. Blushing, she covered her face with one hand and grinned. "I'm going to get you for this, Spencer."

He looked up from the two numerical candles he was lighting on a yellow-and-white frosted cake and winked. They stared at each other a long moment, exchanging questions. *When did you find time to do this? Are you pleased? Why did you do this?* And *Don't you remember how you spent your birthday?*

From behind her Stacy began to sing "Happy Birthday." The others joined in. Glancing around the room, Gina noticed that Barbara had brought along her oldest daughter, Chrissie.

"Okay, make a wish and blow out your candles," Stacy said when the singing was done.

Gina leaned over the table and thought. What should she wish for? What did she want? Oddly, for someone who'd felt so discontented on her birthday, her mind went blank when she thought of herself. She glanced around the table. Okay, her wishes would be for them. For her father, an easy parting. For Stacy, an easy delivery. Barbara and Chrissie—she wished they'd get together with her more often. For Spencer—she hoped Spencer found peace. But for herself, all Gina wanted was the memory of this moment surrounded by friends.

She blew out the candles, first the 4, and then the 0, and everyone cheered. Barbara rushed over and gave her a big hug. "Holy cow, Ginnie. Forty. Did you ever dream you'd see the day?"

Gina stepped out of the embrace, but still clung to her friend's hands, which had grown plump, like the rest of her. "It's great to see you, Barb. And Chrissie. Oh, you became a young lady while I wasn't looking." Gina hugged Barbara's seventeen-year-old daughter, who'd inherited her mother's fair complexion and hair, as well as her humor.

"I hope you don't mind me tagging along with my mother." Chrissie leaned in conspiratorially. "But you know how she drinks at parties. Somebody has to be able to drive home."

Gina shot Stacy a look, hoping she didn't take Chrissie seriously. Stacy was grinning, and Gina got the feeling the two girls had already become acquainted.

Spencer pulled out a chair. "Come sit, Gina."

"Thanks." She looked at the cake and said, "Does this mean I'm not getting swordfish?"

Standing behind her chair, Spencer placed his hands on her shoulders and leaned close. "When I promise a lady swordfish, the lady gets swordfish."

Seated beside Joe, Barbara waggled her eyebrows in an insinuating way. Gina's first memory of those waggling eyebrows was sixth grade, when Billy Martin slipped a Nestlé's Crunch into her desk.   She cast Barbara a look that said, *Don't turn this into something it's not.*

Spencer rolled in a serving cart, then took the seat at the end of the table opposite Gina. Dinner was wonderful. The fish was succulent, the vegetables piquantly seasoned, the bread warm and the wine—Spencer's wine—fragrant and fruity. But Gina hardly noticed what she ate or drank. Her delight came from a set of smiling blue eyes at the other end of the table, from a mouth she knew too well, from a man she realized she was only beginning to know.

After dinner, there were presents. Barbara went all out on the age insults with a T-shirt that read, "Over the hill? What hill? I don't remember any hill," and a pair of heavy-duty support hose.

"What a pal," Gina said, rolling her eyes to camouflage the affection billowing inside her. She'd made lots of friends in her lifetime, but none of them were better than Barbara. No matter how infrequently they saw each other, the minute they they got together time and distance became irrelevant. They were six again and making mud pies; fifteen and trading gym socks; twenty-two and trying on wedding gowns.

Spencer came in from the living room, lugging a large, woven-wood basket whose contents were concealed by yellow tissue paper. "Ma'am," he said, setting the basket on the table in front of her.

"You got me a gift, too? After all this?" Gina waved a hand at the table.

Stacy beamed. "It's from me and my dad and your dad."

Gina lifted the paper and sighed. "Oh, my." The basket was filled with garden supplies: new hand tools, sturdy gloves, copper plant markers and a sign reading Welcome to My Garden. She set those on the table and continued digging. There was a hand-care kit, a bird feeder, birdseed, and at the bottom of the basket, a pair of pewter earrings shaped like dragonflies.

Gina meant to say, "Thank you," but her eyes filled and her throat closed so tight that nothing came out.

"Our pleasure," Spencer murmured as if he'd heard her, anyway. "We had fun shopping for you."

"He's *wonderful*, Ginnie," Barbara whispered later as they were walking into the living room. "Why didn't you tell me?"

Gina settled her father in a chair and said with weary exasperation, "There's nothing to tell."

"Yeah, right. You two've been eating each other up with your eyes all night."

Spencer walked in with a tray of coffee just then. Gina gave her friend a warning look and said, "So how's Tom?"

"Probably not too happy tonight, home with the kids."

Spencer set the tray on the coffee table. Stacy, close behind him, brought in the cake. "Gina told me you've got five. Quite a houseful." He handed Gina a cup.

Barbara's eyes twinkled. "Going on six. I'm two months along."

Gina's jaw dropped. So many feelings scuffled and skirmished inside her she couldn't utter a word.

"Congratulations," Spencer said.

"Yes," Gina finally got out. "All the best to you and Tom."

Her thoughts suddenly took an unexpected leap. "Barb, you've been through birth-preparation classes, haven't you?"

"Honey, I've been through everything. Saddle blocks, natural childbirth, Lamaze training. The only thing I haven't done is go into the woods and hug a tree."

"Well then—" Gina glanced at Stacy "—you're just the person we need to talk to."

SOMETIME LATER, Spencer was in the kitchen making a fresh pot of coffee and wondering why he'd put off talking to Stacy about her delivery. Now that Barbara was doing it, it seemed such an easy matter. But his procrastination didn't bother him half as much as did Stacy's need for the discussion. She was a mass of insecurities and misinformation. She was absorbing Barbara's advice and anecdotes like a dry sponge.

Gina came into the kitchen and placed a stack of dirty dishes on the counter near the sink. As Spencer filled the coffeepot with fresh water, he said, "Thanks for getting that conversation started."

"You really don't mind?"

"No. Why would I?"

"Oh—" she shrugged "—because you know everything that Barbara's been telling Stacy."

"I don't feel as if she's taking my place, if that's what you're saying."

"Well, I've noticed you hanging back." Gina rested her hip against the counter.

"Not sulking. Only trying to stay out of the way."

Gina accepted his answer with a slow nod. Then, looking toward the living room, she smiled. "The two girls seem to be hitting it off."

Spencer couldn't help smiling, too. "That Chrissie is something else. Know what her first words to Stacy were?"

Gina covered her eyes and winced. "What?"

"Not two minutes in the door and she said, 'So, I hear you're knocked up and your sweetie took a hike. Bummer.' Then in the next breath, 'Hey, cool earrings.'"

Gina laughed. "Remind me to tell you some stories about her mother."

Something in the way she laughed caught Spencer off guard. He wanted to kiss her, wanted to in the worst way. He opened the dishwasher and channeled his frustration into loading dishes. "Are you having a good time?"

"The best. It's just what I needed." She helped him load. After a thoughtful moment she confessed, "I don't think you realize how down I was."

"Probably not, but I'm glad if I've helped."

"You have." Her eyes met his, and she added softly, "You do."

Control be damned. He hooked his hand around her neck and drew her to him, not caring if anyone, even Stacy, walked in. "You help me, too," he said, brushing his lips over hers. And before she could ask what he meant, he said, "Let's get back to our company."

When they returned to the living room, Stacy was just saying, "I'm sure I'll love them."

"Love what?" Spencer asked.

"Birth-preparation classes."

Barbara added, "They're given at Union Hospital over in Kingfield. I took them, let's see, before I had my Jason."

Stacy looked up at him with new confidence. "I really ought to enroll, Dad. It's time."

"Will you need a partner?"

"Yeah. Barbara offered. So did Chrissie." Stacy grinned, poking the other girl's arm with her elbow. The two girls had been sitting together all evening. "But I was thinking..." Stacy bit her lip, and looked at Gina. "Gina, do you think you'd have the time? Barbara says the classes run for four or five weeks, one class each week."

Gina's face shifted through a dozen expressions, all of them beautiful, Spencer thought. "I...I'd love to, but..." She glanced at her father. Using his walker, he was inching his way around the room, examining familiar, forgotten corners.

"I'll stay with Joe." The words were out of Spencer's mouth before he could think about what he was committing himself to.

"And I'll spell you," Barbara added. "Every other week."

"Well, in that case, I'd love to be your birth partner, Stacy." Gina's eyes were suspiciously bright.

Spencer went over to the piano and sat on the bench. Behind him the conversation about pregnancy and delivery continued. He lifted the cover and fingered the yellowed keys. Maybe he ought to play something.

Maybe they would sing. He hoped so. Busy, he'd be less likely to think about those bright brown eyes and the conflicted emotions he'd just glimpsed within them.

Forty was a tricky birthday for anyone to navigate, but for a single and childless woman, a woman with so much love to give, it had to be doubly complicated. He could only guess what Gina might be feeling as she looked at Stacy, pregnant so early in her life, pregnant without even wanting to be. And what about when she looked at her friend, expecting for the sixth time? Did she feel anger? Resentment?

No, not at Stacy or Barbara. Gina wasn't capable of such small emotions. But she might be mad as hell at the way life had turned out for her. He knew *he* was.

But the question that really bothered him was, what was he going to do about it?

GINA CHECKED on her father one last time—he was sound asleep—then tiptoed through the just barely lit living room to the connecting door. Before the party had ended, Spencer had taken her aside and told her to come knock on this door after her father got settled. When she'd asked why, he'd simply grinned in that lazy way of his that always put butterflies in her stomach.

Her imagination had been galloping ever since, sometimes so hard and fast she lost her breath. Which was just plain dumb, she told herself as she stood at the door, combing her hair with her fingers. It was late. Everyone was tired. Spencer probably just wanted to say something about Stacy's birth-prep classes. Maybe he wasn't even awake anymore. Joe had taken an inordinately long time to fall asleep, wired as he'd been by the excitement of the party.

Thinking of the party, Gina smiled. She couldn't remember the last time she'd had such a genuinely good time. Spencer had taken such care with the evening—the food, the gifts, the company.

Spencer, she realized, was an unusually thoughtful and kind man. Even the irksome way he sometimes handled Stacy rose from something good in him, his desire to protect her and do the best for her. In Gina's opinion he was often wrong, but there was no question he meant well.

And as for his attitude toward Joe, she decided she just couldn't judge him. When he looked at her father, it wasn't aversion to help that she saw in his eyes. It was something deeper, something that had little to do with Joe personally, but a lot to do with Spencer himself.

He had a troubled heart. Gina wasn't sure what was bothering him but knew it went beyond Stacy. The sad part was, she couldn't even ask because she suspected he didn't know, either. She only wished she could help.

Expelling a shaky breath, Gina raised her hand and gave the door three soft taps with her knuckles.

She didn't even hear footsteps. The door just opened and there he was. Spencer, in shadow, leaning against the door frame, tall and virilely handsome. Suddenly she knew she was in deep trouble, in over her head.

His eyes fixed on her, those intense blue eyes that betrayed his facade of reserve, eyes that had been wanting her all evening. Her mouth went dry.

"Is your father asleep?"

She nodded, not trusting her voice. Her gaze flicked downward. A bottle of champagne dangled negligently from three fingertips.

"Mind if I come in?" he asked. "I'd ask you to my side, but my daughter's curiosity is in overdrive tonight."

So is mine, Gina thought. She glanced over her shoulder toward the privacy screen around her father's bed.

"Just for a while," Spencer assured her. He stepped over the threshold and closed the door. "I just want to wish you a happy birthday."

She frowned. "But you already have."

The corner of his mouth lifted, and the shadowy light revealed the upturned creases at his eyes. "Sweetheart," he drawled, brushing the back of his hand over her hot cheek, "I haven't even begun."

CHAPTER TWELVE

GINA'S KNEES WOBBLED. Memories of the last time she and Spencer had been alone together assailed her: the loft, and kisses so potent that even now they made her weak.

Spencer took a step closer, a man with something on his mind. When he was close enough for her to feel the heat of his body all down the length of her own, he bent to the side and set the champagne bottle on the floor. Straightening, he slid his hands around her waist and pulled her to him, slowly, each second seeming an eternity before their bodies met, hard against soft, muscle against curve, heat against heat. Then just as slowly, he lowered his head and touched his lips to hers—touched, brushed, heated with his breath, moistened with the tip of his tongue.

Gina wanted to keep her head—there were problems involved with what they were doing, weren't there?—but in seconds she was sighing against him, closing her eyes and wanting more. He felt so blessedly good. She pressed her hands up over his shoulders, over the smooth, warm cotton shirt, until her fingertips touched the back of his neck. She applied the slightest pressure, and he responded, brushing her mouth one last teasing time, then taking it fully.

She reeled as heat spilled inside her, steamy and arousing. She tried to think back to the early days of her marriage. Had she responded with such spontaneous, instantaneous fire? But memories of her marriage eluded her.

Spencer's kiss registered in every part of her: her swirling brain, her hungry mouth, her tightening center. No, her marital relations had never been like this. She'd been too young. She'd taken her sexuality for granted. But this, this was passion distilled by time and experience, passion appreciated.

Reluctantly Spencer lifted his head and took a steadying breath. "Gina," he whispered, "Gina."

She nestled closer, breathing in his musky male scent. No doubt remained in her mind why he was here, no doubt what she would do about it, either.

His words feathered over her hair. "Gina, I don't want to hurt you."

"I know." She laid one hand on his chest, measuring his need for her in the cadence of his heart.

"You've had enough disappointment with men, and I *will* be a disappointment."

She lifted her head and looked at him levelly. "Only if I set up unrealistic expectations, which I promise you I won't. I'm a big girl, Spencer, eyes wide open. I know this isn't love."

His eyes narrowed as he warned, "September is going to hurt like hell."

She nodded, agreeing. "But the pleasure of our summer will be worth the pain, don't you think?"

His arms tightened. "Please tell me you're sure."

"I am. I really am." She gazed into his troubled eyes. "What about Stacy?"

His brow furrowed. "I feel bad. I told her this wouldn't happen."

Gina ran her fingertips over his brow, wanting to smooth the worry lines. They seemed indelible. "I'm sure she'll understand." She smiled faintly. "In ten or fifteen years."

"What I'm hoping is, she won't ever find out."

"If we're discreet, there's no reason she should."

He nodded introspectively.

"You're not failing her, Spencer. You just made an unrealistic claim."

"That's for sure." Spencer shifted, moving against her, making his point. "Besides, the way I see it, there are needs more important than my being an example to my daughter."

Gina fixed her gaze on the hard-pulsing vein along Spencer's neck. "I'm not sure those needs are more important, Spencer, but they're certainly more urgent. Furthermore, you *are* an example to her, and you'll continue to be."

One corner of his mouth lifted in a smile. He stepped back, took her hand and pressed a kiss to her palm. The kiss seemed a seal on all that had been said. With his other hand, he picked up the champagne. "We'll need a couple of glasses, Gina."

"Right this way," she said, leading him toward the kitchen.

Gina's bedroom was at the top of the stairs, a cozy, slant-ceilinged space with a dormer window facing the back of the farm and a skylight facing the road. An iron bed with lace-trimmed sheets and several pillows was tucked under the skylight. That bed, a nightstand, a wooden chair and a bureau were the room's only furniture. A dark-shaded lamp cast its only light.

Spencer had never been up here before. He gave the room a slow perusal. As stark as it was, he saw Gina's imprint: the vase of daisies on the bureau, the velvet-jacketed volume of Emily Dickinson by the bed, the lace-edged sheets and that familiar faint scent of old roses.

He stood just inside the door, feeling like a visitor who needed to be invited in. He waited, watching her lower the window shade. From there she went to the bureau and stuffed some underwear into a drawer. She seemed nervous, moving with quick, self-conscious gestures that made him want to hold her close and say, "Stop, stop, you're lovely."

She hadn't understood when he'd made that comment about more important needs. Then again, he hadn't meant for her to understand. She might be offended if she did. She might see his lovemaking as pity.

He didn't mean it as pity. He just wanted her to forget her unmet dreams for a while. Wanted her to feel beautiful and young, desirable and desired. Wanted to take her beyond time's reach.

With the room hastily neatened, she turned, hands behind her, palms pressed against the bureau. He watched her watching him, her brows knit just enough to reveal her insecurity, her lips parted just enough to betray her sensuality. So lovely, he thought. So lovely.

Rain drummed on the roof and ran down the skylight over the bed, giving the room a ripply underwater feel. And he thought, *How appropriate,* because he suddenly couldn't breathe. He was drowning in this woman.

"Should I bother to open this?" He tipped the bottle of champagne toward her.

"If you do," she said in a voice made husky by need, "I may never speak to you again."

Spencer heard the catch in his own breathing. He placed the bottle on the floor and crossed the room, trying to take measured steps, trying not to hurry. He wanted the night to last. Wanted her to remember it.

Still an arm's span away, he paused and simply looked at her, the lamplight bathing her face in amber warmth, the reflection of rain-ripples on her breast.

He lifted his hand and slid it upward through the short ruffles of her hair, once, twice and again.

She lowered her eyes. "I know. It's short." As if there was something inherently unlikable about short hair.

"Yes. I love it," Spencer said. "Haven't I ever told you?"

She lifted awakening eyes to his and shook her head.

"I do." With his hand still threaded through her hair, he pressed a kiss to the top of her head. "And your eyes," he added softly, brushing a kiss across each fluttering lid. "And your chin." He kissed that, too. "But most of all—" he stroked her lips with his thumb "—I love this mouth." He thought she swayed a little. He smiled as he lowered his head.

Spencer's lips touched Gina's, and she thought, *He's going to be disappointed.* He'd been married for thirteen years. He'd probably tried everything, while she . . . well, her life wasn't exactly brimming with sexual experiences. She might appear worldly-wise, but she was nothing more than a well-wrapped package. And that cellulite on her thighs? He was going to take one look at it and run. Maybe this wasn't such a good idea, after all. Maybe she ought to stop.

But she couldn't. Oh, how the man could kiss! Hot, deep kisses that turned her body to liquid and her brain to mush. Kisses so drugging she was hardly aware of clothing coming off, one piece after another. Hardly noticed him guiding her toward the bed. Hardly cared that she was sinking into the mattress.

Spencer sank with her, kissing her all the way. He feared he wasn't in control anymore. He'd climbed the stairs with every intention of keeping his control tonight. He'd planned to lead Gina along a course of sensual pleasures, "lead" being the operative word. He'd intended to give.

But somewhere between the stairs and the bed, he'd lost himself in her. Now he was taking as much as he was giving, an equal participant in this glorious coupling.

But how could he not have lost himself in her? Gina *was* beautiful, and oh, so desired. *See how desired?* his body was saying. And he was beginning to think he could go on being lost forever, making love to her here in this rain-rippled room.

On the periphery of his fevered brain, that thought troubled him. Why, he was uncertain. He and Gina understood what they were doing. Both knew it was only sex. But then the troubling moment passed, burned off like fog under a hot, rising sun, and before long nothing remained of rational thought, nothing of intimations that this could be more. There was only sensation, this magnificent drive, this gathering ache with Gina at its center.

Gina lay still as Spencer pulled a package of condoms from his jeans. He sheathed himself and then entered her, inch by slow inch. She tried to quiet her rising need, as well. But the coils of heat at her center continued to contract and twist. And when finally he'd filled her, he made an unexpected thrust that brought a cry to her throat and shattered whatever control she'd thought she had. And then he began to move, long surges that swept her away, deep thrusts that fevered. Before long she was moving with him, caught up in his rhythm and fire.

How long they made love, ten minutes or two hours, she didn't know. The intensity of their passion burned off all sense of time. She was vaguely aware of the room that enveloped them, its dim light and dampness, the tapping of the rain against the window. Yet she felt far removed. With his hands and his eyes, his body and his whispers, Spencer had carried her off to a place where only they and their passion existed.

Gina wanted to stay there forever, yet thought she might die if she did. "Please, Spencer. Now," she whimpered. And then they were there, caught in the tight gathering heat of climax, riding the breathless drive, upward and tighter and finally over, she and Spencer together, shuddering and shattering and calling each other's name.

Spencer felt the last delicious echo of pleasure fade from his body, then collapsed beside Gina with a surprised laugh. He hadn't expected *that*. Was it abstinence that had caused such a cataclysmic ending? Was it the romance of the rain drumming on the roof?

He groped for the sheet and drew it over them, then nuzzled closer into Gina's warmth. Her hair tickled his eyelids, her womanly scent tickled his nose. He felt boneless, utterly boneless, floating in a peaceful lethargy of body and mind.

Too peaceful. He had to stay awake, had to get up in a little while and get back to his own side of the house. But not yet. Just a few minutes more.

Gina lay quiet in Spencer's heavy embrace, his forehead pressing her ear, his breath warming her shoulder. "Are you awake?" she whispered.

"Mmm-hmm."

She smiled, wrapping him more comfortably to her.

Against her neck he began to chuckle. "Helluva way to get through a midlife crisis, kid."

"Mmm." Her smile broadened. This might not be love, but it would do.

GINA SPENT the first two weeks of July in much the same way she'd spent the rest of her time in Bingham: her days, from one awakening to the next, defined by her father's needs.

With one exception: Spencer was now part of her life.

She was reluctant to say she was happy. Joe's health since his ministroke had steadily worsened. He could barely get around on his own anymore even with his walker, he'd developed difficulty breathing, and his memory and reason, as weak as they'd been before, deteriorated even further. As a result, her work in caring for him doubled. So did her weariness and anxiety—he was failing faster than she'd expected.

Yet, in spite of all that, Gina awoke each morning with a heart that felt happy, a heart eager to meet the day, and the reason for that was Spencer.

The morning after their first lovemaking, she'd found a bouquet of wildflowers on her back doorstep. That was the first of myriad gifts he lavished on her. Some of those gifts were just small kindnesses, like bringing in her mail or watering the garden. Some were not so small, like his arranging for a second aide to come to the farm to help with Joe at bedtime.

Some gifts made her laugh: the doggerel love poem she'd found stuffed in her shoe. Some brought tears: the greeting card whose verse about friendship had touched a particularly vulnerable chord. While others, like his relaxing massages, simply made her feel good. But whatever their immediate impact, the gifts had the cumulative effect of turning what could've been a very grim time for her into one that glittered with expectancy.

As much as she enjoyed Spencer's gifts, she was even more appreciative of his company. They'd fallen into the habit of convening on his porch for drinks in late afternoon, after he'd put in his day of painting the house. Sometimes they shared dinner, sometimes their evenings...

But always they shared their nights, and that, Gina decided, was the facet of Spencer that gladdened her the most. As a lover, he was every dream she'd ever dreamed, every expectation met, and as time passed, it became increasingly difficult for her to imagine cutting him from her life at the end of the summer.

Her friend Barbara saw the difficulty almost immediately.

Barbara invited all of them over for a Fourth of July barbecue, and during a rare free moment in the afternoon, while Joe was napping in the house and Spencer and Barbara's husband were engaged in a game of badminton with their children, the two women fell to talking.

"I like the two of you together, Ginnie," Barbara said, looking up briefly from her embroidery. "Is it serious?"

"Of course not." Gina picked up the baby monitor she'd placed beside her lawn chair and pretended the volume needed adjusting. Through it she heard the rasp of her father's labored breathing. She shouldn't have brought him, shouldn't have come. Joe wasn't up to visits like this anymore.

Barbara plied her needle in silence for a while. "A pity," she said eventually. "Spencer and Tom really hit it off."

Gina gazed across the lawn. The two men had only met that day, but Spencer had already agreed to join the local softball team Tom played on.

The men weren't the only ones who got along. Since meeting at Gina's birthday party the previous week, Stacy and Chrissie had become good friends. Chrissie, who had her driver's license, had come by the farm several times. She'd also taken Stacy on a tour of the town's more important landmarks—if you were a teenager—the high school, the diner where she worked part-time, her boyfriend's house.

With a sly glance, Barbara added, "Imagine what fun we'd all have if you and Spencer—"

"Don't," Gina cut in. "Stop right there. Spencer and I do not have a future. I've told you that again and again."

"So why are you sleeping with him?"

Heat streamed into Gina's face. "Who says I'm . . ."

Barbara gave her a knowing smirk.

Gina groaned. "Do you think Stacy's picked up on it?"

"If she has, it doesn't seem to be bothering her."

Gina focused on the badminton game once more. Out on the sunny lawn, Spencer and Stacy were just regaining their balance after colliding with each other. His arms were around her, and they were laughing. Gina's heart tripped at the sight.

Barbara slip-stitched a knot, then cut the thread. "So I repeat, why are you sleeping with him if you're not serious? Do you enjoy getting hurt?"

Gina swallowed, realizing her friend was worried about her. "It isn't easy to explain, Barbara. All I can say is, I need this relationship. I need *him*." To her complete dis-

may, her voice caught and broke. "This is such a difficult summer."

Barbara set aside her embroidery and turned. "Oh,
Ginnie, I'm sorry if I sounded like I was lecturing. I just
don't want to see you get hurt. Of course I understand.
When my Kayla was in the hospital last year..." She
glanced toward her husband, then lowered her eyes. "Of
course. Whatever gets you through the night."

Barbara returned to her embroidery, and the subject
didn't come up again.

Gina thought about it, though. She knew the end of
the summer would be difficult. But from the vantage
point of early July, the end of summer seemed a long way
off. She decided she would address the problem of saying goodbye when goodbye was upon her and not a day
sooner. In the meantime she would just enjoy what she
had.

And what she had was a lot.

Besides Spencer, there was her garden. She loved
working in her garden, especially in the early morning.
Sometimes she went out before her father was awake,
taking the monitor with her. She loved the stillness of that
hour, the dew on the vines, the rising scents of the plants:
tomato, basil, marigold. Sometimes she found Spencer
already there, his blue stoneware coffee mug sitting on
the gatepost, and he'd be hoeing. Those mornings were
the best. She'd thought he didn't like gardening, but she
found him there so often she decided he must've changed
his mind.

And then there was Stacy. With each new day, Gina
grew to appreciate Stacy at a deeper level. Although
Chrissie had entered Stacy's life—and that meant movies and sleep-overs and afternoons shopping—Stacy
continued to set aside time to help Gina with her father.

What Gina especially enjoyed about Stacy, though, was watching her enthusiasm mount as her first birth-preparation class approached. And that was exactly what Gina was doing the afternoon the letter from Whitman Prep arrived.

It was mid-July, and the weather had turned misera-bly hot. Having decided to try her hand at making ice cream, Gina had set up her father's old ice-cream maker outside in the shade of the oak tree on the east side of the house. She was busily churning a concoction she hoped would turn out to be strawberry ice cream; Joe was snoozing in a nearby chaise; and Stacy, sitting beside him, was reading, yet again, the directions to the hospital in Kingfield, two towns away, where she and Gina would be attending their first class that evening.

Just as Gina was about to reassure her she knew where the hospital was and they wouldn't be late, Spencer came around the corner of the house with the mail.

Looking up from her churning, Gina allowed herself just one quick scan. His hair was speckled with white paint, blending with the gray, and his skin, though he wore sunscreen, had turned a deep rich bronze. One quick scan—and her insides were as churned as the cream and berries and ice in her father's old ice-cream maker.

"Look what just came," he called, waving a long en-velope.

"What is it?" Stacy smiled as he approached.

"According to the return address, I'd say it's word on your application to boarding school."

Gina watched Stacy's face drop. Her own heart sank with it. Life at the farm had fallen into such a pleasant groove she'd forgotten all about Spencer's idea to send Stacy away to school. In fact, she'd thought he'd given up the idea. He certainly never talked about it anymore.

"Don't you want to see what the letter says?" Spencer frowned.

"Not really. But since you do, why don't you open it?"

Spencer flicked a self-conscious glance toward Gina. She gave the handle of the ice-cream maker a desultory turn, then quit again.

"Hey! You've been accepted!"

She thought his enthusiasm sounded forced.

"Yippee," Stacy drawled, her face hardening.

Gina ached with disappointment. Should she try to intervene? But what would she say? And if she did say something, would he think she was interfering?

Without knowing she was doing it, she lifted her eyes to Spencer's and gave him a look that said, *Talk to her. Don't walk away. You and your daughter have come too far.*

Spencer sighed, then hunkered down beside Stacy's chair. "Stace, I know you don't want to go away to school. I understand. It's a big change, and change is frightening."

Gina thought that idea sounded familiar.

"But I think a lot of your fear is coming from the fact that you're pregnant and close to delivery. That's an even scarier prospect, and what I'm thinking is, facing the unknown waters of childbirth is coloring your entire outlook. After the baby is born, you're going to feel a lot better, more your old confident self. I'm sure boarding school isn't going to look half so frightening then."

Gina said nothing, but she thought Spencer had missed the mark. Apparently Stacy did, too. She levered herself out of the chair and said, "It must be great knowing everything. Excuse me. I told Chrissie I'd give her a call."

Gina wiped her hands and gave Spencer a smile and a shrug. But it seemed he didn't want to stick around and talk. He lowered his eyes, stuffed the acceptance letter back into its envelope and returned to painting the house.

GINA HAD NEVER BEEN involved in anything quite like a birth-preparation class, and she was as wide-eyed as the teenager she accompanied. The class was run by a registered nurse and included three married couples, one pair who were unmarried, and a mother/daughter team. All the women were due in August or September. By far, Stacy was the youngest participant.

Class was equal parts physiology lecture, relaxation exercises and discussion of personal experiences. To her dismay, Gina found herself feeling self-conscious during the relaxation session. Sitting on the floor with her arms around Stacy and Stacy leaning against her for support, she thought, *I don't belong here. This is too personal, too important.*

But soon her self-consciousness receded into a far stronger emotion—her affection for this girl. Stacy needed her help, needed her to be calm and mature, and so, following the nurse's instructions, Gina laid her hands on Stacy's stomach and began a slow circular massage in rhythm with her breathing.

She was just beginning to relax, herself, just getting the hang of the exercise, when suddenly Stacy's stomach lifted and shifted. Gina gasped and drew back her hands.

Leaning against her, Stacy laughed. "Awesome, isn't it?"

Gina continued the exercise, but her mind was awash. The baby had suddenly become real to her, not just a mound under a maternity blouse.

Sitting as she was, she also had a vision that made her smile, a vision that probably came from watching too many cartoons when she was a child: a large fish opening its mouth and a smaller fish coming out, followed by an even smaller fish coming out of that fish. Gina, Stacy, baby. All in a row.

But of course Stacy had not come from her. Though Gina was old enough to be this girl's mother, old enough to be the baby's grandmother, she was neither. An unanticipated ache opened within her, an ache she automatically attributed to her recent birthday and the accompanying sense that life had passed her by.

But she knew that wasn't it. Not tonight. Quite simply, she'd come to love Stacy and wished the young girl *was* her daughter. She wanted to help her beyond her delivery, wanted to watch her grow and mature into the wonderful young woman she was sure Stacy was going to be.

But she wouldn't be there, wouldn't be part of Stacy's future, and the idea of not seeing her again after this summer saddened Gina almost as much as the thought of not seeing Spencer.

Later that evening, on the drive back to Bingham, Gina decided that maybe there *was* a way she could help Stacy beyond her delivery.

They'd just pulled onto the highway when she said, "Stace, I'm reluctant to interfere in the problem you're having with your father—" in the pale light from the dash, Gina saw the animation leave Stacy's face "—but I just can't sit on the sidelines and watch you two drift apart again, especially when you could probably work out a compromise."

"We're never going to work this out. He wants to send me away to boarding school, and nothing's going to change his mind." From her tone, Gina suspected Stacy was still thinking her father didn't want her in his life.

"Stace, do you know why your father wants you to go away to school?"

Stacy sighed. "Yeah. He thinks I can make a new start." She sounded bored with the idea.

"Has he ever talked to you about Todd?"

Stacy swung around. "Todd?"

"Mmm."

"Todd's the reason?"

Gina shrugged. "I'd bet my bottom dollar he's half of it."

Stacy sat stiff, breathing fast. "Is Todd also the reason my father moved me to Bingham?"

"I'd say he's a major reason, yes. Your father was also pretty worried about the people you were hanging around with."

"Why didn't he tell me that himself? What, is he a coward or something?"

"No, Stacy, only a man. Give him a break." She glanced across the front seat and caught a budding smile. She added, "Maybe he thought you wouldn't understand and you'd resent him more for it." She paused. "Do you?"

Stacy propped her elbow on the window and dropped her forehead to her palm. "What's to understand?"

"Your father's motives, for one thing. He knows you're still in love with Todd."

Stacy's jaw dropped. "How does he know that?"

"I guess he overheard you calling Todd before you moved here. He also got the idea you used to try to meet him."

Stacy moaned, a weak sound of embarrassment.

"Your father was afraid that if you stayed in Boston, you'd continue trying to see him, and Todd would keep hurting you and making a fool of you. Your father loves

you, Stace. It kills him to see you hurt. He thinks the only
way you're going to stop hurting is by moving on. He's
just trying to help."

Stacy's lips quivered. "I know I made a fool of myself
calling Todd. I thought he loved me, though. I
thought..."

Her voice wavered so badly she had to stop. Gina
reached over and squeezed her arm. "It's okay. Let it out.
God knows how many buckets I've shed over men. I
won't be grossed out or anything."

Stacy smiled a little, then pulled herself together. "No,
I'm not going to cry. I've done enough of that, and if you
want to know the truth, Todd isn't worth it."

Gina relaxed.

"If I tell you something, Gina, will you promise not to
tell my father? He'd probably go back to Boston and tear
Todd limb from limb."

"Sure. It's a promise."

"I really didn't want to have sex with Todd."

Alarms began to go off. "Did he force you?"

"Oh, no, nothing like that. But it was definitely his
idea. He kept bugging me about it, and my friends—"
she emitted a huff of scorn "—my friends told me I
should. They'd all been sleeping with guys for ages. They
said if I didn't, Todd would go looking for somebody
else."

Gina's hands tightened around the steering wheel.
"Remember that conversation we had the day I moved
to the farm, the one about knowing who you are and
what you want and being true to yourself?"

"Yeah, I remember." Stacy grimaced ruefully.

"It's too late now to change what's done, but—"

"I know, I know. And in the future I'll try to be more
careful."

Gina was taking the Bingham exit when Stacy said, "I still don't see what this has to do with reaching a compromise over boarding school."

"Kiddo, it might have everything to do with it."

Stacy sat straighter. "How so?"

"What I think you should do is tell your father you'll promise not to see Todd anymore, not call him or write him or anything, in exchange for his promise to let you stay at home with him in Boston."

"You mean, use Todd as a bargaining chip?"

"Sort of, though I don't mean you should be manipulative. Just be reasonable, Stace. Present your idea as a logical solution. Men love logic. They love solving problems. Meet him on his level."

"Hmm." Stacy sank more comfortably into the passenger seat. "Reasonable, huh?"

"Yep."

"I suppose I could argue that keeping me home would save him lots of money."

"You could."

"I'd be happier at home, too, and therefore be more likely to study."

"Good one!"

Stacy sighed. "I'm still not sure it's going to work."

"How about adding that you'd be willing to transfer to a different school? Do you think you could do that?"

"And get away from my friends? Yeah, I could do that easily."

"Well, then." Gina smiled.

"Okay, I'll talk to him. Just as soon as we get home."

LATER THAT NIGHT Stacy lay in the darkness of her bedroom, grinning. Gina's ploy had worked. She'd made her father sit and discuss the issue of boarding school, and he'd agreed to relinquish the idea.

It hadn't been an easy discussion. He'd come back at her with a host of logical reasons boarding school was in her best interests, but in the end she'd prevailed. She'd won, not through sulking or sarcasm, but through talk. Stacy kicked away the sheet and stretched luxuriously. She felt great.

She also felt like a furnace. She *always* felt like a furnace, now that she was almost due. She rested her hands on her stomach and smiled. Her baby had the hiccups tonight.

"Easy does it," she whispered, stroking what she believed to be the baby's back. "They'll be gone soon."

She continued to murmur and pet, and after a while the baby did settle. "Nightee-night," she whispered, finally letting her hands rest, too.

Her baby had become such a vivid reality to her that at times she got the feeling she was already taking care of it. The food she chose to eat, the walks she took, the sleep she made sure she got—everything was for her baby's benefit as much as for her own. Maybe more so. She disliked broccoli, yet ate it.

Know who you are, Gina had said. *Know what you want and need, and above all be true to yourself.* Easy words to say. Not so easy to follow.

For Stacy knew what she wanted. She'd known for months. But she also knew how impossible her dream was.

Her father would never agree to her keeping the baby. And even if he did, how on earth would she manage? She had no time. Years of schooling still awaited her. She had no money, wasn't even old enough yet to work. On top of that, she was too ignorant. She knew nothing about taking care of a baby. No, she couldn't think of a single logical reason for keeping it. In that way, she was in total accord with her father.

But that was thinking with her head. Her heart, unfortunately, beat to an different rhythm. She only hoped she could keep ignoring its message until the baby was adopted.

THE NEXT MORNING Gina awoke as she usually did, with Spencer's scent on her skin and remembrance of his lovemaking in her heart. She stretched her arms high and smiled.

As she came more awake, she recalled Spencer's visit more fully—the news he'd brought with him that he and Stacy had worked out their problem. Gina's smile broadened. Her heart overflowed with such happiness for Stacy and with pride for Spencer. She sat up, throwing off the covers, eager to see them both and celebrate.

She was reaching toward her nightstand to turn off the monitor when suddenly a small sound drew her attention. She retracted her hand and listened harder. It came again, a low raspy groan. Her heart stopped—and then began to speed.

Recalling the last time she'd awakened to the intimation that something was wrong, she flung on her robe and raced down the stairs.

She found her father still lying in his bed, eyes closed. Relief sluiced through her. She'd overreacted. The moan she'd heard had just been a noise he'd made in his dreams.

She was backing away, trying not to wake him, when his eyes opened a crack. "Sorry, Dad," she whispered. "I didn't mean to disturb you." She turned, took a step and heard the moan again. She froze, turned slowly, ordered herself to breathe. "Do you need something, Dad?"

Her father didn't move. Only his eyes. Only the tips of his fingers, lifting from the bedspread.

She stepped closer. "Want me to put on some coffee? Can you sit up?"

She thought he nodded. He slowly crooked one arm and grunted, but that was as far as he got.

Gina placed her hand on his head, smoothing his crisp gray hair. He looked different. His gentle smile was gone, and in its place was an expression that chilled her. He seemed . . . distant, as if he'd withdrawn into a place so deep and misty there would be no returning.

"I'll be right back, Dad." She patted his arm. "Right back."

Once she was outside the privacy screen, she pressed her fingers over her mouth to stop a sob. It had happened. Her father had had a stroke. Not one of his minor "episodes." A full-blown stroke.

She'd always known this day would come. Dr. Abrams had warned her. And knowing, she'd convinced herself she'd be prepared. Right now, however, she felt she was flying apart.

Pull yourself together, Gina, she ordered herself. *Think this through calmly. Clear your mind.*

But her mind refused to clear. All she could see was her father, lying there mute and unmoving. He was having difficulty breathing, and his blood pressure was probably sky-high. Or would it have dropped? She didn't know. She didn't know anything.

Her gaze sped across the apartment. She ought to be doing something. But what? What? Her breath seized up on her. Where had she gotten the notion she could handle this?

She zeroed in on the phone. Should she call Dr. Abrams? No, of course not. It was only six-thirty in the morning.

The hospital, then? Gina moaned, remembering how arrogantly she'd told Spencer she'd never take Joe to a hospital. Who, in her right mind, didn't take a parent to the hospital when he was this sick? A grossly irresponsible daughter, that's who.

Gina took two unsteady steps toward the phone, then stopped. *I promised I'd care for him myself. I promised he'd die at home.*

But was keeping her father home really what was best for him? Was negligence best? Was suffering best? In a hospital he'd have modern technology on his side, drugs to ease his pain, professionals who knew what they were doing. Maybe it was wrong to keep such a promise. Besides, as Spencer had once mentioned, her father probably wouldn't even know where he was.

Her gaze returned to the phone. On one of her more difficult days, she'd jotted down the number of the local ambulance service and posted it by the phone. It was there, right there. So easy. Within minutes others would be here, helping out, taking over.

She closed her eyes, fighting back tears. "I'm sorry, Dad," she whispered as she headed for the phone.

CHAPTER THIRTEEN

SPENCER STOOD in the early-morning stillness watching the medics carry the stretcher out through Gina's front door. Stacy, in pajamas and robe, clung to his arm, gulping back tears.

He still couldn't believe Gina had decided her father should be taken to the hospital. Not that he thought the decision was a bad one. That had been his argument all along: Joe belonged in professionally supervised care. He just thought she would've wanted his advice first, or at least his company while she made her decision. It had to be the hardest one she'd ever faced. But by the time she'd knocked on the connecting door, the ambulance was already on its way.

Stacy pressed closer. "Gina looks scared."

She *was* scared, he thought, watching her follow the stretcher to the rear of the ambulance. Before waking Stacy, he'd been alone with her for a while, and although she'd kept up a stoic front, he'd seen the darkness in her eyes; he'd felt her trembling when he held her.

"Dad, can't you do something?"

Spencer knew what Stacy was hinting at. He kept his eyes fixed on the ambulance. "It's Gina's decision."

"Yeah, but only because she thinks she can't handle this."

"She can't. Joe's needs far exceed what she can do for him now."

Stacy seemed about to contradict him when Gina called, "Are you coming in the ambulance, Spencer?"

Grateful for the distraction, he said, "No, I'll follow in my car. You'll need a ride back later."

"Okay. See you there then."

He nodded, then focused his attention on his daughter. "You'll call Chrissie now, right?"

"Please, Dad, I'd rather go with you."

"No, baby. It's going to be a long, tiring day. Nothing you can do, anyway. The only reason I'm going is to keep Gina company. It's better for you to stay here and take care of yourself. But I don't want you staying alone."

"Dad, I'm fifteen." She huffed.

Taking her by the shoulders, he turned her away from the scene at Gina's door. "Stace, I don't have time to argue. Gina needs me." At the edges of his vision, he saw Gina climbing into the passenger seat beside the ambulance driver. "But I won't leave until you promise me you'll—"

"Okay, okay, I'll call Chrissie."

"Good. Now go have some breakfast."

She sighed and rolled her eyes. Yeah, he knew. Fifteen.

"And *you* call *me*," she ordered, pointing a stern finger at him. "Keep me posted."

"I will."

He was already headed for the garage when she said, "Dad?" He turned, puzzled, as she crossed the dew-damp yard. Rising up on tiptoe, she blessed his unshaven cheek with a kiss. "Hang in."

Spencer swallowed over an unexpected tightness in his throat. "You, too." He gave her hair a ruffle, then bolted for his car.

MATTERS HAD SLIPPED out of her hands.

Gina sat beside the ambulance driver, thinking the same thought that had been running through her mind from the moment she'd hung up the phone. Out of her hands. Out of her hands. Out of control.

With a twist of her shoulders she could see her father, strapped to a stretcher, an oxygen mask over his nose, two EMTs hovering over him.

Looking back was too painful. Gina faced forward and watched the side mirror, instead. Spencer following in his car. She desperately needed that image right now, needed to know she wasn't alone.

Joe was taken to the same hospital where she attended birth class with Stacy. When the ambulance turned in at the gate, her mind momentarily jogged. The driver must've made a mistake. This was a place linked with life and joy, not . . . what was happening to her father.

Hospital staff met the ambulance, and Joe was whisked away with what seemed to Gina the speed of magic. By the time Spencer had found a parking spot and run to the emergency entrance, she was alone.

"Where's your father?" He took her arm and escorted her through the automatic glass doors.

Her voice trembled when she replied, "Gone for examining and testing." Abruptly she dug in her heels. "I should be with him." She looked around the reception area, not knowing which door to take, which corridor to follow.

Spencer wrapped his arm around her and kept her moving toward the admissions desk where the ambulance driver was handing in a report. "He'll be fine. Your job right now is to shuffle a few tons of paper. The sooner the better, too. You don't want to still be filling out forms when they say you can see him, do you?"

She looked over her shoulder one last time, straining to find the father who'd been taken so quickly away. "Spencer, I think I made a mistake bringing him here."

Spencer gave her shoulder a gentle squeeze. "You did the right thing. He's had a serious stroke, Gina. He'll get care here you couldn't possibly give him at home. This is the only place for him to be."

Her shoulders sagged. "Of course. You're right."

She and Spencer sat in the waiting room for an hour. She'd finished filling out the various forms given to her, and the only word was that Joe was still being examined.

Spencer bought her a magazine, but she was unable to focus on reading. What were they doing to her father? she wondered. How was he responding to strangers poking and prodding him? Was he distressed over his inability to move? Panicked because he couldn't speak? Joe had the emotional and mental capacities of a child, and she felt she'd abandoned that child.

After two hours, a nurse came and sat with them. She apologized for the delay, but a heart attack victim had come in just before Joe, taking precedence. Then she explained the tests he was undergoing: a full physical, a CAT scan, checks for mental alertness and muscular weakness.

"Yes, but how is he?" Gina asked the nurse as she rose to leave.

"I can't really say yet. A neurologist will meet with you later." She gave Gina's arm a reassuring squeeze. "It won't be much longer. Would you like the chaplain to come sit with you a while?"

"Chaplain?" Gina didn't think she needed a chaplain. Parting with her father wasn't the issue. She'd resigned herself to that long ago. It was parting in this manner. "No, I'm okay. But thanks for asking."

The nurse had been kind. Everyone was kind, especially Spencer. He rubbed her knotted shoulders. He talked. He brought her coffee and a Danish. He walked with her as far as she dared range. Yet time passed so slowly she thought she might go crazy.

After three hours had elapsed, even Spencer was muttering complaints.

"I imagine time goes by a lot faster when you're on the other side of the curtain."

"It sure does," he said.

"It's a good thing you persuaded Stacy to stay home."

"Mmm. That reminds me, I should give her a call."

But Spencer hadn't even gotten to his feet when a nurse approached and told them Joe had been taken to his room and they could finally see him.

The three hours' wait should've prepared her, but it didn't. Gina walked up to Joe's bed, so weak-kneed that she weaved. He lay in a tangle of intravenous tubes and oxygen lines, and his arms were discolored in several places from blood work. Gina flinched under the sting of guilt. She felt as if she'd inflicted those bruises herself.

She placed a tentative hand on his head. His eyelids fluttered. "Is he awake?" she asked the nurse who was checking his IV drip.

"He's been drifting in and out. But don't expect much. He's having trouble talking, and even when he does speak, he's pretty incoherent."

Gina stood by the bed, gazing at her father's ashen skin and lost eyes. "Hi, Dad," she said, fighting to keep her voice from breaking. He moved his head and tried to speak. His Adam's apple bobbed and he winced.

Gina felt Spencer standing behind her, felt his breath on her hair, his strength in her heart. *Don't leave me, Spencer,* she begged. *I need you now more than ever.*

As if he'd heard her plea, Spencer remained with her throughout the long day, an anchor in a sea of strangers who swirled around her father's bed. One of those strangers was the neurologist who'd attended Joe's admittance.

"I'm sorry I can't tell you with more certainty how long your father will be hospitalized," he said. "Ten people could have the same stroke, but each will bounce back differently. Dozens of factors come into play. We'll just have to wait and see how your father responds over the next few days."

"Bounce back?" she repeated after the neurologist was gone. "He thinks my father is going to bounce back?"

Spencer didn't say a word.

Late in the day Stacy dropped by with Chrissie. They'd spent the afternoon baking lasagna and came bearing two warm covered dishes for Gina and Spencer.

"It'll be a break from hospital food," Stacy explained before approaching Joe's bed. Gina could see she was nervous from the way her fingers clenched the rail, yet she was able to make her voice lilt with spiritedness. "Joe, what *happened?* You look like hell."

Gina didn't know who she felt worse for, Joe, who did look like hell, or Stacy, who apparently didn't realize how damaged he was. She probably expected him to answer her. But suddenly the old man chuckled. Gina couldn't believe it. Even in his near-comatose state, he'd recognized Stacy's voice and responded to her teasing.

Stacy remained by his side for nearly half an hour, filling him in on her lasagna-making and how the garden was doing. Gina was sure he didn't understand a word, but he was still responding to something, her cheering voice, a vaguely remembered affection, perhaps.

Gina curled up in her chair by the window, knotted with remorse. Just as she'd figured, Joe retained an emotional memory, and if he remembered Stacy's affection, then he remembered his fear of hospitals. Did he also remember his daughter's pledge not to bring him here?

When a nurse came in to check Joe's blood pressure, Stacy finally sat down. Her ebullience was gone, utterly drained away, and Gina realized that her cheerfulness had been a conscious kindness. Once again she was struck by how mature the teenager could sometimes be. She wondered if Spencer had noticed, if he'd been as moved as she was.

"He looks awful," Stacy whispered, her forehead puckered. "Is he going to make it?"

Gina didn't answer. Couldn't answer. Until now, everyone had been talking therapy and recuperation time. But with the swift directness of youth, Stacy had struck at the heart of the matter.

"We're not sure, Stace," Spencer said. "It was a serious stroke, and he's awfully old and frail. His heart is pretty weak, too."

The teenager's eyes filled. She looked toward the bed. "He can't die. Not yet. I wanted him to see..." She ducked her head and swiped at her eyes.

To see what? Gina wondered. The garden? Her sunflowers? She ached for the girl. Stacy might be mature in some ways, but her maturity existed alongside an innocent and quite vulnerable romanticism. She was relieved that Spencer didn't press his daughter to finish her thought.

"The hospital staff is doing everything they can, babe."

Stacy nodded, lips pressed tight. "I know."

The girls stayed until Gina and Spencer had finished their supper. When they were gone, Gina pulled her chair close to the bed and, imitating Stacy, kept up a running monologue. Her father fixed his eyes on her, and, depthless though they were, they were her incentive to go on. Eventually he drifted off to sleep.

"Gina, it's time to go home."

She turned, amazed anew by Spencer's presence. That had been happening to her all day. She'd rise out of herself and suddenly realize he was still there. And each time, her heart billowed with relief and gratitude and a host of other emotions she wasn't inclined to examine at present.

"Thanks for being here, Spencer."

His eyes were bloodshot and a day's growth of beard darkened his jaw. "No big deal. Come on. We've stayed past visiting hours."

"No, I'm not leaving."

"Gina, you can't stay here."

"Yes, I can. If my father wakes up during the night, he'll be terrified."

"You'll serve your father better if you go home and get a good night's sleep."

"I can sleep here."

"In that chair?"

"Yes." She lifted her chin.

Spencer growled. "You're the most pigheaded woman I've ever met."

"Please, Spencer. I won't get any sleep at home, worrying."

He growled again, but his growl was combined with a sigh of resignation. "Okay, but try not to kink up your neck."

He stood with her by the bed and placed a hand, light as a dream, on her father's head. "Good night, Joe. Sleep well." Then he took her in his arms. "I'll see you tomorrow morning."

She gazed up into his weary eyes, lifted her hand and brushed at a wayward lock falling over his brow. Her heart swelled with emotion again. What a good man, she thought, as he bent forward and kissed her—a tired, loving kiss.

"Good night, Spencer."

He held her against him tightly, held her there as if absorbing something of her through his skin, then with a sigh released her and stepped back. "Good night." He turned and left.

GINA LOOKED as if she hadn't slept a wink. Her eyes were small and pouchy, her face pale and drawn. Spencer could see she'd also been crying. She was sitting tense and upright in the same uncomfortable chair she'd occupied most of yesterday. In her lap lay a mess of shredded plastic foam, which her jittery fingers persisted in shredding further. When she noticed him at the door, her hands stilled and she smiled a quivery smile. "Spencer."

He stepped into the room. It was quiet. Joe was asleep. "I brought you some coffee and muffins. Coffee's mine. Stacy made the muffins."

"Oh, how sweet." She scooped up the foam pieces and dropped them into a nearby wastebasket. "How is she?"

Worried, he thought. "Fine. I persuaded her and Chrissie to go to the movies today."

"Good." Gina yawned, scrubbing at her eyes and then her head, leaving her short dark hair sticking up in swirly peaks. He'd missed her at the farm last night, more than he cared to think about right now.

He set the coffee and muffins on the bedside table, gave Joe a quick study, then rolled the table over. "What happened last night? Did Joe try to remove his IV?"

Gina glanced at her father's securely taped arm and nodded. "He just doesn't understand." Her lower lip trembled.

Quickly Spencer changed the subject. "Who are the flowers from?"

She looked behind her at the basket of carnations on the wide windowsill. "Barbara and Tom. They came this morning." She smiled, yawning at the same time.

"After you eat, go home, Gina. Take my car." He dropped his keys on the table. "You need some sleep."

"But my father—"

"I'll stay with him." Spencer lowered himself into the chair beside hers. He's sleeping, anyway."

"No surprise." Her face hardened. "A physical therapist was in here this morning. It was . . . tiring."

Spencer was sure she'd meant to say something far more condemning. "What did she do?"

"Tested his reflexes and muscle strength. Then she did his memory."

Spencer watched her tug at the same wisp of hair again and again. "I know those tests can seem dumb and degrading, Gina, but she was just doing her job."

"Yeah." She forced a smile. "That's what she said, too. Personally, I don't see the point, but I suppose it's necessary. They want to put my father in therapy." Her gaze wandered to the bed, and despite another try at a smile, her eyes filled.

Spencer felt pretty miserable himself. Joe looked played out, exhausted right to the bone.

"I made a mistake, Spencer." He heard her voice wobble. "I shouldn't have brought him here."

Spencer had been telling her no, she'd done right, from the moment she'd called him over yesterday morning. Each time, he'd felt a little less sure of himself. Now he didn't know what to say.

He slumped in his chair, torn with guilt. If he hadn't criticized her plan to take care of Joe at home, would she have chosen to call the ambulance? Had his being a doctor added weight to his criticism? Was she waiting for him to suggest they take Joe home?

Did she even know she *could* take him home?

At a loss for what to say, he reached for the coffee, uncapped it and held it toward her. "Here. Get something in your stomach."

She took the cup and sipped dutifully, and he felt worse. Coffee wasn't going to cure what ailed her.

She set the cup down and was quiet a moment. He watched her face. Emotions, like cloud shadows on the hills, shifted in her eyes and across her mouth. "Why did I promise I'd never bring him to a hospital?" she asked. "Why did he ask such a thing of me?" She looked toward the bed, her eyes momentarily hardening with resentment. "It was so unfair of him. It's...too much. Who does he think I am, Superwoman?"

No, just his daughter, Spencer thought. He suspected the same thought crossed her mind. He could see her brief flare of anger cooling, sliding away under a much stronger wave of remorse. He wanted to gather her in his arms, but made do with a soft stroking of her cheek.

She looked at him, her eyes pleading for understanding. "I should've had the fortitude. He's my father. He was always there for me. Always."

"And you're here for him."

She shook her head. "No. I gave him over to others. I was afraid. I didn't know what to do for him. All at once it hit me, how much special care he needed. I felt inadequate, and I panicked. What if I did something wrong, something harmful? Who was I to deny him whatever a hospital could provide." She paused, chewing on her bottom lip, her eyes becoming even more haunted.

After a while she said, "I was also afraid of the sadness."

"The sadness?" Spencer scowled.

"Mmm. Seeing him suffer, seeing him degenerate, knowing he's dying and that I'll never see him again. Such intense emotions, such a painful experience. I didn't want to face all that. I thought if I brought him here, maybe it wouldn't be so bad. Other people would dilute the experience. Silly of me, I know." She gave a little smile and turned away, but he'd already seen her tears.

"Gina." He squeezed her arm, aching for her. "Those are just natural reactions, very human. I wish you'd stop beating yourself up over them."

"I can't help it. I failed him. I'm his daughter, and I went back on my word. God, I can't even look at him. Every time I do, I feel him accusing me."

Spencer hated to see her hurting. But there were no glib words to ease her pain. He knew. He'd failed loved ones, too.

"At least you're here," he said.

She made a small, self-deprecating sound, but then abruptly asked, "What do you mean, at least I'm here? Weren't you with your father when he died?"

He shook his head. "When my sister called to tell me he'd had a heart attack, I offered to fly home right away. But she knew I had responsibilities—my clinic, my patients—so she said it wasn't necessary. He was getting good care, and there was nothing I could add to it. Besides, he was a relatively healthy person. Everyone expected a recovery.

"So I stayed in Boston, thinking I'd fly out the following week. But two days later Lisa called back with the news that he'd passed away."

Spencer didn't realize that Gina had placed her hand on his forearm until she moved it, stroking and caressing him. "As deaths go," she said softly, "he was lucky. It was fast. You should take comfort in that."

Spencer tried to say yes, but he couldn't even nod.

"Must've been hard on you, though," she added. "You must've been so unprepared. I think I almost prefer this." She cast a glance toward Joe's bed. "Not for my father, of course. His ordeal has been much too long already. But for me."

Spencer grimaced wryly. "Boy, do I know how to cheer a lady or what?"

She brushed her fingers over his knuckles. "Yes, you do."

He turned his hand over and, clasping hers, brought it to his lips. "Go home, Gina. You really need some sleep."

Sighing, she looked at the untouched muffin.

"Take it with you."

She nodded. "I could use a shower and change of clothes, too."

"I've been meaning to say something about that."

She smiled and got to her feet. "Are you sure you want to do this?"

No, he didn't want to, but he would. For her. "Joe and I will be fine. When he wakes up, I'll see if he wants to play some seven card stud or something."

This time, he got her to laugh. "Thanks. I owe you."

After walking Gina to the elevator, Spencer returned to Joe's room. He paced. He read Joe's chart. He sat on the windowsill and watched the open doorway, waiting for someone else to come in, a nurse, an orderly, anybody. Being alone with Joe made him nervous. Too much time with his conscience, he guessed.

Bringing Joe here had been an ordeal for Gina, one she'd felt guilty about ever since. Guilty? Her decision was eating her up. He felt to blame. He'd planted the idea in her head and never retracted it. Worst part was, he wasn't even sure he was right anymore.

Spencer pushed away from the windowsill, turned and looked down on the parking lot where visitors were coming and going. He imagined himself one of them, getting into a car, switching the ignition.

Running away.

But there would be no hiding from the voice that said he could ease Gina's guilt. He could unburden her heart of its anguish and anger. He had the power.

But at what price?

Spencer turned from the window and glowered at Joe, wishing he didn't exist. This summer would be so much easier if he wasn't around.

God, the old man was looking back, a mute plea in his sunken, slitty eyes. Spencer suddenly felt like an ass for his selfish thoughts. Reluctantly, he stepped closer.

"Hey, Joe." He reached for his legendary bedside manner. "How are you doing? You're looking better today." He thought he sounded about as consoling as an empty bucket. "Probably not feeling better though, huh?"

Joe's eyes moved, taking in the strange room. Did he understand where he was? Poor guy, he did look frightened. Spencer's uneasiness grew. Until now, he'd thought Joe's hospitalization bothered him because Gina was bothered by it. He'd thought it was her pain hurting him. But now he realized he hated seeing Joe here simply because of Joe himself. Somehow, despite his best efforts to stay uninvolved with him, the old man had worked his way into Spencer's affections.

Spencer noticed Joe's lips working. He leaned over until he felt the whispered name against his ear. "Gina?" Spencer repeated. "She just went out for a cup of coffee." No sense in upsetting him any more than necessary. "She'll be right back." Spencer lay his hand gently on Joe's bony shoulder. The hospital gown looked ridiculous on him. Spencer wanted to see him in a plaid shirt and suspenders. "In the meantime, I'm here, Joe. I'll stay with you."

Spencer pulled a chair over beside the bed and sat. What had Gina done yesterday, all that time she'd sat here by her father? Ah, yes. She'd talked.

And so did Spencer. He talked about the weather. He talked about the Red Sox. He talked about what he'd had for breakfast and what he planned for dinner. Gradually Joe's eyes drifted shut again.

Relieved, Spencer slouched in his chair and closed his own eyes, as well. For a while, he lost himself in the hospital sounds swirling outside him: doctors being paged, food carts clattering by, bursts of laughter at the nurses' station.

But when he'd ridden those distractions as far as they'd go, he opened his eyes and discovered he was back where he'd started, sitting by a dying man's bed and trying not to think about his own father's passing.

Spencer let his gaze roam Joe's hospital room. Had the walls of his father's room been painted off-white, too? Had his sister and mother kept watch in uncomfortable vinyl chairs? He didn't know. He hadn't been there. Where memories should've been, Spencer only had blanks.

He hadn't been there for any of it. Calling the ambulance. Consulting with doctors. Pacing the corridors. And he hadn't been there to sit by his father's bed. He'd escaped the anxiety and the anger, escaped the tears in the night. For a time, he'd considered himself lucky. Now he wasn't so sure.

The only images he had of his father's death involved the funeral—the minister's voice, his sister's sniffles, snowflakes on the casket. The next day, he'd returned to Boston and resumed his life. Until now, he'd assumed his father's death was behind him. Apparently it wasn't.

Spencer suddenly understood why he'd tried to keep Joe Banning from moving to the farm, and, once the old man had moved there, why he'd wished Joe were in a nursing home.

He hadn't gotten the chance to say goodbye to his own father. Hadn't had the opportunity to grieve.

Spencer looked at Joe and swallowed. Maybe it was time.

DURING THE NEXT COUPLE of days, Joe's health declined steadily. Yet, hospital staff continued to bustle around him with a cheerful disregard for what was happening. At least that was how it seemed to Gina. Death wasn't in their lexicon. Couldn't be, she supposed. But it was painful to watch.

More than ever, she wanted to take her father home, but didn't see how that was possible. He had a feeding tube. He was getting injections, oxygen, IVs. There were orderlies to lift him and change him. And he'd developed pneumonia. How did you remove a parent from a hospital when he had pneumonia?

Five days after his admittance, Gina walked into his room to find him gone. "He's having another CAT scan," an orderly informed her.

"Why? He had one when he was admitted."

The young man gave her an explanation, but all Gina could think was that the test was unnecessary. How many images did they need of him, anyway? Why put him through the anxiety and the discomfort of being moved? And why, above all, couldn't they see what was so obvious to her—that he was dying?

After Joe had been wheeled back to his room and settled in bed, Gina stood by his side and stroked his hair. He hadn't spoken coherently in days, yet he looked up at Gina at that moment and whispered, "Enough."

Her heart splintered.

Standing behind her, Spencer put his hand on her shoulder. Not once during the week had he said anything critical about the care Joe was getting, which led her to think he approved.

Therefore, it came as a great surprise when he said, "Let's take him home."

CHAPTER FOURTEEN

STACY WAS FOLDING laundry on the dining-room table when the phone rang.

Before this summer she hadn't done much house-work—her mother had a cleaning woman in three times a week—but she was discovering she really enjoyed it. Chrissie's mom called it a nesting instinct. She called it pitching in. These days, her father didn't have time for such things.

She dashed to the kitchen phone as fast as her girth would allow. "Hello?"

"Stace, it's Dad."

"Hi! What's up?"

"Well—" he sighed "—there's something important I have to discuss with you."

He sounded too guarded. "Go on," she said, bracing herself for the worst.

"We're going to be bringing Joe home this after-noon."

"Oh." Her breath whooshed out in abrupt relief.

"And I have a favor to ask. What we'd like to do is settle him in a room where both Gina and I can tend to him. The most likely spot is the spare room, the one next to yours. That is, if you don't mind giving up your room to Gina and moving into her place for a while."

Stacy was about to say sure, she didn't mind, but her father rushed on. "I know it's another change, and it's coming at a time when you least need the upset."

"Dad—"

"You might find it lonely over there, too, so we'll keep the connecting door open at all times. Feel free to have Chrissie sleep over anytime, too."

"Listen, Dad—"

"And remember, we're only a shout away if you need—"

"Dad!" she hollered on a laugh.

"Yes?"

"It's okay. I'll be fine. I love Gina's place. And remember, *I'll* be just a shout away, too."

The line hummed with silence for several seconds before her father said, "You're one in a million, kid."

"Glad you finally noticed. Is Gina there?"

"No, she's off talking with the discharge planner. Which reminds me, some equipment is going to be delivered to the house this afternoon—a hospital bed, a portable oxygen unit, stuff like that. It'll probably arrive before we get home, so could you show the delivery people up to the room?"

"Sure enough. Are you going to be taking over Joe's care?"

Her father's sigh crackled over the line. "Not officially. Before we leave, the nurses here are going to teach Gina everything she needs to know to take care of him, but of course I'll help as a friend."

Stacy relaxed. "That's great, Dad."

"Do me another favor, Stace?"

She heard something odd in her father's voice. "Sure. What?"

"My bag's in my closet. Will you get it out for me please? Put it in Joe's room?"

"Okeydoke." A bell went off on the stove. "Oh, my brownies are done."

"Better get going, then."

"See you soon. And tell Gina I'm glad Joe's coming home."

She was about to hang up when she heard, "Stacy?"

"Yeah?"

"Stace, our bringing Joe home doesn't mean he's getting better."

"I know," she said with false brightness. "How...how long does he have?"

"Not long."

"A few weeks?"

"Not likely. More like days."

"Oh." Disappointment slid through her. She laid a hand on her stomach. She wasn't sure why she so wanted Joe to see her baby. Maybe it was because Gina didn't have kids. She felt a need to give him something—the idea that he would live on in a new generation. Which was crazy, of course. They weren't even related. She just felt they were. What made the notion even crazier was, she wasn't keeping the baby. She'd barely get to see it herself.

"Are you going to be okay, hon?"

Stacy pulled in a fortifying breath. "Sure. We'll just take it one day at a time." She was pleasantly surprised to hear her father laugh.

"How old did you say you were, kid?"

GINA TURNED ON the monitor by her father's bed, then tiptoed out of the dimly lit room. The farmhouse was quiet and dark. In the hall she listened for Spencer moving about in the rooms below. The silence, disturbed only by the chirping of crickets, told her he was still next door checking on Stacy for the night.

She gave the small spare room one last glance. The amount of equipment and medical supplies that had come home with Joe still staggered her. She hadn't known this type of help was so readily available until today.

Relieved as she was to have her father home, Gina was still uncertain about her ability to care for him. The nurses at the hospital had given her careful instructions, but she still felt queasy about certain things. Suctioning his windpipe, for example. In fact, when she'd found out the extent of her responsibilities, she'd almost changed her mind. But Spencer had pulled her aside and assured her that he'd help.

Yawning, she stepped into Stacy's room, which she'd commandeered, and switched on the overhead light. In that brief moment when the room went from dark to light, she unexpectedly experienced a flash of déjà vu. This had been her room when she was a girl, and although the furniture was different, it was placed in the same position as hers, giving the room an uncanny sense of sameness.

She pried off her shoes and padded to the dresser where earlier she'd placed the receiver end of the monitor. She turned it on and jumped. The volume was too high, and her father's breathing hit the room like a blast of static. Quickly she turned the knob down.

With her pulse returning to normal, she leaned toward the mirror to take off her earrings. The image looking back startled her almost as much as the static had. It seemed a stranger. How tired she looked. And old. That was the shock of it.

But then the moment passed and she laughed, feeling foolish. That image was just *her,* how she normally looked. Had walking into this room prepared her subconscious to expect an eighteen-year-old in the mirror? Had her mind played a trick on her?

She laughed again, took off her silver earrings and laid them beside the monitor. Hesitantly, she glanced in the mirror again, taking in the deepening crow's-feet at her eyes, the flecks of gray in her hair, the skin that was no longer shiny-taut. Dread crawled over her.

She whirled from the mirror, intent on making herself busy. From a cardboard box on the floor she dug out her nightgown and tossed it on the bed. Next came her slippers, her robe and a book. Then she went to the window to pull down the shade.

Outside, a nearly full moon was pouring its milky light on the world. She lowered the shade halfway, then paused and lifted it again. Her enraptured gaze roamed.

Was there anything more beautiful than moonlight on those hills, carving them, curving them, making of their woods a veritable Arden. She braced herself on the sill and drank in the view, from the hills to her father's fields, from the greenhouse and sheds to the garden below. Moonlight silvered everything, every leaf and shingle, every blade of grass. Shadows poured from lawn chairs and hollyhocks, clotheslines and fence posts, a tracery so fine Gina thought she might cry.

How did a person leave all this? How did a person die?

You're not the one who's dying, she reminded herself. But a voice replied, *We're all dying, from the day we're born.*

She yanked down the window shade, disgusted for allowing herself to get so maudlin and self-pitying.

But it's not self-pity. It's fear.

Gina dropped onto the bed, wrapped her arms around herself and rocked. During the month since her birthday, she'd managed to distract herself, with gardening, with birth classes, with Spencer. She'd thought the fear was gone. But, oh, it wasn't.

"Gina?"

She jerked around. Spencer was standing in the hall, watching her. "Hi," she said stiffly.

"I made you some tea. Camomile." He was carrying a tray with a steaming cup and a plate of cookies. There was also a glass of beer. "Come on across the hall." He glanced at the monitor. "My room's more comfortable."

Gina followed him into his room where he set the tray on the unmade bed and handed her the teacup. She settled into the chair by the window and looked out on the moon-washed night. From a nearby tree, she heard a bird singing. "What time is it?" she asked, confused.

"Nine forty-two."

She continued to frown. "What *day* is it?"

"Tuesday. July twenty-fourth."

He could've said December twenty-fourth for all the sense of time she had. All the usual markers that kept her days ordered seemed to have been leveled.

She heard the mattress squeak and turned to see Spencer arranging himself on the bed. He propped pillows against the headboard, reached for his beer and settled back. Glancing at her, he smiled, and her heart expanded. She was beginning to think she'd never really known friendship before she'd found this man.

At the moment, lying there, he appeared so strong and alive she wanted to cry out—in joy? Or was it relief?

His eyes narrowed. "How're you doing?"

"Oh, hangin' in." The teacup rattled in her hand.

He continued to look at her. "Come here," he finally said, setting aside his beer and raising one arm.

She put down her cup, hiked up her skirt, crawled over the bed and sank into his embrace with a shudder. Under her cheek, his chest was firmly muscled, his heartbeat steady and strong. Against her palm, his arm was taut and tanned and warm, so warm. She fit herself along his side more closely, wanting to soak up his vitality, wanting to drown in it. He rearranged the pillows, slipping lower to accommodate her...

Which was probably the wrong thing to do, Spencer considered.

At first he thought she just needed comfort. A shoulder to lean on. An ear to pour her worries into. But he could feel a tension in her body that went beyond those needs. He stroked her hair, letting his caress continue down her back, and felt the tension heighten. He gathered her closer, rested his lips on her sweet-scented hair and shivered when she worked the tips of two fingers inside his shirt and began to stroke his breastbone.

She was telegraphing needs he felt inadequate to handle. Contradictory needs, of body, of soul. Lord knew he was no expert on matters of the soul, but he knew something of the other. Tonight he hoped that was enough.

Gina stroked the hot skin of Spencer's chest with her fingertips and suddenly wondered, *What am I doing?* Her father was dying. How could she be feeling sexual stirrings now? It wasn't right.

But it wasn't wrong, either, she thought. It was a need too obscure to label. She simply had to touch this man, had to inhale his scent, had to fill her eyes with him. He... quickened her.

Lifting her head from his shoulder and bracing on an elbow, she gazed into his eyes, eyes that had seen everything, and was reassured that he understood. Slowly she brought her lips to his. They kissed with a steady, unmoving pressure devoid of sexuality. Why, she couldn't have explained. It just seemed the right beginning.

Easing the pressure, she brushed her lips across his, delighting in their softness, a softness made even sweeter because of the rasp of beard surrounding them—like this sweet moment carved out of sorrow.

She worked her way upward to his eyes. He closed them and lay still, letting her kiss each lid. Pulling back, her gaze roamed, taking in his dark, rumpled hair, the strong planes of cheek and jaw, the small birthmark above his left eye. On a sudden move, she returned to his mouth, kissing him with an urgency that surged, a desperation that rose from the deepest part of her.

Spencer slipped his arms under her and lifted her over him. She settled, knees planted on either his hips, and parted his lips. Under her, his body tightened as if minute charges were exploding in various sensitive parts of him. She circled his tongue with hers, stroked it, reveling in her power to ignite those explosions.

He groaned deep in his throat as heat built between them. She knew he was tired. After the week they'd had, it was patently unfair of her to be doing this. But instead of deterring her, his tiredness spurred her on. She wanted to flood this weary man with arousal, wanted to overwhelm his senses.

She sat up, skirt rucked up over her thighs, and wantonly unbuttoned his shirt. She spread it open and ran her hungry hands over his muscle-ridged chest, sliding her fingers through the crisp hair that covered it. He closed his eyes and swallowed, and her heart gladdened.

She pulled her blouse from her skirt, and before he could start to unbutton it, she had it off. She was wearing a functional white bra that momentarily dismayed her. But Spencer quickly banished her disappointment by slipping the straps off her shoulders and cupping her breasts.

No, it wasn't just his cupping her breasts that made her forget her dismay. It was the raggedness of his breathing.

And the way he spread his fingers to get more of her.

And the hard ridge of arousal under the placket of his jeans.

Ah, sex. What an invention! She threw back her head and laughed. What a glorious mystery, this drive that fused bodies and souls and sometimes cells.

Spencer rasped his palms across the hardened tips of her breasts, bringing on a flood of full body heat that pooled at her center. She closed her eyes, tightened her thighs around his hips, her center seeking his.

She hadn't forgotten her father. Nor had she forgotten her own fragile mortality. Yes, she was going to die. Sadly, so was Spencer, and Stacy, and even the baby Stacy was carrying. The reality was inescapable.

But she wasn't dying today, nor tomorrow probably. Her time hadn't come yet. For now, she was alive. Very much alive. *See how alive?* her heated body seemed to shout.

Spencer tried to unbuckle his belt, but Gina's hands were there first, pushing his aside. He let her take over. She seemed to need that tonight, he thought. He didn't mind, even though she didn't appear to be too aware of him. Didn't mind? Actually, she was driving him right to the edge of crazy.

Probably sensing how aroused he was, she moved off him and, with his help, tugged off his jeans and shorts. Next went her own skirt and underpants. When she was totally naked, she sat back on her heels, her gaze skimming him like a physical stroking.

Odd, how they didn't talk, he thought. They usually did.

No, not odd. Not tonight.

He reached for her and she came to him, moving over his body like an erotic dream. He lay back and let her explore, first with her hands and then with her mouth. His back arched and his head pressed into the pillow. He gritted his teeth, trying to forestall the pleasure, but she persisted, and it seized him, anyway, with great emptying shudders of near-painful delight. When he'd finally stopped quaking, she dropped to his side and let him rest.

But then it began again, her kisses, her heat, her irresistible seduction, and he came back to life with a force greater than before. He needed it. She made love with an energy that was ferocious and frenzied. And when she peaked, her cry was a high thin sound that could've been mistaken for keening. Then, without a word, she folded against him and went to sleep.

JOE FADED FAST. Once home, he seemed to relax into an ease of mind and heart that had been impossible in the hospital. Although he was unconscious most of the time, Gina was sure he knew where he was.

Days were long, nights even longer, and they would've been longer still if it hadn't been for the companionship of others. Barbara, who brought over her cheer and home-cooked food. The nurse assigned to Joe's case. Stacy, who insisted on helping, too, although both Gina and Spencer tried to keep her involvement to a minimum.

Eight months pregnant, she shouldn't have to subject herself to such a grim chore as a death watch. But she insisted, sitting with Joe and reading to him, while his favorite music played in the background. Youthfully sentimental, she even potted up a three-foot-high sunflower and set it on the bureau where he could look at it anytime.

"I know there are no flowers yet," she said, apologizing for the tight buds, "but that'll just give him a reason to open his eyes every morning, don't you think?"

And then there was Spencer. What to think of Spencer? He not only checked Joe's vital signs every few hours, but he performed all the other tasks the nurses had taught her to do. Gina didn't think doctors usually did those things. Their specialized skills put them above monitoring IV drips and clearing breathing passages. But Spencer performed those chores without any prompting, gently and with patience.

He did all the heavy work, too, the lifting and changing and bathing. Those things she was *certain* doctors didn't do. Gina was grateful, but more than that, increasingly curious.

Why did he insist, especially when home-health aides were available? Was he deliberately giving himself a lesson in humility? She didn't understand, didn't have a clue, until one afternoon when she was carrying towels to the bathroom and noticed Spencer in the spare room, sponge-bathing her father.

She paused in the doorway, unnoticed, as he swished the washcloth in a basin and wrung it out. Then he lifted the cloth and began to wash her father's face. He was humming softly, a tuneless phrase that nonetheless imparted a sense of well-being, of being in good hands. Strange, that humming. Every so often Spencer swiped at his eyes.

In that moment she knew that whatever Spencer's reasons, he seemed to need this personal caring for her father. He was walking some mysterious journey of the heart, and all she could do was watch and hope he reached his destination.

ON THE AFTERNOON of Joe's fifth day home, Gina was in the garden, clawing at the dirt around her tomatoes, wondering if she'd been out here a sufficient amount of time to constitute a break, when Spencer came out of the house. He was the one who'd insisted she get some air and pay some attention to her garden. She couldn't have cared less. All the time she'd been out here, she'd kept looking toward the house, thinking she should be getting back.

Spencer strode across the yard and opened the garden gate. He'd forgotten to take off his stethoscope. He often did, she'd noticed. He stepped between the rows of vegetables and flowers and hunkered down beside her.

Her cheeks were wet with tears she hadn't had time to hide. He lent her a handkerchief and waited until she'd mopped up before saying, "I think you ought to go up and talk to your father."

She gave her eyes another dab, then bunched the damp linen in her fist. "Talk to him?"

"Mmm. He's ready to go, but I sense he's fighting it."

Gina stood up slowly and glanced toward the second-floor window. "But he's unconscious. Would he hear me?"

Spencer stood up, too, and shrugged. "Some people claim it's possible. I'm not sure, but it's worth a shot. The least that'll happen is, he'll sense you're there. That alone might bring him the peace he needs."

She twisted the handkerchief. "What should I say?"

"Whatever's in your heart."

Gina looked up at the billowing cumulus clouds raised by the summer heat. Everything in her resisted the reality of the moment, everything wanted to run and run and run...

"Okay," she said on a long sigh, and nodded. "Okay."

GINA STOOD BESIDE her father's bed and took his hand in hers. His eyes were closed, his skin looked gray and his breathing had an unsettling rattle.

"Hi, Dad. It's me, Gina," she said, leaning close. His fingers gave the faintest flutter. "I was out in the garden just now. Everything's coming up great. I already picked a few small cukes." With her free hand she stroked his hair, hoping he felt her touch and at least got a vague sense of being loved and cared for.

"It's a nice day," she continued with a glance toward the window. "Lots of sun, big white clouds. It's July twenty-eighth, by the way, late afternoon, and you're home at the farm up in the spare room." She paused again, wondering why she was talking such nonsense. Did she really think her father cared about the temperature or where he was lying? Was she trying to give him a mental image of the time and place of his death, a set of coordinates to navigate by? Or was she just reassuring herself he *was* still a part of time and place?

Better to move on, get to what was important.

"Spencer told me you're feeling pretty tired, Dad, so I'll be brief. I just wanted to tell you I love you." What she really wanted was to ask him if he was scared. But she couldn't bring herself to ask and he couldn't answer, anyway, so she merely repeated, "I love you and I'm here."

His eyes opened to the merest slits. Did he see her? Did he hear? His mind had deteriorated so much he probably saw only shadow and light, heard only indiscriminate noise, much the way a newborn did.

"I also want to reassure you I'll carry out your wishes regarding the funeral. There will be no wake, no one gawking at you in your casket and no hoopla in church. Just a small service at McCrory's and the burial beside Mama. If you don't mind, I also thought I'd have your friends over for brunch afterward."

Spencer quietly slipped into the room. He hoped he wasn't intruding, but he didn't want Gina to be alone at this difficult time. She looked over, her head tilted at a sad, piquant angle, and nodded. He took that as an invitation to stay and lowered himself into the chair by the door.

Gina returned to her attention to her father, glad that Spencer was there, but forgetting him almost immediately. She stroked her father's head—he felt too warm—and pressed a kiss to his brow. What else could she say to put his mind at ease?

"You've been a wonderful father to me, Dad, and I'm going to miss you terribly. But I'll be okay because you'll always be with me. You're leaving me with so many memories, so much of a legacy."

Stacy tiptoed in at that moment. She looked at her father, asking him with her eyes if it was all right for her to be there. He nodded and she melded into the shadowy corner.

"I always knew I'd picked up my love of literature from you," Gina continued. "Remember reading me *The Five Little Peppers* in the evening after supper? I'm not sure I ever thanked you for that. But I need to thank you for some other things, too, things like your optimistic outlook on life, your joy in the seasons and in planting and seeing things grow. I love gardening, and I love seeing things grow." Suddenly she paused, her eyes opening wide at a dawning realization. "That includes my students."

Sitting by the door, Spencer thought about the legacy left him by his own father—a name, a passion for medicine, a lethal over-the-head jump shot and a mental scrapbook bursting at the binding with memories, some bad, a lot good. But he'd never told his father, never relayed his gratitude, never had the satisfaction of telling him his life had been worthwhile.

Gina stroked her father's warm head. What else could she say? What else *needed* to be said?

"I'm sorry you had to sell the farm. I know you had bills. If I'd come home after college, I could've helped you financially. But I was young and needed to make my own way. Can you forgive me?"

Spencer, too, was sorry. He'd spent so little time back home, starting with his early college days. He'd even stayed away some summers, picking up jobs near campus. There would be time later, he'd always thought.

Gina lifted her father's hand and kissed his knuckles. "I'm also sorry I'm not married and don't have kids. I know you worry about leaving me this way." Unexpectedly she felt a resurgence of the anxiety that had been dogging her throughout the summer. *Oh, God, to die alone, no one holding my hand. That was what this fear was about.*

For her father's sake, however, she set her fear aside. He needed reassurance that she could get on without him. Watching Spencer this summer with his daughter, she'd learned how deep that vein of paternal protectiveness ran.

"I know you worry because I don't have a family." She smiled. "Believe me, I'm not too crazy about it myself. But I'll be okay. Financially I'm doing fine. I earn a good living wage, and I have my condominium and a retirement plan. On a more personal note, I've got good friends." She felt the urge to glance over her shoulder. "Besides, I'm only forty, Dad. You didn't have me until you were forty-three. Who knows what the future will bring?"

Leaning against the wall in the corner, Stacy asked the same question. What would the future bring? Where would she be in a year? Where would her baby be? And how about her father and Gina? She hoped they found a way to stay together. She didn't ever want this circle of love to break.

"So you see, Dad, you shouldn't feel bad about leaving me," Gina said softly. "I'm going to be okay." She took a shallow breath and decided, "I guess that's all I've got to say. That, and I love you. Take care of yourself now, Dad. All your life you've worked hard. You deserve to rest. Thank you for always being there for me. Now . . . rest."

Gina kissed his brow once more and took the seat by the bed.

She sat for what seemed an eternity, although the angle of the sunlight coming in the window hardly shifted. During that time Joe receded deeper into unconsciousness, then deeper still.

She stroked his head. She continued to hold his hand. And when she could take the intensity of her anxiety and sadness no longer, she watched the gauzy curtain, lit with sunshine like a Chinese lantern, alternately billowing and flattening against the screen. After a while her mind dulled with the soft ebb and flow, and thoughts bumped helter-skelter.

She brought herself back with a shake of her head, feeling guilty for having wandered. She looked at her father and felt even worse. In just the past few minutes, something had happened. His face seemed to have changed physically. Not a bad change really. He'd taken on a peaceful repose, his skin almost a radiancy.

Gina gazed at him, bemused. He looked almost... happy.

Joe suddenly filled his lungs so deep he arched, then expelled the breath with a long, noisy exhalation. Gina waited in stunned disbelief, but he never breathed again.

She looked up, around the room, the very room where he'd been born. She felt him all around her. "Godspeed," she whispered. His spirit hovered a moment longer and then just faded through a keyhole in time. She imagined it as the same keyhole through which he'd entered. Then she bowed her head, touched it to his and let the tears flow.

Standing in the corner, Stacy cried, *It isn't fair. You never saw my baby.*

Sitting by the door, Spencer shaded his eyes and whispered, "Goodbye, Dad."

CHAPTER FIFTEEN

THE DAY AFTER THE FUNERAL, Gina packed a small bag, got in her car and, with only the vaguest of plans, drove away from the farm. She drove all that day and all the next, with just a brief stay at a motel the intervening night, the constant movement separating her, body and mind, from the sorrow and anxiety of the past two months.

Although she knew she needed this break, she'd been reluctant to leave the farm. Stacy had taken Joe's death hard, something Gina still felt guilty about. One of Spencer's earliest objections to her father's moving to the farm had been that he'd upset Stacy. Gina had thought the teenager would handle him just fine as a neighbor. And she had. What Gina hadn't anticipated was how she'd handle him as a deceased friend.

She and Spencer had talked to her after the funeral, reminding her that Joe had lived a good and long life and that he'd died as well as anyone could, surrounded by people who loved him. They'd rephrased ideas from the psalm that Gina had read at the service, ideas about there being a time for everything in life, for sowing and reaping, for sadness and joy. They'd also assured her that death was just a part of the cycle.

In the end, Gina thought the talk did her and Spencer as much good as it did Stacy. For certainly Gina felt more at peace.

She realized there was nothing in her father's passing to be angry about except maybe in how he went. But even that had brought her closer to him, made her more loving, so maybe it had had its purpose, too.

As she drove through the peaceful green hills and valleys of western New England, Gina also realized she'd come away from her father's death with a strength she hadn't had before. She couldn't explain it yet. Perhaps she would in time, but for now she only knew she was no longer afraid of dying or being alone. Although she'd been right by her father's side, he'd died alone. Alone was the only way anyone ever went. Yet he'd done it, and maybe that was part of the cycle, too—parents dying to prepare their children for their own passing.

In any case, by the third day she felt over the darkest part of her grief. Spencer had predicted she would, that her grief would pass quickly because she'd already been grieving for months.

Spencer also had told her not to worry about anything while she was gone, the garden or Stacy or her apartment. He'd handle anything that came up.

Driving along those endlessly winding back roads on her three-day journey, Gina began to see that words would never express the depth of gratitude she felt toward Spencer. Because of him, Joe had been able to die at home. Because of him, Gina had been able to keep her promise. Because of him, there was peace in her heart.

And as she wandered, Gina realized something else about Spencer. She loved him. They hadn't wanted to call it love and had named it everything but. But if all the experiences they'd endured, if all the help they'd given each other, and if all the pleasure they'd shared wasn't love, she didn't know what was.

At that moment her wandering came to a halt. It was time to go home and tell him how she felt.

DURING THE FIRST COUPLE of days that Gina was gone, Spencer strapped on a backpack and took to the hills, walking, climbing, sweating, working through his belated grief over his father's death. By the time he returned those nights, he was too exhausted even to shower. He fell into bed and slept the deepest sleep he'd had in months.

On the third morning he awoke refreshed. Although his calf muscles were sore, he felt energized and ready to do something other than hill climbing. Since he'd already finished painting the house, he walked the farm looking for chores. But nothing stirred his interest. Finally he sat on his front porch steps and looked into his heart. What he found was an eagerness to get back to work. Not to repairing sheds or tilling gardens. *His* work.

He didn't understand why the change had occurred. Maybe he never would. He only knew he felt healed, and when the time came to return to work, he'd be ready. He was ready now.

He didn't even mind that the clinic was a two-hour drive away. If he just worked a couple of hours, he could be home between four and five. Stacy would be okay in his absence. Chrissie had become a fixture at the farm, and Stacy's due date was still two weeks away.

He set off for Boston with an eagerness he hadn't felt since he was an intern. God, he hoped Gina would be back that night. He wanted to tell her, wanted to share the things he'd kept locked inside him. She'd understand.

He missed her. Missed having her beside him in his bed. Missed her bright eyes, her insouciant smile, her strength. And he couldn't imagine not having her in his life after this summer.

Maybe he ought to tell her how he felt. The prospect was unnerving. She'd made it clear she was holding out for commitment of the permanent kind, and he still wasn't sure he could talk about that. But who knew what the future would bring? Maybe they'd work something out. He hoped so. God, he hoped so.

GINA GOT BACK to the farm a little after noon. She parked her car by her door and was instantly dismayed to see the garage empty.

Maybe it was better Spencer wasn't here, she thought as she stepped into her kitchen. She had an unpleasant chore awaiting her, sorting through her father's clothing, bundling it for Goodwill and deciding what to keep of his furniture, what to give away.

But first things first, and that meant lunch.

While she was organizing the fixings for a BLT, a knock sounded on the connecting door, which had remained unlocked since Joe's return from the hospital.

"Hi," she greeted Stacy in surprise. "I didn't know you were home. Where's your dad?"

"Would you believe he went to work?"

"At the walk-in?"

"Yep." Stacy climbed onto a counter stool with difficulty.

Gina banked her curiosity and invited Stacy to join her for lunch. While they prepared their sandwiches, they talked about inconsequential matters, but from the very beginning, Gina sensed that something was worrying Stacy.

When they were seated at the kitchen island, Gina finally asked, "Are you okay, Stace?"

"Yeah, sure," Stacy answered too readily. "Well, not really. Sleeping through the night's become impossible. But," she said with a shrug, "that's only normal at this stage." She took a small bite of her sandwich and stared at the plate.

"Stace, are you concerned I might be moving back to Syracuse and forgetting about being your birth partner?"

The girl glanced up. "Oh, you're not, are you?"

"Of course not. I wouldn't leave you in the lurch like that."

Stacy's shoulders sagged with relief, but the worry lines on her face remained.

"What is it, kiddo?"

For a moment Gina thought the teenager was going to cry, but she quickly composed herself. She wiped her mouth and squeezed the paper napkin.

"I don't know how else to say this, so I'll just say it. Gina, I want to keep my baby."

The moment froze for a few fathomless seconds, then fractured into a thousand tiny arrows piercing Gina's heart. Before she'd managed to regroup, Stacy read her reaction.

"I know. The adoption is all arranged." Tears glistened in her haunted eyes. "But I figure it's not final till...till it's final. Right?" She gazed at Gina through her tears, needing her to agree.

"I guess. Sure. But...oh, Stacy, are you serious?"

"Yes."

"This is going to kill your father." The statement was out before Gina could edit herself.

"I know." Stacy's voice cracked on a sob. "He's upset enough over the fact that I got pregnant. Keeping the baby..." She shook her head. "He'll go ballistic. He's hoping I'll put all this behind me and pick up my life as if nothing happened. But I can't do that. It did happen, and I'll never be the same. I'll never forget."

"Of course not, but does that mean you have to keep the baby?"

"I don't have to. I want to."

"But are you sure? Have you thought about how difficult it's going to be?"

"Yes." Stacy glanced aside. "I've always wanted to keep the baby, but my father never let me even talk about it. Adoption was his idea, not mine, and I went along with it because I'd already disappointed him enough. I can't do that anymore, Gina. As you say, a person's got to be true to herself."

Gina flinched, hearing her words come back at her.

"Stace, I know you've agreed not to see Todd anymore, but does this have anything to do with him?"

Stacy's eyebrows knit. "How so?"

"Well, are you hoping, if he sees you and the baby together, his paternal instincts might be moved?"

"Moved? You have to *have* paternal instincts first. Sometimes I think that guy isn't even carbon-based." Her eyes gleamed with a disillusionment that simultaneously heartened Gina and saddened her.

"Then, if Todd isn't the reason, is it so you'll have someone you can call your very own? You know, someone who'll love you and need you and never leave you?"

Stacy exhaled a sharp laugh. "Boy, you don't pull any punches, do you?"

"This is too important an issue to do otherwise."

Stacy slumped. "I'd be lying if I said that wasn't part of it. But it's not the entire reason. I already love this baby, Gina. I know it sounds crazy, but I do. And I want to keep on loving it." She placed her right hand on her stomach in a way that Gina could only think of as maternal. "What especially convinced me was seeing you with your father these last few weeks. I never knew family could be like that, so close, so devoted, and I want to create that same sort of relationship in this baby's life. I think I can...I'm not saying an adoptive parent wouldn't love it, too, but nobody's gonna love it better."

Gina had been sitting in a daze, fingers over her mouth, head slowly shaking. Now she sighed and said, "Oh, Stacy, I understand your feelings. Honestly, I can't imagine giving a baby up for adoption, either. But you're so young. I don't think you understand the amount of time and attention a baby needs from a mother."

Stacy grew serious. "I know it's going to be hard. I've done enough baby-sitting to have an idea of what it'll be like. I also know I can't raise a baby on my own. But all my instincts are still telling me to keep it, anyway."

"You say you can't raise it on your own. What do you have in mind, then?"

"What I'm hoping is, my father will help. I'd like to keep on living with him—me and the baby. If I can just get him to agree to that, I'm sure the rest will fall into place. Maybe I can go to a school like yours that has a new-mothers program, or maybe Dad'll agree to hire a part-time nanny." She traced a pattern on the tile counter with her thumbnail. "Or maybe you and Dad'll get married, and you'll decide to stay home and baby-sit your grandbaby."

Gina's jaw dropped and she stammered for several seconds, going hot all over.

"I'm kidding, I'm kidding." Stacy laughed.

Gina wasn't so sure. Scrambling for composure, she decided it was best just to move on. "You do realize, don't you, that what you're asking your father to do is raise another child?''

Stacy nodded, wearing a deep, sad frown.

''By your own admission, it'll be a child whose existence he'd rather not even acknowledge, a child he believes has robbed you of your innocence and youth, and if you keep it, he thinks it'll ruin your future.''

Stacy's mouth quivered, but just for a moment. Gina could see she was making a tremendous effort to stay calm.

''That's why I was wondering if you'd do me the favor of speaking to him for me.''

''Me?''

''Yes.'' Her eyes pleaded.

Gina dropped her head to one hand. Under her nose lay a half-eaten sandwich that would stay that way. ''I can't ask him that, Stace.''

''Sure you can. If anybody can convince him, it's you.''

''You vastly overrate my powers of persuasion.''

''Gina, you have to. I don't have anybody else. He'll listen to you.''

The silence spun out while Gina thought of all the ramifications of Stacy's choice. The ramification she thought about most was Spencer's reaction. It would be negative from beginning to end.

On the other hand, Stacy seemed determined. She was going to present her decision to Spencer with or without help. The confrontation might go more smoothly if Gina was there to mediate.

''Okay, this is what I'll do, Stace. I'll go with you for moral support, but that's all. I can't possibly take sides. For one thing it's not my business. For another, I can't. I sympathize with both of you.''

Stacy looked disappointed, but Gina didn't see how she could commit to anything more.

"When would you like to talk to him?"

Stacy shrugged. "Dinner?"

"In that case, we'd better prepare something he really, really likes." Gina smiled reassuringly. Maybe it would work out. Raising a daughter and a grandchild together wasn't an unheard-of occurrence, and maybe Spencer would surprise them.

SPENCER LAUGHED. "You want to do *what?*"

They were eating in the dining room of the farmhouse, Spencer at the head of the table, Gina to his right, Stacy to his left.

Stacy swallowed and repeated, "Keep my baby."

Spencer slowly lowered his fork, the smile simultaneously leaving his face as if it were connected somehow to his hand. "You're serious?"

Stacy glanced across the table at Gina. She was so pale Gina grew alarmed. "Yes," she whispered, lowering her eyes.

Spencer swiveled, pinning Gina with his incredulous gaze. This wasn't how she'd envisioned their evening unfolding. She'd wanted to tell him she loved him. She'd wanted them to figure out a way they could make their relationship work. So far, they hadn't had a minute to themselves.

"Did you know about this?" he asked her.

"Yes. She told me this afternoon."

Spencer emitted a sound that was somewhere between exasperation and despair. "And what's your opinion?" His eyes were hurt yet hard, asking Gina to unite with him, daring her not to.

"I think she's serious and you ought to listen to her reasoning." Although she'd meant to stay neutral, Spencer reacted as if she'd taken sides. The muggy summer air between them chilled.

"Reasoning? What reasoning can there possibly be for such an unreasonable statement?" Spencer threw down his napkin.

"Dad, please."

"Please what? I thought this was settled. The adoption agency already has a couple picked out."

Gina searched his eyes. Her skin crawled with foreboding. This was not going to end well.

"But nothing's finalized," Stacy argued. "This is still *my* baby."

Spencer closed his eyes and expelled a long, gusty sigh. "Don't even think it, Stacy."

"Why not? I'll make a good mother."

In disgust, Spencer bit out, "You're a child yourself. You've got most of high school ahead of you yet, dances, football games, going out for cheerleading, college after that. How can you even think about being a mother?"

Stacy went red and her nostrils flared. "This is how," she said, standing up and placing a hand on her stomach.

It was apparent to Gina that Spencer wasn't going to listen. He was on the wrong track, hurtling toward a disastrous argument. Maybe just a few words from her would get him to slow down.

"Spencer, you know what struck me most when Stacy told me about wanting to keep the baby? Her sense of responsibility." Gina received a glower for her effort. She continued, anyway. "At a time when everybody has an excuse for their mistakes, when nobody is willing to accept blame, your daughter is trying to take responsibility. I think that's remarkable, and you ought to be proud to have such an admirable young woman for a daughter."

"Oh, I'm busting my buttons." Spencer turned to Stacy. "Honey, I know the idea of a baby is nice. They're small and cute, and you get to wheel them around in carriages and dress them in cute clothes, sort of like playing with dolls. But they're not dolls."

"Duh! I didn't know that," she said, mocking her father.

A muscle jumped along his iron jaw. "Just for kicks, you wanna tell me how you expect to do this? Raise this child?"

Stacy fumed. Her gaze avoided his, and her mouth got tighter and smaller.

"She was hoping you'd let her live with you," Gina supplied. "She thought she might find a school with a new-mothers program so she could take the baby to school with her, or maybe you'd hire a nanny." Gina spoke as reasonably as she could, trying to impart the sense that this issue could be handled, and *was* handled every day.

Spencer looked as if she'd betrayed him. "Have you been feeding her those ideas? Is that why she . . . ?"

"No!" Stacy fired back. "Gina had nothing to do with it. Keeping the baby is my thing entirely."

"Since when?"

"Since always. I've always wanted to keep it." Her chin began to quiver. Gina ached for the girl. "I just couldn't bring myself to tell you because you were already—" the quivering overtook her lips "—already so disappointed in me."

Spencer sagged like a punctured balloon. "I'm not disappointed in you. I'm disappointed *for* you. This isn't how I wanted your life to turn out."

"I know, and I'm sorry. You had lots of hopes for me that probably won't be fulfilled. But so did I, Dad." A tear shimmered on Stacy's eyelashes. "I'm disappointed, too. This is my deepest regret, this mistake I've made."

Spencer ran a hand over his mouth again and again. Trying to gather his own composure? "Then why put yourself through any more unnecessary pain? You can have all your dreams back in a couple of months. All you have to do is—"

"No. It's my baby, my responsibility. My flesh and blood. I can't abandon it."

"You wouldn't be abandoning it. You'd be entrusting it to a mature couple who'd raise it in a comfortable, stable environment."

Stacy swiped at her tears. "That's why I need your help. I know I won't always be able to make the best decisions or know what to do. I need your maturity. I need you to back me up."

Spencer shook his head. "Sorry, Stace. I still say no."

Gina reached across the table and touched his arm. "She really wants to keep her baby, Spencer," she warned again as forcefully as she could. "Maybe you ought to start exploring ways to help her."

He sat back, pulling himself out of Gina's reach. "She'll get over this. It's just teenage sentimentality and romanticism. *My* baby, *my* flesh and blood."

Gina had to make an effort to keep her temper. "Was it sentimentality that got her to take meals to us in the hospital? Was it romanticism that kept her by my father's bed?"

Spencer averted his eyes. "I can't see a single good consequence in her keeping the baby. Not one."

"A baby can bring lots of joy."

"Exhaustion and bills, too, to say nothing of short tempers. Sorry, I'm not going to let that happen. I backed down on the boarding-school issue, but this is one point I can't bend on."

Stacy had been sitting by quietly, but now she said, "You don't get it, do you? I'm not asking your permission to keep the baby. I'm just asking for your help."

"And what I'm saying is no, I won't give it."

Gina flinched. "Spencer, caution. 'No' brings down houses."

"Stay out of this, Gina. It's between me and Stacy."

Gina gritted her teeth, feeling an onrush of disaster.

"I only want what's best for my daughter. Maybe she doesn't appreciate it now, but in the future she'll thank me."

Stacy shot up from the table, knocking over her chair. Tears magnified her eyes. "Sometimes I really hate you," she cried before storming out of the room, sobbing.

In the stunned silence that followed, Gina said, "You love her? Just look what your love has done."

She started to get up, too. She wanted no further part in this, but Spencer caught her wrist.

"Wait." He looked at her, a plea in his eyes. "Please, sit."

She returned to her chair. After a moment he said, "Gina, try to understand. I'm her father. Protecting her is the deepest instinct I have. I already feel as though this situation's my fault, because I wasn't around to prevent it. I refuse to let it go any further."

"You really believe you're doing what's best."

"Yes, I do. And apparently you don't."

"That's right. I wish she wanted to give up the baby, too, I honestly do, but she doesn't, and that's the bottom line. What you or I think really doesn't matter. She has to find her own way, Spencer, the way I did, and probably the way you did, too. Of course she'll make mistakes. Of course you'll be disappointed. It's only natural."

"That's crap, Gina. I realize life isn't perfect, and there are disappointments along the way, but we do what we can to minimize the damage."

"Of course. I agree. Only, we're looking at this from different angles. You think you're saving her, and I think you may be doing more damage than you're preventing."

Spencer leaned on the arm of his chair and looked at her a long, silent while. His eyes were sad, and before he even spoke she knew what he was going to say. Her heart splintered.

"I'm not angry with you, Gina. This has been an unforgettable summer." He swallowed, lowered his eyes. "But it would probably be best if Stacy and I were alone for a while. It'll be easier to bring her around."

Around to what? Gina wondered. His way of thinking? *Ah, hubris. Downfall of greater men than you, Dr. Coburn.*

She nodded, lips pressed tight to still their trembling. "Well, we never did expect it to go on forever. Maybe it's better to end it now."

He scowled, saying nothing.

"I'll leave tomorrow. I've been away from my house too long as it is. But I still intend to be Stacy's birth partner."

"That isn't necessary."

"Yes, it is. She's depending on me." Gina got up from her chair and started for the door.

He walked behind her out of the dining room, through the kitchen. At the connecting door, she paused. "The baby would be your grandchild, you know."

"Yes, of course."

She shrugged. "I wasn't sure you'd ever thought of it in that way." She looked into her darkened apartment. A sense of finality hung in the air.

"What difference would it make?"

"Well, it occurred to me that maybe you just don't want to be a grandfather."

"No. I'm not too concerned about that." He punctuated the remark with a quick smile.

"I wasn't referring to aging. I meant loving." She scratched her eyebrow, speculating. "Maybe you don't want a grandchild around because you'll grow to love it."

Spencer laughed dryly. "You're not making much sense."

"Oh, I believe I am. Think about it." She reached up and brushed at a lock of hair that had fallen over his brow. "Don't let fear paralyze you, Spencer. You might succeed in protecting yourself from the bad, but you'll also deprive yourself of the good."

"I'll keep that in mind."

"Well, whatever happens, good luck, Spencer. I mean that."

"To you, too."

There seemed nothing else to say. She stepped over the threshold and closed the connecting door. On the other side the lock slid shut.

CHAPTER SIXTEEN

STACY STILL COULDN'T believe Gina was leaving. From the end of the front porch, she gazed across the courtyard and watched Gina arrange her luggage in the trunk of her car. She'd decided to simply close up the apartment, and all her father's things with it, and go back to Syracuse for a while. Sorting through and cleaning out could wait for another time, she said. When feelings were less raw. Right now, she and Spencer needed to put some distance between them. Stacy felt awful. She'd known her father would be angry about her decision to keep the baby, but she hadn't expected him to split with Gina over it.

Gina closed the trunk, looked up and noticed Stacy on the porch. She made an effort to smile, but it didn't come out her usual big "Gina" smile. She jogged over and stood looking up at Stacy at the rail. "You have my phone number, right?"

"Yeah," Stacy said downheartedly.

"If you happen to go into early labor, call me immediately."

"I will."

"But I should be back well before your due date."

"Are you all packed and ready to leave?" Stacy looked from her to the car.

Gina pressed her lips together and nodded.

Stacy turned, crossed the porch and started down the steps. Gina met her at the bottom and they fell together in a tight hug.

"I'm so sorry, Gina. This is all my fault."

"Shh, I don't want to hear it."

"But it is."

Gina held her at arm's length. "It was bound to happen eventually. Your father and I have different ways of looking at things."

"I like your way better."

Gina's fingers tightened on Stacy's upper arms. "Listen to me, Stacy. Your father truly believes he's doing what's best for you. He thinks he's sparing you years of hardship. A lifetime of it, in fact. You may disagree with his choices, but don't ever, ever doubt that he loves you."

Stacy gave a nod, but she didn't feel it inside. Inside, she felt angry and mean and so very sad.

"Okay, well, I should hit the road and try to beat the commuter traffic." Gina looked past her toward the open door. She pulled in a shivery breath and climbed the porch stairs.

"Spencer?" she called through the screen.

From some distant corner of the house came the casual reply, "Yes?"

"I'm leaving now."

They were acting as if nothing in the world was wrong, as if she was just running into town and would be back in half an hour. Stacy hated what they were doing. Hated it.

"Take care," he called, still from his distance.

"You, too." Gina descended the stairs, walked to her car and drove away.

THAT NIGHT Stacy lay awake on her bed, hands on her stomach, feeling the baby kick and squirm. It was restless tonight. It had dropped into position, Chrissie's mom said. Probably knew it, too, and was eager to get out.

Stacy, on the other hand, was miserable. She didn't want to give birth. She still had misgivings about the process—the pain and possible complications—but mostly she was afraid of what would happen once the baby was delivered. Delivered to whom? Given her age and total dependency on her father, would she have any say in the matter? Would she be unconscious and never know what happened to it? She closed her eyes tight and tears squeezed through her lashes.

She had to get away from here. She didn't want to stay with her father anymore. He was going to force her to give up the baby. But where would she go? She rolled carefully onto her side and tried to rub her aching back. Who could she run to?

Todd immediately sprang to mind, and she booted him out just as quickly. No, definitely not Todd. They were through.

Chrissie? Chrissie was a relatively new friend but one of the best she'd ever had. Surely Chrissie would help.

But how? Stacy couldn't very well expect her to ask her parents to let her pregnant friend move in with them. With five kids already and another on the way, Chrissie's parents weren't exactly in a position to take in one more. Two more, after the baby was born. They probably wouldn't want to come between Stacy and her father, anyway.

Okay, so if not Chrissie...maybe her mother?

Stacy gave a little laugh that turned into a sob. Her mother had thrown her out. She wanted nothing to do with her or this pregnancy. Besides, she was getting married. She had no time for a daughter left over from another life.

Gina, then. She could go to Gina. Gina understood her better than anybody, even Chrissie. She was strong. She'd fight for Stacy's right to keep the baby. And afterward, maybe she'd let Stacy and the baby live in her condo. Maybe Stacy could go to Gina's school.

On the other hand, getting Gina involved to such a degree was a surefire way to keep Gina and her father from ever reconciling. He'd never forgive Gina then, and Stacy did hope they'd get back together someday. Gina was good for her father, and whether they knew it or not, they were in love.

So was there nobody she could turn to? Her heart ached with the answer. She felt more alone than she ever had in her life. Without friends, without family, cut utterly adrift. Stacy sat up, suddenly accepting her fate. Well, fine. She was alone and on her own. But so were lots of other young women, and they survived. She would, too.

She got out of bed and walked quietly to her closet where she pulled a nylon gym bag off the shelf and began to pack.

WHERE IN GOD'S NAME was she? Spencer ran to the back door and called out her name. A flock of startled sparrows lifted from Gina's bird feeder and took to the air. "Stacy?" he called again.

He listened to the stubborn silence, hearing the truth in the pounding of his heart.

He turned, intent on calling Chrissie. That was when he noticed the note, anchored by a saltshaker, on the kitchen counter.

"Dad," it read, "I've left. I'm sorry if this causes you any grief, but I see no other way. I'll call in a few weeks. Don't worry. I'll be safe. Stacy."

The shakily penned words swam before his eyes. He didn't understand. When he'd left for the clinic that morning, she'd been sitting on the living-room floor, practicing the breathing and relaxation exercises she'd learned in class. When he'd asked her what she planned to do with her day, she'd wrinkled her nose and said she'd clean her room. It had seemed a perfectly normal start to a perfectly normal morning.

When had she left? Right after he had? That was eight hours ago. How had she left? Where had she gone? Where? That was the question.

No, *why* was the question. Why? Spencer dropped the note, pressed his hands over his eyes and pushed his fingers into his hair. The walls closed in on him. The bright summer afternoon swirled. *I see no other way,* she'd written. No other way.

Okay, calm down and think this through logically, Spencer told himself. This was not an unsolvable problem. Where would she go? Where *could* she go?

A number of faces sprang to mind. The first and most persistent belonged to Gina. But then, Gina was always on his mind. He glanced at the phone. Her number was posted on the corkboard beside it. He ought to call, see if Stacy was there.

But if she wasn't, Gina would know the consequences of that damn argument. She'd know what a fool he was for not understanding how important keeping the baby was to his daughter, for not understanding that Stacy saw it as a choice between him and the baby, with no middle ground. She'd know what an arrogant imbecile he was.

He'd leave calling Gina for last.

He picked up the phone and punched in Chrissie's number. While he was waiting for the call to go through, he opened the cabinet where he kept the jar of grocery money. He didn't keep close tabs, but he figured roughly sixty dollars was missing.

Barbara answered the ring, said Chrissie was at work, and, no, they hadn't heard from Stacy all day. Spencer didn't want to alarm Barbara or get her involved, but he couldn't think of a single believable excuse for his odd call. So he made none, said Stacy was probably out for a walk and ended the call as quickly as possible, leaving Barbara totally befuddled, he was sure.

Reluctantly he called Maureen next. For that call, he armed himself with an excuse. Since Maureen would be getting married in two weeks, he wanted to make sure she understood that alimony payments would be ending. It was a weak excuse, because of course she did understand. Their lawyers had been conferring. But at least he was able to call without confessing he'd botched up with Stacy. He asked about the new house Maureen was having built, discussed the sale of the old one, and when he was convinced Stacy wasn't there and hadn't called, he ended the strained conversation.

The next call was equally unpleasant—to Todd. Todd wasn't home, his mother said, and she didn't expect him back for about a week. Spencer's antennae immediately went up. Had he and Stacy taken off together? When he started to ask questions, though, the woman got defensive. Before he could find out much of anything, she'd hung up.

Then Spencer called a couple of Stacy's old school friends, but no one had heard from her lately. Finally he admitted that his back was to the wall. There was no one left to call but Gina.

He punched in her number, wondering if he should even try to make an excuse. Better not. She'd see through anything he said, anyway. Besides, he didn't want to dissemble with Gina.

She answered on the fourth ring, breathless. "Hello?"

"Gina, it's me."

Her breath hitched. "Oh."

After a length of prickly silence, "Is this a bad time?"

"No, I was just doing laundry." She sounded guardedly polite. "What's up?"

Her voice brought to mind her face, her scent, her warmth. *I love you,* he thought. *That's what's up.* The realization knocked him speechless for several awkward seconds. He loved her, and he had all summer. Why hadn't he admitted it sooner? Why had it taken separation to bring him to his senses?

But there was no time to think of that now. Nothing he could do at present, maybe nothing he could do ever.

"Gina, has Stacy called you today?"

"No," she said, puzzled. Then, "Oh, no! Has she gone into labor?"

"No, nothing like that. Gina, I..." He swallowed over a baseball-size lump of pride. "I think I messed up— bad." He waited for her to jump on him with an I-told-you-so lecture.

"Go on," she urged.

"Stacy's taken off. Run away."

Gina emitted a shaky breath. "Do you have any idea where she went?"

"None. She left a note, but it doesn't say much. Here, let me read it to you." When he had, he said, "I called everyone she might've run to, but nobody's heard from her."

A span of silence thrummed between them. Then, "You mean I'm the last person you called?"

Spencer shrank under the injury he heard in her accusation. "Sorry," he muttered.

"Never mind. Now isn't the time for recriminations. Do you want me to drive home? Back to Bingham, I mean."

"As much as I'd like your company, you'd better stay there. Stacy might call on you yet. For all I know, she might still be en route. I'm not sure what time she took off."

"Okay. I won't budge. I'll call you as soon as I hear anything." And in a smaller voice, "*If* I hear anything."

"Thanks. I'll keep you posted, too."

"Spencer? This is just a suggestion, but how about calling Town Taxi and asking if one of their runs today was to the farm. I can't imagine how Stacy left otherwise. If the dispatcher says yes, ask where she went. If it was to the bus station, take a snapshot of her there and ask if anyone sold her a ticket, and if they did, to where."

"You're right, dammit. But I'd prefer not to leave the house, in case she calls."

"Get Barbara or her husband or Chrissie to help, then."

His sigh must've revealed his reluctance, because she said, "Spencer, this is too important for pride to interfere."

"You're right. Of course."

"If the bus station turns out to be a dead end, well, I don't know... The police?"

"Yes, I've already thought of that."

"Good. They'll know best how to track her."

Spencer knew the moment to hang up had arrived, but too much still seemed unspoken. Now wasn't the time, though. "Thanks," he said simply. "Talk to you later."

After hanging up, Spencer called Town Taxi. He was stymied when the dispatcher said no run had been made to the farm that day. How on earth had his daughter left? The farm wasn't on any bus line.

Spencer phoned the diner and talked to Chrissie, hoping she harbored some secret she hadn't divulged to her mother. Maybe she was the one who'd driven Stacy from the farm. Maybe she was even sheltering her somewhere. He thought he'd be able to discern a cover-up in her tone.

What Spencer discerned in Chrissie's tone was shock and distress. "Oh, my God," she kept repeating. "What can I do?"

"Nothing. Just, if you hear anything, or remember anything she might've said..."

"I'll call you. Right away. Oh, my God."

"Sorry I disturbed you at work."

After hanging up, Spencer called Barbara's house again. Her husband was home from work by then, and it was Tom who made the run to the bus station. His news upon returning was disheartening. No one could recall seeing a pregnant teenager come through that day.

Spencer spent that night on the living-room couch, the phone at arm's length. It never rang. He dozed fitfully. It seemed the longest night of his life.

Upon rising, he made a pot of coffee, showered, shaved and called the state police. They said they'd send an officer out later in the morning to get more information. At present, it didn't seem to be an emergency.

He was upstairs searching Stacy's room for clues when the phone rang. He shoved the bureau drawer closed and dashed out to the hall. "Yes?"

"Spencer, I found her." It was Gina. She sounded as if she'd been running.

Spencer's entire being shot to attention. "Where? Is she all right?"

"Yes, she's fine," Gina rushed on. "But she's gone into labor."

Spencer's blood thundered in his ears.

"She's at Union Hospital now. She asked someone to call me."

"Union?" he asked in a confused daze.

"Yes. That's where she and I attended birth-preparation classes. It's the hospital where she planned to have the baby all along."

"Then she never wandered very far."

"No. She went to a women's shelter in Kingfield, just two miles from the hospital. They came and picked her up at the farm. That's where she spent the night."

Spencer exhaled in an explosion of relief and self-derision. A women's shelter. Why hadn't he thought of that? Did he think his daughter had no sense at all? Did he think, without his help, nothing but harm could come to her?

"Listen, Spence, I don't have much time to talk."

"Oh, that's right. You're her birth partner. I'll head over there now, keep her company till you arrive."

"Oh, wait. Uh..."

"What's the matter? She is all right, isn't she?"

"Yes, yes. It's just...you might not be let in to see her."

From the sound of her voice, Spencer could almost see Gina wincing. "Why the hell not?" he demanded.

"Stacy doesn't want . . . She'd rather you . . ."

His heart sank, leaving an aching hollow in its place. "I see. You don't have to spell it out, Gina." He closed his eyes and squeezed his brow under the span of his thumb and fingers. His daughter didn't want him near her during the birth of her baby. That was why she'd run away. She was afraid he'd make her give it up.

"Spencer, go to the hospital, anyway. No one can stop you from sitting in the waiting room."

He began to nod, encouraged. "I'll do that. Yes."

"Good. I'll meet you there."

GINA ARRIVED at the maternity ward out of breath. She felt as if she'd run the entire distance from Syracuse to Kingfield. She spotted Spencer immediately. He was sitting on a blue damask divan in the waiting area, hunched over, elbows on knees and head in hands.

"Spencer?"

He looked up with a start. A smile transformed his face, and suddenly she couldn't imagine why she shouldn't embrace him.

He leapt to his feet and instantly they were holding each other. "I thought you'd never get here," he whispered.

Over his shoulder she checked her watch. It was nine-thirty. She'd made the drive in record time—two hours and fifteen minutes. "Have you seen Stacy?"

Spencer released her. "No." Frustration vied with anger and sadness in his eyes. "I've been told everything's proceeding normally, though. Evidently, she came in around five. Contractions were twenty minutes apart then."

"Five?" Gina looked around the reception area in a panic. It was quite possible Stacy had gone into the final stages of labor. "Has she been alone all this time?"

"No, someone from the women's shelter is with her, the woman who drove her in. She said she wouldn't leave until you got here."

Gina nodded, in a daze. "How about the obstetrician?"

"She's in the building somewhere."

She went on nodding. "Good. Okay. Oh, God, I'm scared."

Spencer held her again, pressing her against the strong beating of his heart. "We're all scared."

"Yes." Thinking of Stacy, Gina became filled with resolve. She pulled away and took a step toward the nurses' station.

"Gina?" Spencer called. She turned. He looked distraught and tired. "Gina, see if you can get Stacy to agree to see me, even if just for a few minutes. All I want to do is tell her I love her."

She nodded.

The nurse who was attending Stacy escorted Gina to the birthing room, filling her in on the way. Stacy hadn't gone into hard labor yet, but she was close.

"And the baby's positioning?"

"Perfect. I have to warn you, though, she isn't having an easy time of it."

"Oh, God. Is it her size? Is she too small?"

The nurse frowned. "She's tense. She knows her father's here and refuses even the mildest medication to relax. She's afraid she'll get groggy and the baby will be taken away from her. I've tried to reassure her that won't happen, but she still won't take anything."

Gina passed a shaky hand over her brow. "I was going to ask permission for him to visit with her awhile."

"He's already asked to come in several times. But when I presented the idea to Stacy, she became adamant. I think it would be better if he didn't see her until after the baby was born."

"He's really a wonderful man. He's a doctor, did you know that?"

The nurse's eyebrows rose. She glanced down the corridor as if trying to get a second look at him. "I'm surprised he didn't say something or try to throw his weight around to get in."

"He isn't your ordinary doctor."

"Guess not. Well, you'd better get to work."

Gina shivered. "I've never done this before."

"Neither has Stacy." The nurse pushed open the door to the birthing suite.

Stacy stifled a cry when she saw Gina.

"Stacy, hi. Sorry I'm so late."

Stacy, dressed in a blue hospital gown, sat squatting on a birthing stool. Gina knelt in front of her, brushing the hair out of her eyes. "How are you doing?"

"Oh, just peachy." Stacy sniffed, stifling a sob, then tightened all over as a contraction overtook her. Sweat beaded on her brow.

Gina didn't know what to do. Her first instinct was to call for a doctor, the nurse, anybody, and demand they make the pain stop. Stacy was too young, too tiny. She shouldn't have to be going through such a big, grown-up experience.

Gina suddenly became aware of another woman in the room, kneeling behind Stacy, bracing her. "Easy, easy, try to relax," she said.

When the contraction had passed, she introduced herself as the woman who'd brought Stacy in, the same woman who'd called Gina, in fact.

"Well, I guess this is my shift," Gina said, forcing a bright smile. "You're officially off duty."

"I'll stay if you'd like."

"No, we'll be fine."

The woman looked to Stacy, who nodded in agreement.

"Thanks for staying with her, though."

"My pleasure."

The woman wished Stacy well and left.

Stacy turned her glance aside. "I'm sorry."

"What on earth for?"

"For running off... Oh, wait." She panted and made small crying sounds as another contraction gripped her.

Gina scooted around behind her to brace her. "Inhale, Stace. Hold it. Now slowly breathe it out, all the tension."

Stacy wasn't listening. She was lost somewhere in the pain.

"Gina, I can't do this. It's too hard!" she cried.

"Yes, you can. Think of my cousin, the wimp."

A faint smile touched Stacy's pale lips.

Gina got her to her feet and walked her around the room. "Would you like to take a bath? That might help."

The nurse overheard. "I've already asked."

"I've changed my mind," Stacy said, giving Gina's arm a squeeze. "My partner's here."

Several minutes later, Stacy sat immersed in a warm, deep tub in the bathroom adjacent to the birthing room. "How does that feel?" the nurse asked, swishing the water with her fingertips.

"Heavenly." Stacy sighed. "Even the contractions aren't as bad now."

Gina sank into a chair and blew out a breath of relief.

With Stacy more relaxed, Gina decided to broach the subject of Spencer. "Stacy, you know your father's here, right?"

The girl's eyes darkened. "Still?"

"Yes, and he's not going to go away. He wants to see you."

"I don't want to see him. Please, Gina, don't let him near the baby. Please. I'm depending on you."

"Honey, calm down, calm down." Gina stroked Stacy's hair. "Nobody can take your baby from you."

"I don't believe it. I signed adoption agreements. Dad'll find a way to make them stick." Her hands whitened over the rim of the tub and she gritted her teeth.

Gina waited until the tightness melted from her face. "Okay, relax. You can count on me."

The bath seemed to soothe Stacy enough for Gina to leave with the nurse for a few minutes. She hurried out to the waiting room and quickly informed Spencer of his daughter's condition.

"She'd still rather not see you, though." Gina watched the hope die in his eyes. Dejection replaced it, dejection so black she took him in her arms.

"There's nothing to do, then, but give in," he said against her hair.

She went still, frozen in disbelief. Jerking back, she searched his face. "What?"

"Tell her I'll support whatever decision she makes."

In some corner of her mind, Gina thought she ought to be whooping in joy, dancing in triumph. But the slump of resignation in Spencer's stance squelched the impulse. The small creases of worry on his brow told her that keeping the baby remained the last choice he'd ever make for his daughter.

"Are you sure?"

He nodded. "I've had nothing to do these past couple of hours but think about it. If it means getting Stacy back and keeping her with me, yes, I'll take in the baby too."

"I think she needs to know that."

"Yes. Go tell her."

"No, you tell her. I think she needs to hear it from you."

"But . . ."

"Of course she wants to see you. Haven't you figured it out yet that the sun rises and sets on you as far as she's concerned? She just doesn't want her baby taken from her."

Hope glimmered in his eyes. He glanced toward the doors marked No Admittance—Staff Only.

"She loves you, Spencer," Gina persisted. "And she needs you very much right now."

Spencer's granite chin wobbled once before he lifted it high, pressing his lips together. He nodded, reached for Gina's hand and said, "Lead the way."

Gina went into the room, leaving Spencer in the hall. Stacy was sitting up in bed, her face to the monitor that measured her baby's heartbeat.

"Stacy, your father has asked to speak with you. He's outside the door."

"Here?" The sweat sleeking Stacy's face told Gina she was just coming off another contraction.

"Let him say his piece." Gina felt a smile rising from deep inside her. "I think you're going to like what he has to say."

Tilting her head, Stacy bit her lower lip, which slowly fanned out into a hopeful smile. "You're kidding."

"Would I kid you at a time like this?"

"Let him in."

Spencer stepped to the bed and, before he'd thought about it, kissed his daughter's brow. Surprisingly, she didn't resist him. She looked so tired. "How are you doing, baby?"

Better not call her baby, he thought. *Those days are gone.*

"Hanging in. Gina tells me you have something to say. I don't mean to rush you or anything, but...but... Gina!"

Spencer stood by, clenching and unclenching his fists, as Gina rushed to Stacy's side. Gina helped her through the contraction, murmuring assurances, rubbing her back, being her usual strong self. She wiped Stacy's face with a cool cloth, gave her some ice chips to suck on, then stepped aside to let the conversation between father and daughter continue.

"I'll be quick," he said, holding Stacy's hand in one of his, stroking it with the other. "I want you and the baby to come home with me."

Stacy closed her eyes and whispered something. *Thank you,* he thought.

"I'm not sure about any of the details, but we'll work them out," he said. "The important thing now is for you to know I want us together."

Stacy's smile trembled. "Okay," she said weakly. "You've got us."

He patted her wrist. "Stace, we're a family. You're not in this alone."

"Oh, really. Then you take the next contraction."

Spencer wanted to tell her how much he loved her, how proud he was of her, but just then the obstetrician swept into the room. "I hear we're having a baby today," she sang.

Stacy smirked. "I wish *we*."

"I'm going to be examining her now, Dr. Coburn," the obstetrician said.

Spencer nodded, only vaguely aware of Gina taking his arm, leading him to the door.

"Thanks, Spencer," Gina said. "I can see a change in Stacy already."

In the corridor he looked back. "It's going to be so difficult for her."

"Raising the baby? Yes. But she'll have you to help her. I never thought I'd be saying this, but money can solve a lot of the problems facing you—paying for diaper service, tutors, baby-sitters, that sort of thing."

"Yes, I suppose you're right."

"You're not going to regret this. I have a feeling this baby is going to bring you joy and blessings you can't even imagine now."

Spencer nodded, but halfheartedly. Out of love for Stacy, he'd take in the baby and support it, but his heart really wasn't in it. He doubted it ever would be. There was a sadness inside him that wouldn't lift, a knot that wouldn't untie.

Gina glanced over her shoulder and gave him a small shove. "Okay, I've got to get back."

"I feel so helpless."

"There's nothing you can do. In this case, you're not a doctor. You're an expectant grandfather. Go pace."

As usual, Gina left him in a better frame of mind. He returned to the waiting room and followed her directive.

But gradually his pacing slowed, and he found himself standing by a window, staring out, looking inward. He knew why he persisted in feeling sad. What he was experiencing was so similar to what he'd felt for his father, how could he *not* recognize it? He was grieving. He was mourning the passing of Stacy's youth and innocence. While all around him people were pressing forward, excited about what lay ahead, he was still trying to say goodbye.

CHAPTER SEVENTEEN

IT WAS THE LONGEST morning of his life. By eleven-thirty Spencer thought he might lose it, just start tearing down the corridors, demanding someone do a C-section and get this ordeal over with. He hadn't eaten anything, which probably contributed to his bad humor.

He was standing at the desk, asking for yet one more update, when the No Admittance doors squealed open behind him.

He swiveled, heart stopped, and found Gina standing there. Her short dark hair stood up in disorderly swirls, blood smeared her green hospital smock, and lines of stress etched her face. But she was beaming, and Spencer thought he'd never seen anyone more like an angel in his life.

Gina looked at Spencer and wanted to cry, in jubilation, in pride, in pure release of tension.

"Yes?" he asked, eyebrows puckered in caution.

She nodded. "Yes. It's a boy."

She was vaguely aware of other people cheering—the desk nurse, a flower-delivery person, an expectant father. But their cheers got lost as Spencer rushed forward and crushed her to him.

"Thank God," he muttered against her ear. "Thank God." When he finally set her down, he asked, "How is she?"

"She? I said it's a boy, Spencer."

He laughed. "I'm talking about Stacy."

"Oh." Of course, he'd want to know about his daughter first. It was only natural. There was no reason to feel disappointed. None at all. "She's fine. A little spacey. She had a shot of Demerol toward the end."

"Can I see her?"

"Yup. The baby was born half an hour ago. We've just been cleaning up since." Gina grinned. "Oh, you should see the baby, Spencer. He's absolutely beautiful. Seven pounds, five—"

"Great." He smiled vacantly. "Great." Then headed for the birthing room.

The maternity nurse was still with Stacy when Spencer got there. So was the obstetrician, although she seemed ready to leave. Spencer sidled up to the bed. Stacy was awake but looked exhausted, and so pale. His panicked gaze sought out the obstetrician.

"She did really well, Dr. Coburn. She was a trooper." Turning to her patient, she said, "Okay, Stacy, you take it easy now and rest. You've earned it. I'll stop by and see you tomorrow morning."

Stacy smiled wanly, then looked at Spencer. "Hi, Daddy."

His chest tightened. She hadn't called him Daddy in years.

"Hi, Stace."

"I'm glad you're here," she whispered.

"Where else would I be at a time like this?"

A tear beaded at the corner of her eye. "I feel like I was hit by a bus."

"I know." He pressed a kiss to her forehead. "Don't expect to be feeling yourself for a while, either. But eventually you will. Two weeks from now you'll feel like a new person." He brushed her matted hair off her forehead, her uneven, unruly hair. Why had it ever offended him? Couldn't he see the wonderful person beneath?

She smiled again. "It was awesome. Totally awesome." Then she closed her eyes. Gina stepped to the other side of the bed and nodded, agreeing.

"Stace, would you like to sleep?" he asked.

"Oh." Her eyes opened. "Not yet. They've taken the baby to the nursery—you know, to have him measured and tested."

"Yes, that's routine."

She raised herself up on one elbow. "I know, but could you do me a favor, Dad? Could you go and stay with him during the tests, keep an eye on him?"

Spencer was about to protest that no harm was going to come to the baby in the nursery.

"Please, Dad. I barely got to hold him before they took him away. That isn't right. Newborns shouldn't be taken from family so soon. The world is all so new and cold and strange. They need to know they've landed in a safe place."

Spencer was about to protest again when Gina caught his eye. *Do what she asks,* her stern expression said.

Feeling outnumbered, he murmured a gracious "Of course" and went in search of the nursery.

He found it easily, down the corridor and around a corner, a relatively quiet place, cheerfully decorated with ducks and birds. He stood in the open doorway, watching a masked-and-gowned pediatric nurse hovering over an incubator, her back to him. He scanned the rest of the room. Sitting in a rocker, another nurse was bottle-feeding an infant. Two other babies lay in their bassinets. One was crying.

The pediatric nurse turned. "Oh. Can I help you?"

"Yes. Is that Stacy Coburn's baby?" He nodded toward the incubator.

"Yes, it is." Above the mask, her eyes crinkled.

"Do you mind if I step inside?"

"I'm sorry." She shook her head. "You can watch from the viewing window, though."

He was about to comply when she moved and the incubator came into full view. Inside, pinkly lit like a museum treasure on display, lay a newborn baby with deep blue eyes, open and exploring, and hair the color and texture of peach fuzz. His lilliputian hands were fisted and waving. His thin legs kicked and folded. He had long feet, a sturdy torso, healthy coloring, and a perfectly shaped head.

Suddenly Spencer's entire being centered on that one small person. He was beautiful. He was absolutely beautiful. *And he's my grandson,* Spencer thought in awe.

"The incubator is just for warmth while I'm checking him," the nurse explained hurriedly, misreading his reaction. "There's nothing wrong."

"Yes, I know," he answered, mesmerized. "He seems so alert. And he isn't crying."

"Mmm. Looks like he's happy to be here." The nurse cooed and ran her index finger over the sole of one pink foot. "Are you related?"

"Yes," Spencer was about to say he was the mother's father, then laughed. "I'm the baby's grandfather."

"Oh, congratulations."

"Thank you." He hitched his shoulders and grinned, ear to ear. He felt so weird. Floaty. Expanded. Transformed on a molecular level.

Then Spencer noticed the nurse approach his grandson with a bulb syringe. His voice leapt into another register when he asked, "What are you going to do with that thing?"

She turned, frowning. "Please, I can't allow you in here."

He hadn't even realized he'd stepped into the room. "I'll leave. Just tell me what you're doing."

Her laugh was muffled behind her mask. "I'm going to clear some mucus from his mouth."

Mucus. Oh, right. Spencer retreated with a chagrined smirk. At the same time he was struck with amazement. Just like that, he'd wanted to snatch up his grandson and run with him, protect him from all of life's harms, big and small.

"My daughter sent me here," he finally explained. "She requested that I stay close by the baby so he'd know he, um, was safe."

"Oh." The nurse's eyes crinkled again. "In that case…" She inclined her head toward a tube of masks on a supply cart. "Put one of those on and hand me a fresh diaper."

Sometime later Spencer was swaddling the baby in a soft flannel receiving blanket when a tap sounded at the large viewing window. He looked up and Gina waved. Just when he'd been thinking he'd reached his absolute peak of happiness, his spirits rushed and reached a new height. He finished wrapping the baby, picked him up and carried him to the window, eager to share his joy.

"Is that the baby's grandmother?" the nurse inquired as she readied a bassinet.

Spencer's heart lurched at the thought. "No. A very close friend. She was my daughter's birthing partner."

"Oh." The nurse opened the door and invited Gina inside.

"Isn't he precious?" Gina whispered, standing close by Spencer's side and brushing a finger over the baby's soft cheek.

Spencer didn't know what to say. Yes, the baby was precious. Yes, a miracle. But suddenly words seemed totally incapable of expressing all that this baby was.

"Stacy's finally decided on a name."

From the nasally tremor in Gina's voice, Spencer thought he knew what she was going to say. His sentimental daughter was going to name the baby Joe.

"Spencer."

"Yes?"

Gina laughed softly. "No. She's naming the baby Spencer. Spencer Coburn the third."

Spencer couldn't find his breath. Spencer? This little guy was going to be named after him?

"But she says, if you don't mind, she's going to call him Joey. Joseph's his middle name."

Grinning, Spencer nodded. "Somehow I knew *Joseph* would get in there."

With the baby held in the crook of his left arm, Spencer pulled Gina close with his right. "Holding him like this," he admitted, "I find it hard to keep feeling disappointed for Stacy, to keep thinking of her future as ruined."

"That's because it isn't." With her head against Spencer's shoulder, Gina brushed Joey's cheek again. "It'll just be different from what you expected."

Spencer nodded. Yes, her life would definitely be different. But maybe different wouldn't be so bad.

The baby turned his head and rooted at Gina's knuckle. "I think he's getting hungry."

The nurse came over then. "He sure is. Come on, sweetie. Time to go see your mom."

THAT AFTERNOON, Chrissie burst into Stacy's room with a huge balloon bouquet and an effervescent "Oh, my God, we had a boy!"

Gina, who hadn't given up the baby for the past hour, agreed. "We" had indeed had a boy, for Joey did feel rather like a communal baby. Certainly he wouldn't be raised in a conventional manner. Stacy was going to need help from lots of people.

But would she be one of them?

She carefully passed the newborn to Chrissie who, as the oldest of five children, handled the slumbering bundle with experienced ease.

"Spencer, it's nearly four o'clock." Gina rubbed her bleary eyes. "I think I'm going home. To the farm," she added for clarity, although to her there was no obscurity. The farm *was* home.

Spencer rose from his chair by the bed where he'd been compiling a shopping list of baby things with his daughter. "Of course. You look tired. I should've suggested it sooner." He gave the two girls a backward glance. Chrissie was sitting on the bed, the baby between her and Stacy. Stacy seemed to have caught her second wind and was proudly rushing on about the birth in exuberant detail.

"I think I'll go home, too." He kissed his daughter and told her he'd be back after dinner.

"Thanks for everything, Dad," she said, then went right on talking.

They drove home in their separate cars, one behind the other. Finally alone, Gina steadily sank into a state of anticlimax. After so much excitement, she told herself, it was only natural to feel let down.

But as she rode along, rethinking the day, she eventually conceded that anticlimax wasn't what she was feeling at all. It was dejection, and the reason had nothing to do with what had transpired that day. Rather, it had everything to do with what hadn't transpired.

Spencer hadn't mentioned a word about where they stood. He'd made some fairly monumental decisions about the future today, but apparently he didn't see Gina figuring into that future. Not once had he even hinted at her being included.

She told herself the hospital was an inappropriate place to hold such a discussion. The day had belonged to Stacy and the baby. But couldn't he have said something to indicate that she, Gina, had a place in this newly merged family, even if just as a friend who occasionally visited?

When they reached the farm, the westering sun was gilding the towering maples on the front lawn and splashing its bright gold across the newly painted house. Never had the farm looked lovelier, she thought. And that, too, saddened her. Three weeks was all that was left on her rental agreement. Three more weeks and the farm would be a memory again. She would be back in Syracuse preparing for another school year.

Spencer pulled to the side of the driveway in front of the house and waved to her to park ahead of him. She had already prepared herself for an evening alone, just in case he considered the eight hours he'd already spent with her enough for one day. But no sooner had she brought her car to a stop than he was opening her door and saying, "I think the baby has my chin. What do you think? I'm not trying to say he looks like me or anything, but let's face it, I am his grandfather, and it wouldn't be unreasonable for him to inherit something of my looks, right?"

Gina stood on the driveway gazing up into Spencer's handsome, animated face and laughed. How could she have thought she'd be spending the evening alone? Spencer needed someone to talk at about his new grandson.

"Yes. He definitely has your chin. Do you have any plans for dinner?"

He scratched his jaw. "I haven't thought it through in any detail, but I know there's stuff in the pantry we can throw together." He touched his hand to her back and started for the porch. "Actually, dinner has been the farthest thing from my mind."

"I know. You've been too preoccupied with your grandson."

He breathed out a quiet laugh. "Not totally."

When they reached the front door, he paused, a thoughtful expression in his eyes. "Why don't you have a seat here and relax a while. I'll get us something to drink."

"Oh, I can help." She reached to push in the door.

"No, really," he protested, blocking her way. "I'd rather you...I mean... Please, won't you let me pamper you a bit?"

"Well, if you insist." Gina thought he was acting odd but said nothing more. She plumped a cushion on one of the porch rockers and sat.

Although the sun had wheeled around to this side of the house, the porch felt gloriously cool. She rocked, closing her eyes, listening to the bird songs and the rackety-rackety of the rocker against the uneven floorboards. She tried to relax but couldn't. Spencer was up to something.

The screen door opened and Spencer stepped out, a tall glass of iced tea in each hand. He handed one to Gina, then sank into the rocker next to hers.

"What I've been thinking about mostly," he continued as if there'd been no break in their conversation, "is how different my life's going to be from here on." He sipped his tea. The rockers went rackety-rackety. "Different and difficult. I'll have to move. That's the first change I'll have to make. My place in Boston is close to my clinic and it's suited my needs until now, but I wouldn't want to raise a child there."

Gina screwed her attention on the road and the occasional car that passed. "Do you have any idea where you'd like to go?"

"Well, see, that's the thing." He braced his foot against the rail. "I'd rather not take Stacy back to the Boston area at all. Why put her through the agony and humiliation of explaining herself to relatives and old friends?"

Gina's heart began to lift. "So what do you intend to do?"

He sipped his tea, barely wetting his lips, she noticed. "Living here seems to have agreed with her. It's peaceful and safe, and she's made new friends." Spencer abruptly dropped his foot and turned to her. "So I've been thinking of buying the farm."

Gina went still. She didn't have to ask the question. It rang between them as loud as thunder.

"That'll mean leaving the clinic of course. I can't very well commute from here to Boston." He set his glass down on the floor, lurched to his feet and paced to the end of the porch where he gripped the rail in two tensed hands.

Gina could imagine the turmoil he was suffering. The clinic was his life's work, the product of years of dedication and love.

"Is there someone who can take over for you? Someone you can sell it to? What *do* you do with a clinic?"

Spencer turned and leaned back against the rail. "Yes, there's someone. I don't foresee that as a problem."

"Is there work for you here?"

"I think so." His eyes lit. "Bingham could use another family practitioner. Maybe even a walk-in clinic. I don't know about you, but I found the drive to Kingfield absurdly long."

"You mean you'd have the energy to start over from scratch?"

"Yeah." His confident, spreading smile spoke volumes. "Someone once told me a person ought to change direction every twenty years. It keeps you fresh. I'm only beginning to see the wisdom in that advice now."

He retraced his steps, drank his tea thirstily and set down the glass. "Care to stretch your legs?"

"Mmm."

Gina went ahead of him down the steps. They walked at a lazy, meandering pace along the driveway, across the courtyard, by her door.

Gina plucked a rose off the bush at the corner of the barn. "The baby's going to love growing up here," she said.

"I hope so." Spencer laughed. "A baby—God!" And he laughed again.

"Scary, isn't it?"

"Terrifying."

They walked on, around the barn, to the back of the house. Gina was beginning to get the feeling they weren't just walking. She was being led.

He said, "It's such an unconventional setup, raising a teenage daughter and her son simultaneously. I have no guidelines to follow. I mean, who has the last say when the kid wants to stay up past his bedtime, me or Stacy? What do I do when she discovers boys again? Do I tell her her responsibility is to stay home with her son?''

Spencer paused, turning to Gina. ''But you know what really scares me? What happens when Stacy's, say, twenty-three and ready to move out on her own?''

''Are you afraid she'll saddle you with her son?''

Spencer looked surprised. ''No. Just the opposite. After I've changed his diapers and taught him to fish and waved him off to kindergarten, how the hell am I supposed to give him up?''

Gina reached up and brushed her fingers over the frown lines on his forehead. ''You worry far too much, Dr. Coburn.''

''Well, what would you do, facing what I'm facing?''

Gina didn't hesitate. ''I'd make every minute count. I'd pour all the love and attention I could into Joey and Stacy. Then I'd trust in that love to keep us all close.''

Spencer flattened his lips in a stoic line and nodded. They continued walking.

''The garden's doing well,'' she commented, her gaze sweeping the vines heavy with yellow summer squash and the leafy towers of runner beans. ''And wouldn't you know, the sunflowers are opening.''

They arrived at the gate. Spencer had forgotten a coffee mug on the left post, she noticed with a smile. In the next instant her gaze flew back to the center of the garden.

''What's that?'' she asked. But even as she spoke she knew what the new object was. A sundial. ''Oh, what a lovely addition,'' she said, reaching for the gate latch. ''When did you put it there?''

Spencer rubbed a hand across his brow, shading his guilty eyes, and grinned. ''About ten minutes ago.''

"What?"

"That's why I asked you to stay on the porch."

Gina laughed uncertainly. "I'm not sure I follow this."

Spencer shrugged. "Nothing much to follow. I have a confession to make. I bought that sundial over a month ago for your birthday, but I felt strange giving it to you then. It's been in the basement ever since."

Gina thought she understood. A month ago they hadn't been close enough to warrant such an expensive present. Eager to get a closer look, she opened the gate.

"How did you know? I love sundials. I've always wanted one." She came to an abrupt, embarrassed halt. "I'm sorry. Obviously you mean to keep it." She lowered her eyes.

"Well, yes. But I mean for you to enjoy it, too." He took her arm and urged her forward until they were standing on either side of the sundial.

Reluctantly Gina gave it an admiring look. It was made of heavy metal, seasoned to a ripe verdigris, with Roman numerals and an encircling inscription: *Grow old along with me. The best is yet to be.* She swallowed.

Don't be silly, she told herself. That was a common inscription on sundials. Spencer didn't mean anything by it. In all likelihood, he probably hadn't even had a choice.

But no matter how hard she worked at keeping the inscription from reaching her heart, she failed. *Grow old along with me.* Oh, how she would love that, to share Spencer's days now and tomorrow. And yes, she was sure the best was yet to be.

She lifted her gaze to his, too fearful to hope. The look in his eyes did not disappoint her.

"I don't know how to ask, Gina. You have your life, and I have no right to expect you to sacrifice it."

She gripped the edge of the sundial with her tremulous fingertips. A heady giddiness rose inside her.

"I just want you to know I wouldn't ask you to leave your job or your condo. Just as long as you come home to me on occasion, weekends perhaps." He pressed his hands on the face of the sundial and leaned in, intensely beseeching. "What I'm offering is a hell of a life, Gina, a ready-made dysfunctional family, and if you'd prefer to not get involved, I'll understand perfectly. But you should also know that I'd do my best to make you happy. I love you, and if you want to know the truth, I don't think I can handle what lies ahead of me without you. I need your help. I need your strength and compassion. I even need your occasional brassy attitude. In short, I need *you*, Gina. And if you can find it in your heart to say yes to this crazy life I'm offering, you'd make me the happiest man on earth."

Gina inched her hands over the sundial until her fingertips were touching Spencer's. "Yes," she answered. "Oh, yes."

CHAPTER EIGHTEEN

IT SNOWED on Thanksgiving Day, lending the farm-house a cozy, sheltering feel. Mulled cider, roasting turkey and pumpkin pie scented the air. Flames crackled and hissed in the living-room fireplace.

Spencer's family—his mother, sister, brother-in-law and two nieces—had flown in from Illinois the previous afternoon, leaving only two other guests, Doug Ferguson and his current girlfriend, to travel the snowy roads, but even they arrived in plenty of time to pitch in with the potato-mashing.

The house was noisy and full, all five bedrooms occupied, and if Doug stayed over tonight, he and his friend would have to make do with the pullout couch in the family room, which was what the living area in the barn had become.

Gina felt thankful, indeed.

She and Spencer had gotten married the second week of September here at the farm in a quiet ceremony surrounded by family and friends. That same week they'd signed papers on the house. They hadn't gone away on a honeymoon. With Joey added to their lives, the thought hadn't even crossed their minds.

Untying her apron, Gina shouldered her way through the crowded kitchen and slipped through the doorway to the barn.

"Stacy, I'm ready to seat people."

"And I'm ready to be seated. I'm starved." Stacy was sitting on the couch that Spencer had brought from his place in Boston. Lying in her arms, Joey was clapping his chubby hands against his near-empty bottle. Stacy's cousins, Amy and Molly, age six and eight, crowded in on either side. She lifted Joey to her shoulder and he immediately gave a loud burp. The enraptured girls fell over themselves giggling.

Gina returned to the kitchen and moved on to the living room. "Gentlemen?"

Spencer, sitting back with his elbows on the piano, turned from a conversation with Doug and his brother-in-law. His eyes, meeting hers, took on a private brilliance. "Is dinner ready?" Ordinarily, Spencer pitched in with meal preparations, but Gina had been overassisted today. In fact, getting the men *out* of the kitchen had been a blessing.

"Yes, it is. If you'll turn off that football game and open the wine."

From the doorway to the dining room Spencer's mother was saying, "Gina, do you have another bowl? We forgot to put out the turnips." Behind her, the voice of Gina's new sister-in-law answered, "Oh, here's one."

Spencer's family had come for the wedding and had stayed three days, allowing Gina to get to know them. This visit, she was getting to love them.

From their various corners of the house, people converged on the dining room and took their places at the long mahogany table that Spencer had found on one of his now routine stops at Buffington Auction Barn. Gina hadn't realized she was marrying an antiques zealot, but she certainly wasn't complaining about it.

Spencer sat at one end of the table, Gina at the other. Murmurs of "What a lovely table" and "Mmm, smells good" drifted between them. But then the murmurs subsided. So did the rustlings of linen napkins, leaving an uneasy space, a question hovering in the air. Gina looked at Spencer, uneasy herself. It was their first Thanksgiving together, all new ground.

Spencer nodded reassuringly, knowing what she was thinking. "At our house in Illinois—" he gave his mother a smiling glance "—it was customary to join hands, bow our heads and, in the privacy of our own hearts, express our thanks for our blessings. I'd like to continue that tradition here."

He reached for his mother's hand to his right, his sister's to his left, and all around the table the chain continued until they were an unbroken circle. Even three-month-old Joey was included, since Stacy had propped him in his carrier seat on a chair between herself and Gina.

Then, like everyone else, Gina lowered her head and closed her eyes. Thoughts crowded in. *I'm thankful for little Joey, the light of my life. I'm thankful for his health, his sweet disposition, his gummy smiles. It's also pretty nice that he's finally sleeping through the night.*

At the other end of the table Spencer thought, *I'm glad Stacy likes her new school and is acing her classes*. He regretted she didn't have time for extracurricular activities and making a lot of friends, but as Gina pointed out, that seemed only to be strengthening her. *She's becoming such an individual, a young woman with uncommon focus and drive. I love her and I'm proud of her.*

And Gina thought, *Thank God my condo just sold.*

And Spencer thought, *Thank God Doug took over the clinic*. Although he still held ownership, Doug was handling the everyday administration.

Gina, at her end, was glad she finally had the opportunity to be a full-time homemaker. She knew Spencer worried that she would become bored or, worse, resentful for the sacrifices she was making—giving up her career, taking care of Joey while Stacy was in school. But after eighteen years of teaching—high school, no less—she was ready to stay home and bake cookies for a decade or two. In fact, she was reveling in it.

Spencer, at his end, was happy for his new practice, for the four-room suite above the real-estate office in the white frame house next to the library. It would do very well—for a while.

Thank you for this sturdy old house, Gina thought, *which has sheltered six generations of my family.* She hoped they didn't mind, but she was planning to do some remodeling.

Thank you for this town which I found by pure chance, Spencer thought, *and for the people in it who are becoming my patients, my neighbors, my friends.*

Gina's thoughts roamed to the land outside, the fields, the hills, the woods. *I'm truly lucky,* she thought.

Spencer thought of his grandson, and he grinned.

Gina thought of the memories she had of her parents, and she blessed them, then opened her heart to memories yet to be made.

Spencer thought of the life growing inside his wife's body, a life so new they hadn't told anyone yet, not even Stacy, and his heart overflowed.

Heads were still bowed, when Gina lifted hers. Spencer, too, was just looking up.

Thank you for Spencer, the foundation of my happiness.

Thank you for Gina, the source of my strength.

In the hush of that moment before the others raised their heads, before wishes of happy Thanksgiving got exchanged and platters were passed, Gina and Spencer gazed at each other over the bounty of their table and silently said, *I love you.*

Outside, the snow continued to fall.

Inside, Spencer and Gina smiled.